WEDDING BELLS AT GOODWILL HOUSE

FENELLA J. MILLER

Boldwood

First published in Great Britain in 2023 by Boldwood Books Ltd.

Cover Design by Colin Thomas

Cover Photography: iStock, Alamy and Colin Thomas

A CIP catalogue record for this book is available from the British Library.

Paperback ISBN 978-1-80162-875-4

Large Print ISBN 978-1-80162-874-7

Hardback ISBN 978-1-80162-873-0

Ebook ISBN 978-1-80162-876-1

Kindle ISBN 978-1-80162-877-8

Audio CD ISBN 978-1-80162-868-6

MP3 CD ISBN 978-1-80162-869-3

Digital audio download ISBN 978-1-80162-871-6

Boldwood Books Ltd
23 Bowerdean Street
London SW6 3TN
www.boldwoodbooks.com

For our wonderful and collapsing NHS and the dedication of all the staff who work in it.

1

JANUARY 1941

Lady Joanna Harcourt heard the telephone jangling in the icy grand hall of Goodwill House and hoped someone else would venture from the kitchen to answer it. She was snug in the small sitting room with her mother-in-law and was reluctant to leave this comfort and brave the chilled corridors and hall.

Her adopted son and daughter, the twins, Joe and Liza, had walked into the village for their morning lessons as Mr Kent, their tutor, was too elderly and decrepit to make the journey with several inches of snow on the ground and temperatures well below freezing.

'I'd better answer the telephone, Elizabeth, as the land girls in the kitchen are pretending not to hear it.'

'Biggins has gone to Ramsgate on the bus, otherwise she would have answered it.'

Maureen Biggins was her mother-in-law's recently appointed personal maid-cum-companion. She was a quiet middle-aged lady who had been a nanny to an aristocratic family and been let go when they'd emigrated to America for the duration of the war.

'Heavens, you shouldn't have sent the poor woman out in this weather!'

'She had a personal errand to run. I am more than satisfied with her so was happy to give her the morning off.' Elizabeth frowned. 'I do hope the buses are still functioning. I'd hate for her to be marooned somewhere today.'

'Don't worry, if they weren't she'd be back already, wouldn't she?'

Joanna had to step over the dog in order to reach the door. Lazzy, now fully grown and the size of a pit pony, was flopped in front of the fire and raised his head briefly as she got up but didn't bother to follow her. He might be a big hairy dog, but one would think he didn't have a thick fur coat of his own, the way he hogged the fire.

'Do you think it could be Lord Harcourt? We've heard nothing from him since you saw him in London in October.'

Joanna hoped she'd never hear from that particular man again. He'd had the gall to suggest she become his mistress and, in his arrogance, had been certain she'd agree. At least he'd not contacted her again after she'd abandoned him in his car last year.

'It won't be him. I'll close the door as I don't want to let in the cold air.' She pulled her thick woollen shawl around her shoulders and hurried down the icy passageway, into the hall, and snatched up the noisy telephone.

'Goodwill House, Lady Harcourt speaking, how can I be of help?'

'Good morning, my lady, Mrs Ramsbottom speaking. How many of your girls are actually working today?' The area organiser for the land girls was extremely efficient.

'The three who work in the dairy farm, obviously, have continued despite the appalling weather. However, the other nine are here. They have all been told by their respective employers that they're not needed until the weather improves. Unfortunately, as you know, if they don't work then they won't be paid.'

'Exactly so. And you still have to feed them; I'm assuming this is at your own expense?'

'It is, but I've no intention of turning them out,' Joanna said. 'They are part of the household. I'm prepared to have them here even if they can't afford to pay for their board and lodging.'

'That's very kind of you, my lady, but these girls cannot be allowed to sit around doing nothing. They must work somewhere and I'm looking into that. Would you be kind enough to tell them they must make themselves useful at Goodwill House?'

'That's already in hand, Mrs Ramsbottom. The ladies from the village are unable to get here because of the snow and the girls have been doing all the domestic chores, including the laundry, as well as helping in the kitchen.'

'Good, good, I'm glad to hear that. I do understand that they can't get on with hedging and ditching at the moment. I pray that this dire weather will abate very soon.'

Joanna bid Mrs Ramsbottom goodbye and replaced the receiver in the cradle and, her breath steaming in front of her, made a mad dash for the kitchen. This was the warmest room in the house as the range was always alight. There just wasn't enough coal to have fires in the upstairs rooms. There had been icicles on the inside of the windows in the ballroom the last time she'd looked inside, which was now too cold to be used as a recreation space by the land girls.

In the kitchen, there were five of her boarders sitting at the table playing cards. Three would be taking their turn doing chores and the other three were dairy maids at Brook Farm. Charlie was the only one missing. Her two friends, Sal and Daphne, immediately stood up on Joanna's entrance but the other three continued with their game.

'Is there anything you'd like us to do, my lady, we feel a bit guilty enjoying ourselves in here,' Daphne said.

'No, my dear, that's not why I've come. I've just been speaking to Mrs Ramsbottom.'

She gave them a brief resumé of what she'd been told and now had the attention of everybody in the kitchen. Even Jean, the housekeeper, and a good friend, stopped stirring whatever it was she had been cooking on the range in order to listen.

'The fog's so thick, we'd get lost just trying to find our farms,' Daphne said, and the others agreed.

'I reckon the only good thing about this blooming awful weather is that them Germans ain't been over dropping bombs for a few days,' Sal said.

'How true. I notice that Charlie's missing – has she volunteered to help those on the domestic rota this morning?'

'She has, my lady,' one of the other land girls said. 'She's been fetching in logs from the barn for the past hour or so. We're going to have fires in three bedrooms – we drew straws to see which rooms these will be – and then we can spend a bit of time upstairs and get out of Jean's hair.'

There was a plentiful supply of timber in the woods bordering the house and Joe had been felling dead trees and collecting them all summer. Her elder daughter Sarah's mare, Star, had proved invaluable by pulling the cart back and forth and there were now enough seasoned logs for the winter as long as they didn't have every fire burning.

'What a good idea, I should have thought of that myself.'

'There will be a fire in your bedroom and Lady Harcourt's, my lady,' Daphne said. 'Joe and Liza said they didn't want one.'

Jean tipped boiling water into a large brown teapot. 'I'll get one of the girls to bring in your tea, my lady, and there's some lovely jam tarts to go with it this morning.'

The last of the coffee, sadly, was finished and Joanna doubted there would be any more until after the war was over.

'Thank you, that will be most welcome.' She returned to her sanctuary and this time, her dog did lumber to his feet in order to greet her with a slobbery kiss.

'Tea's on its way, Elizabeth. Even better, we're to have a fire in our bedrooms from now on. Charlie is bringing in the logs.'

'I should think so too. A lady of my age should not be obliged to dress under the blankets. Even Biggins said as much. At her previous employment, all rooms had a fire lit night and day.'

'There wasn't a fuel shortage or a war on, Elizabeth, things are different for everyone nowadays.'

Elizabeth was right, life was different and it was difficult for everyone with fuel shortages and rationing. They'd said the war would be over by Christmas 1939 and it was already 1941, with no sign of it stopping.

* * *

Charlie didn't like sitting around when she could be doing something useful. She'd been the first to volunteer to take down the paper decorations on Twelfth Night and now, two days later, was eager to be back at Fiddler's Farm.

All work had stopped, apart from at Brook Farm, which was all dairy, since the week before Christmas because of the fog, snow and sub-zero temperatures. Most of the girls had been given permission to go home to spend time with their families. Charlie had no family – well, to be more accurate, she had relatives but had no wish to be associated with any of them.

Fortunately, Daphne and Sal had remained at Goodwill House, too, so they'd had a jolly festive season with the Harcourt family. Dr Willoughby had been invited to Christmas lunch as he was on his own, as his loyal and hard-working housekeeper, as well as his maid of all work, had been given a few days' holiday.

Charlie was returning from dumping her fifth wheelbarrow full of rock-hard, cold logs outside the back door when Joe and Liza crunched up to her through the snow.

'You shouldn't be doing that on your own, Charlie. We'll help you. It'll warm us up a bit more after our freezing walk from the village,' Joe said.

'I just need two more loads and then I'll start taking it up to the bedrooms. What we really need is kindling to start the fires as these logs will be damp.'

Liza agreed. 'Leave the last two lots to my brother and we'll go in search of dry twigs and scraps of paper. We never had any sort of heating at home apart from the range in the kitchen and a small fire in the front room for high days and holidays – not that there were many of those.'

'The weather's being absolutely beastly at the moment. The only positive is that there's been a slight lull in the bombing,' Charlie said. 'I can't wait to get back to work, even if it's only pulling up brussels sprouts and clearing ditches.'

'Mr Kent said that someone told him that Manston's fully operational again. He said he'd heard there's going to be squadrons based there. That'll mean the Germans will start dropping bombs on it and we might well get one dropped on us by mistake,' Joe said, but he didn't seem particularly bothered by this grim news. 'Two years from now, I hope to be on a fighter squadron.'

Charlie sent a quick prayer to the Almighty that this wretched war might, by some miracle, be finished before he was old enough to volunteer.

On that cheerful note, he took the wheelbarrow from her and, whistling a lively tune she almost recognised, he vanished behind the barn, and she could hear him throwing logs from the pile into the wheelbarrow.

'Right, I found two log baskets and I've left them just inside the back door. Are you quite sure you want to help? *I* volunteered to do this.'

'Some of the lazy lumps drinking tea and playing cards in the kitchen should take a turn,' Liza said.

The two of them made so much noise that Sal and Daphne came out to join them and were only too happy to help. By the time lunch was ready, the five fires upstairs were laid and ready to light.

'Imagine, the luxury of having a warm bedroom tonight,' Daphne said as she blew on her cold fingers.

Charlie was distracted by what sounded like a large car arriving outside their window. She hurried across and rubbed the ice from the inside of the glass with her elbow so she could peer out.

'Goodness, it's not a civilian car, it's an army vehicle and imagine who's getting out?'

Her friends joined her. 'The only officer we know who comes here is Lord Harcourt,' Daphne said.

'That's what I thought, but we're both wrong. There are two very grand officers heading for the front door. Neither of the Lady Harcourts will be pleased to have their lunch interrupted. Let's open the door for them ourselves.'

The three of them pounded downstairs and skidded in an ungainly heap to a standstill in front of the door. It was so cold in the massive entrance hall, there seemed to be a film of ice on the parquet floor.

Whilst they were untangling themselves, one of the officers knocked loudly and authoritatively on the door. Daphne and Sal pushed Charlie forward.

She pulled the door open and greeted the two impressive gentlemen with what she hoped was a polite smile. 'Lady Harcourt is unavailable at the moment. Can I be of assistance, sir?'

'No, young lady, you can't.' The speaker, with a terrifying moustache, prepared to step around her. 'I'll speak to Lady Harcourt, and I'll find her for myself if necessary.'

Charlie was about to warn him that the floor was lethal but too late. He charged into the hall, his feet flew from under him, and he ended up on his backside in the centre of the hall.

The other officer had followed with equal disregard for courtesy and although he didn't lose his balance, he was in such a hurry, he stumbled headlong over his superior officer.

Sal was screaming with laughter; Daphne covered her ears as the language from the two floundering about on the parquet was appalling and Charlie was biting her lip. Someone really should try to remain composed. Then Lazzy, hearing the commotion, bounded in to join in the fun.

'No, bad boy, they don't need your help,' Charlie said despairingly but the dog ignored her entreaty and, barking loudly, jumped on top of the unfortunate officers, sending them sprawling for a second time.

The ruckus brought everyone else into the hall to see what was going on. Lady Harcourt and her mother-in-law, the other Lady Harcourt, appeared and stood, eyes wide and mouths open, viewing the ridiculous scene.

Then Joe stepped in, grabbed the dog's collar, and hauled him away. Once freed from the boisterous attentions of the mutt, the two very irate visitors managed to recover their feet but not their composure.

The moustachioed man straightened his uniform and glared at Lady Harcourt. 'Are you responsible for this outrage, madam? Do you know who I am?'

'No, sir, I do not. As you are uninvited guests to my house, and both your behaviour and language are unacceptable, I suggest you and your companion about turn and quick march out.'

The military references weren't lost on Lady Harcourt's audience and an appreciative ripple of amusement went around the hall for a second time which did nothing to improve the situation. Charlie thought both men might literally explode with rage.

'Young man,' the old Lady Harcourt said loudly, 'why did you come in here so rudely? What is it you want? Speak up or I'll set the dog on you again.'

This was hardly conciliatory, but it did the trick. The officer ran his finger around his collar, swallowed audibly, and then attempted a smile but failed miserably as it was more like a grimace.

'My ladies, I apologise for my language and my intemperate behaviour. Could I possibly have a moment of your time?' Surely this was when the two of them should have introduced themselves?

To Charlie's astonishment, Lady Harcourt the younger smiled charmingly and invited the two bad-tempered gentlemen to lunch. 'We are having a delicious vegetable pottage to be followed by game pie served with jacket potatoes. I believe there might be some sort of dessert as well.'

The mention of a hot, home-cooked lunch was enough to mollify these irascible officers and the two of them followed meekly, as if moments before they hadn't been yelling blue murder, leaving Charlie and her friends none the wiser as to why they'd come in the first place.

* * *

James, Dr Willoughby, the GP for Stodham village and the surrounding area, was holding his weekly surgery at his home. Miss Turnbull, a ferocious and determined lady of uncertain age, acted as his receptionist and guard dog.

'Good grief! It's absolutely packed out there. Start with the old chap, he was here last week complaining of abdominal pain. I'd better give him a thorough examination today.'

Miss Turnbull sniffed. 'If you spent less time cutting people open at the hospital in Ramsgate and more seeing your actual patients, Dr Willoughby, there wouldn't be so many people queueing up to see you today.'

This was a bone of contention between them, so he just nodded but didn't respond as it would only end up in an argument. He'd trained as a general surgeon but when his fiancée had left him for his best friend – who was also a surgeon at the same hospital – James had decided to move on and start again.

He'd bought this thriving general practice from the retiring GP as it was so close to the Royal Free. They had been delighted to add him to their rota, so he spent three days a week operating, one on his surgery and one doing home visits. Then, if there was an emergency at any time and he was available, he attended regardless of the hour or the day.

He'd been living in Stodham for five years and didn't regret the move. His lips curved as he thought of the lovely young lady who might just possibly be the one he'd been waiting for. Charlotte – known as Charlie – was a land girl and living at Goodwill House. He was more than a decade her senior, and this had made him hesitate, but she obviously reciprocated his interest and he was now paying court to her. He was taking things very slowly as she seemed nervous of any physical contact. He had a nasty suspicion she'd been hurt by some bastard and this had made her wary of all men.

The noise from the waiting room reminded him he had a very busy day ahead of him. No time for wishful thinking.

There was a small anteroom next to his surgery where he could wash his hands before starting. His receptionist poked her head around the door.

'The old codger refuses to undress.'

'Get his wife to help him – she was sitting next to him.'

There was the sound of scuffling in the surgery next door and he waited until all was quiet before stepping in. The wife was sitting, hands folded in her lap, on one of the two chairs against the wall. The old bloke was lying stark naked on the examination bed, his clothes neatly folded on the spare chair.

'How long has your husband had this pain?'

'Husband? I've never seen him before in me life.'

James wasn't often lost for words but for a moment he was unable to say anything sensible. 'I see. Thank you for your assistance, ma'am, but I'll take it from here.'

The old lady nodded, not at all embarrassed or put out, and let herself out into the waiting room.

He helped the old chap into his underpants before beginning his examination. After a few pertinent questions, he was confident of his diagnosis. Cecil Reynolds – he now knew his name – had a bowel obstruction and needed urgent surgery.

'Can you get yourself dressed, Mr Reynolds? I'm going to get my receptionist to call an ambulance.'

The old man nodded and with remarkable speed and agility for someone who'd needed to be undressed by a complete stranger a few minutes ago and was suffering from a bowel obstruction, he put on his clothes.

'I know, Doc, but I ain't been undressed by a woman for decades. Wasn't going to say no, now, was I?'

Miss Turnbull assisted the old chap into the small sitting room he kept for just such eventualities and kept an eye on him until the ambulance arrived.

It took James until mid-afternoon to empty the waiting room and he'd not even stopped for a cup of tea. He left Miss Turnbull to get everything ready for the next onslaught and made his way into the kitchen, where his housekeeper had a plate of rabbit stew waiting for him.

He told her about the amusing incident and they both laughed. 'Old Cecil's a bit of a card, but I'm surprised that Mrs Tiverton didn't quibble.'

'I suppose that when given an instruction, particularly at the moment, we just follow the orders without query. I apologised to her, but she just shrugged it off.'

He'd just finished his second helping when the telephone rang and Mary, his housekeeper, as always, hurried off to answer it.

'It's the hospital. They need you. I think it might be to operate on Mr Reynolds.'

'Let's hope I can get there without driving into a hedge. The roads are icy and the fog doesn't help.' The blackouts were pulled but he didn't need to look outside to know it would be almost dark already.

'You will be staying the night there, I assume, Doctor?'

'Obviously, I have a long list for tomorrow. Let's hope there are no babies or other emergencies in Stodham whilst I'm absent.'

2

Joanna was trying not to laugh as to do so would make the choleric major general even more angry. God knows what had possessed her to invite them for lunch, but it was all she'd been able to think of in order to smooth things over.

A major general was two ranks higher than a lieutenant colonel, so this was an important officer; his companion was the same rank as Peter, so it was inevitable that the two of them would know each other.

As Jean had been in the hall when Joanna had issued the invitation, there was no necessity to inform the kitchen. No doubt the land girls would be falling over each other to volunteer to act as waitresses and maybe overhear something interesting.

'As you can see, sir, we've suffered considerable bomb damage and have not been able to reglaze the drawing room windows.' She paused and gestured into the room. Normally the double doors were closed but as the hall itself was arctic, it really made little difference if they were open or shut.

'I'm sorry to hear that that, my lady. Lieutenant Colonel Benson will put in a requisition on our return.'

'That's so kind of you, Major General, but quite unnecessary. We don't have the fuel to heat the room at present. We use the drawing room in the summer months only.'

She hoped this slight delay had given Jean and Liza time to fling a cloth onto the table in the breakfast room. The fire had been lit that morning so it should be a lot more pleasant than the hall or passageways. She led them into the room where they were to eat luncheon and, as she'd hoped, it was laid and ready for the three of them to sit.

By the time they'd done so, Liza came in with the soup tureen on the trolley. They drank two bowls of this and then sat watching the arrival of the main course. The appetising aroma of game pie wafted from the plates and both gentlemen licked their lips in anticipation. The senior of the two strongly reminded her of Lazzy when the dog was fixed on someone eating in the hope that he might be given a morsel too.

There was little chitchat during the meal – Joanna because she had nothing to say but the men because they were too busy shovelling food into their mouths as if they'd not eaten for a month.

She wasn't going to ask the reason for their uninvited visit again and could only hope they would enlighten her soon. It had to be something to do with Lord Peter Harcourt, as she could think of no other reason for them to appear so suddenly. They would get around to telling her eventually.

Liza cleared away the dessert plates and replaced them with cups and saucers.

'I'm afraid we have no coffee and I'd rather do without than drink the disgusting chicory concoction that's available to replace it. Therefore, gentlemen, you must make do with tea.'

'I'll have some coffee sent to you, my lady, bound to be some knocking about at Horse Guards,' the major general offered.

Everything had been served on the best china, the set with the family coat of arms, and that included the tea service. After pouring them both a cup, Joanna added a slice of lemon to her own tea. She much preferred milk but wanted to keep up the façade of an aristocratic gentlewoman.

'Now, gentlemen, perhaps you could tell me why you're here?'

They exchanged glances and she thought that the lieutenant colonel might finally be going to speak but he remained silent and the other one answered.

'This is an enormous house, and we are hoping that even with the land girls staying here, you might have rooms to accommodate some visiting foreign dignitaries and an accompanying British officer.'

This was the last thing she'd expected to be asked. Goodwill House might be the largest house in the area, close to Manston and within fifty miles of several RAF bases, but it was cold and inhospitable and they would be far more comfortable staying in a hotel.

'I'm sorry? How can my being asked to house some extra guests be so urgent that you were prepared to drive from London in this appalling weather?' She stopped – of course they hadn't driven themselves, there must be an unfortunate ATS girl freezing to death outside waiting for them.

She stood up. 'Please excuse me for a moment, gentlemen, there's something I must attend to. I shall be back directly and you can explain exactly who it is you wish me to take in.'

The kitchen was at capacity, every chair along the central table occupied. She was pleased when she saw a lone ATS girl happily tucking into apple crumble. The girl jumped to her feet and saluted, which made Joanna smile.

'Good, I'm glad that you weren't left outside. Do you know if you're expected to drive them back in the dark?'

'Yes, ma'am, I am. Will my officers be ready to leave soon?'

'I'll send them out in half an hour. That will give you an hour of daylight and you should be able to get onto a main road by then.'

The two waiting impatiently in the breakfast room probably thought it was a call of nature that had caused her to leave them so abruptly and she'd no intention of enlightening them when she returned to the table.

'I apologise, gentlemen, you were about to explain who you wish me to accommodate and why?'

'Manston is crucial to our country's defence, my lady, as are all the other bases in Kent. Despite the dangers of travelling into a war zone, Americans are coming to England. These visitors wish to see for themselves how the money they are investing into our war effort is being spent.'

Joanna poured herself another cup of tea, which gave her a few moments to process this information. 'How many foreign dignitaries would you expect me to accommodate at one time and how often? Also, how much notice would we have of their arrival?'

Finally, Benson found his voice. 'We have two Americans arriving in London today and we would want you to offer your hospitality tomorrow. They would be staying for three nights whilst they tour the area. They will be accompanied by a senior officer, and they would all require accommodation – not forgetting the driver, of course.'

'The Americans would have to share a room. This is not an hotel, Lieutenant Colonel Benson. It is the family home of the Harcourts. I have twelve land girls here as I believe it's my patriotic duty to do so. Why do you wish them to stay at Goodwill House? There are excellent hotels in Ramsgate, Dover and Hastings that could look after them far better than we can.'

'They don't have aristocrats or houses like this in the States, my lady, and we wanted to give them the real experience.' He nodded enthusiastically before continuing, unaware that she wasn't impressed. 'The War Office will ensure that you have adequate fuel to heat all the rooms and also get the drawing room windows fixed as soon as possible. Extra rations will also be available so that your guests can dine well.'

'I see. To whom will I have my secretary send the invoice for this service? I can assure you that it won't be inexpensive as it will be putting us to a deal of inconvenience.'

The anonymous major general choked on his tea. Presumably he thought all the extras he was offering would be more than enough to compensate for any inconvenience. Joanna hid her smile behind her cup, knowing that they'd expected her to offer these visitors a luxurious stay mainly at her own expense. A few months ago, she would probably have done so – now she wasn't going to be manipulated into doing something she didn't want to do. It seemed it was acceptable for her and her household to freeze but two Americans must be made warm and comfortable.

'My lady, surely having your house repairs expedited and paid for, extra fuel provided and—'

'Lieutenant Colonel Benson, forgive me for interrupting you but having strangers, however important they might be to your department, foisted on the household is not something I want. Frankly, not having the drawing room windows done and extra fuel provided is preferable to hosting your diplomatic visitors.'

* * *

Charlie tucked into the game pie and joined in the general speculation about why these high-ranking officers had appeared so unexpectedly.

'The old bloke won't forget his arrival in a hurry,' Sal said through a mouthful of pie. 'I ain't laughed so much in years.'

'Sliding on his backside was undignified and then when the other one fell on top of him—' Daphne said gleefully.

Jill interrupted. 'I think Lazzy stole the show. That dog's priceless.'

'Girls, keep it down, please. They'll hear you in the breakfast room,' Jean said.

The ATS girl had joined them but was tight-lipped about why her superiors were visiting.

When the last delicious mouthful of crumble had been devoured, those on domestic duties remained behind to wash up and get the evening meal preparations started but the rest of them headed upstairs to light the fires and enjoy an afternoon of privacy and relative comfort.

The bedroom Charlie shared with Daphne and Sal was at the front of the house and was marginally colder than all the others. Sal put a match to the kindling and after sulking for few minutes, the damp logs began to burn. Each of the three rooms chosen had one basket of logs and one scuttle of coal. It wouldn't last for more than a few hours but should make the rooms bearable overnight.

Whilst they waited, the three of them wrapped a blanket around their shoulders and huddled together on one bed. The blackouts were drawn and this would help keep the heat in.

'Imagine what it'd be like if we'd agreed to go and live on the farm,' Daphne said as she shivered. 'There wasn't a fireplace in the bedroom we'd have had.'

'I'm glad you didn't even consider it,' Charlie said. 'It wouldn't be the same here without my two best friends. Did I tell you James has invited me to Sunday lunch? After church, of course.'

'Blimey, that's somethink, ain't it?'

'Of course, if he's called away to the hospital or another local emergency then I won't be going. He's a surgeon as well as a GP and that means he's on call all the time. I'm not sure getting serious about him would be a good idea as I'd never see him.'

'I don't see my Bob for more than an hour or so at a time and then only every few weeks,' Daphne said. 'Some women haven't seen their husbands since the war started and at least your doctor isn't risking his life every day.'

'That's true. I did ask him why he hadn't volunteered and he said he preferred to do his bit in Blighty. That's why he works such long hours and so on.'

Charlie shuffled across to the fire, making sure she didn't tread on the blanket as she did so. After adding a few lumps of coal and poking the logs, she sat back, satisfied the fire was doing well.

'I reckon it's warm enough to take these off, don't you?' Sal said and promptly removed her blanket and spread it back on her bed. At the moment they needed at least four blankets plus their land girl mackintosh to help keep warm at night.

'I wonder what those officers wanted with Lady Harcourt? I think I heard them leave just now,' Charlie said as she pulled her woolly covering closer.

'I expect someone will know by tomorrow. Shall we play I Spy?'

'It's not warm enough to sit at the table and play cards. Shall I go down and make us a cocoa? I'm sure Jean won't object,' Daphne said.

'No, you stop there, Daphne, I'm already unwrapped. I'll do it.' Sal dashed off, not even bothering to put on her gloves, scarf, or the dressing gown Jean had made her.

'Have you told the doctor about what happened to you, Charlie?'

'No, of course I haven't. Telling a man I hardly know, who I'm already finding rather attractive, I was raped isn't on. I'll have to if things change, but at the moment we're little more than good friends. He's so much older than me and sometimes I feel like his little sister rather than a potential wife.'

'He's a medical man, I'm sure he's picked up on your not liking to be touched. Unless you tell him why, things will never move on. I suppose you want them to, do you?'

Charlie was quiet for a moment, deciding on her answer carefully. 'When I was forced to stay at his house with concussion last summer, I got to know him really well and thought there might be something between us, then when he ignored me afterwards, I assumed I'd imagined it. Only after I was shot and ended up in hospital did he begin to show any real interest in me.'

'Imagine getting close because a Nazi shot you in the leg. Not very romantic,' Daphne said. 'You didn't answer my question. A few moments ago, you seemed a bit lukewarm about him – is that because you know being married involves sharing the same bed?'

'I think it might be. Being raped by my cousin certainly put me off all men. James is different, gentle, not in any way threatening or predatory. He's also handsome, a doctor and exactly the sort of man I imagined one day I might marry.'

'So he could be the one you've been waiting for?'

'I think he might be.'

Charlie leapt to her feet, shedding her blanket and then twirling it around her head.

The trailing ends swept several items off the chest of drawers and both she and Daphne were on their knees recovering them – fortunately, nothing had been broken – when Sal shouldered her way in clutching a tray with three steaming mugs of cocoa.

'Blimey! What's going on here?'

Charlie looked up, smiling. 'I just had an epiphany and, in my excitement, I sent several things flying.'

'Epiphany? Ain't that something they have in the Bible?'

'It is, Sal, but I'm using it to try and explain how I felt when I understood what I wanted.' She scrambled up and replaced the last few bits and pieces to where they should have been. Daphne had put both blankets back on their respective beds.

'I'm in love with James and I rather think he might feel the same way. Next time I see him, I'm going to explain about what happened. I hope it doesn't mean he wants nothing more to do with me.'

Her friends looked at her as if she was speaking a foreign language.

'It weren't your fault, Charlie. It's not like what I did with Den. I lived in sin with that bastard for a year. I'm damaged goods now and I don't reckon any decent man would look twice in my direction.' Sal spilt some of the cocoa as she put the brimming mugs down on the tiles that surrounded the fireplace.

Charlie hugged her. 'Don't be ridiculous, what's in the past is gone. I don't see why you even have to mention it if ever you want to get serious with another chap.'

'Ta ever so for saying that. I'm not looking for a fella, I like being me own boss. If you marry the doc, will you carry on working?'

'Good heavens, that's a long way in the future if it happens at all. Thank you for bringing up the cocoa – let's enjoy it whilst it's hot. Our bedroom's heating up wonderfully. I honestly don't want to venture out into the freezing house again today. I think I'll forgo supper.'

'No need, Charlie, it's the soup we had for lunch with toast and dripping. Jean said she's putting it on trays, and we can fetch it at six o'clock.'

'I'll go down next time, Sal,' Daphne volunteered.

'I ain't bothered about the cold. Now, I know why them blokes came. I'll tell you, shall I?'

* * *

James had scarcely slept for three days as there had been one emergency after another. The senior surgeon was away on his Christmas break, which had left him in charge. Eventually, he drove home on Saturday, determined to catch up on his rest before Charlie came for lunch the next day.

Mary knew the drill, food first, then a bath and then bed. Whilst he gobbled down a heaped plate of stew, she brought him up to speed on local news.

'The blooming Germans are at it again. Never mind the fog and freezing weather, they came in and dropped bombs on Manston this morning. Imagine! Just five days after Twelfth Night and it's started.'

'Any casualties?' None had been brought in for him to deal with and surgical cases always came to the hospital. The sick bay on the base couldn't deal with more than minor cuts, bruises and sniffles.

'No, they were lucky. Vera's boy works in the kitchens and he was here not an hour ago, full of it.'

He thought Vera was a WI friend of Mary's but he'd never met nor heard of any son. As to why the young man had called in to regale his housekeeper with the news, he'd no idea and was too damn tired to ask.

She continued to talk while he ate and listened.

'The Bf 109s dropped two bombs from ever so low. One bounced along the runway before exploding. The Lewis guns got one of the German blighters and only an old Spitfire was damaged.'

She paused and waited for him to comment. 'That's good.'

'A new squadron arrived from Biggin Hill on Thursday. I expect there'll be bombs going astray very likely, now the base's operational, and we'll get one dropped on us.'

He scraped the last of the gravy from his plate and dropped his cutlery. 'I think it unlikely, but we have a perfectly good Morrison shelter in the kitchen for our use.' He stood up, needing the support of the table to do so, he was so tired. 'Thank you, Mary, that was delicious as always. I'm going to bathe and sleep. I don't want to know if there's an emergency. I'd be more likely to kill a patient than help them at the moment.'

'The members of St John Ambulance Brigade take care of all the minor complaints whilst you're busy at the hospital. Is Miss Somiton still coming for lunch tomorrow? I need to attend the eight o'clock communion service or evening prayers if she is.'

'I bloody well hope so. It's that that has kept me going the past three nights.' James rarely swore but after three gruelling days and most of the nights, too, he was shattered and didn't even have the energy to apologise for his slip of the tongue.

He'd love to have the water up to his chin, to luxuriate in it, lie back and relax for half an hour but with only the regulation five inches, it was too cold to hang about. He was lucky to have a bath at all, indoor plumbing was rare in Stodham.

He ducked his head into the bath water and gave it a swirl about. That would have to do. He was too fagged to bother with soap. He shook his head like a dog emerging from a pond, gave it a cursory rub with an already wet towel and tugged on his pyjamas. They clung to his damp skin and he was cold just dashing across the passageway to his bedroom.

There was a fire, which was a bonus. Mary had drawn the blackouts and put two hot water bottles into his bed. He tumbled in, kicked the bottles out onto the lino, and was asleep in seconds.

* * *

He was woken next morning by the sound of rattling crockery as Mary put down his early-morning tea on the bedside table.

'Good morning, Doctor, the weather's still miserable, but at least it hasn't snowed again. There's hot water in the jug for you to shave.'

The temperamental boiler in the cellar that heated the hot water was only lit a couple of times a week. The rest of the time, he washed in cold or if he was lucky, Dolly, the maid, provided him with a jug of hot water.

'Thanks, did the siren go off last night?'

Mary shook her head. 'It didn't, I doubt I could have woken you if it had, so that's a good thing. Breakfast will be ready in half an hour.'

James had a spring in his step this morning. He ignored the ache across his shoulders, the heaviness of his legs having stood for so long at the operating table, and bounded down the stairs whistling 'Fools Rush In', a recent ditty by Glenn Miller. Today was to be a turning point in his pursuit of Charlie. After lunch, he intended to tell her how he felt and prayed her reaction would be favourable.

3

Joanna had made the point about expecting a substantial payment for having foreign dignitaries staying in the hope that the officers would change their minds. A year ago, she'd been asked to host a French family and that hadn't been at all enjoyable, even though it had proved lucrative.

The major general had, to her surprise, acquiesced to her terms, so now she was committed to having unwanted diplomats living in the house. The first contingent would arrive sometime Monday. This gave Jean only one day to arrange things. She, Jean, Liza, and Elizabeth congregated in the small sitting room to discuss how things would work.

'Will their driver eat with the land girls?' Jean asked.

'Yes, I assume that's how the protocol works. Americans are used to central heating, have no rationing or blackouts at home. I fear they won't be impressed with Goodwill House.'

Elizabeth had been listening avidly. She was the only member of the household excited by the prospect of having these unwanted people staying. 'They will have to use the study as their drawing room. They cannot share this room as it is far too small.'

'Jean, the driver can use the spare room on the nursery floor. Let's hope it's a female driver as I wouldn't dream of foisting a man on you and Biggins.'

Joe and Liza had occupied this floor when they'd first come to live with her and had always referred to these rooms on the third floor as 'the attics'. The attics were, obviously, on the floor above.

'That means more work, more fires to lay and clear. Joe has cycled into Stodham to see if Aggie and her chums will agree to brave the elements. Hopefully, with the enticement of extra wages, they will come to help.' Joanna had been very generous in her offer.

An extra pound a week to each one of them was more than she received from each girl for their board and lodging. In fact, as only three of the girls were still paying anything at all, it was fortunate she was now a relatively wealthy woman.

The house shook as fighters roared overhead and Joanna waited, holding her breath, for the wail from the siren, but it remained silent.

'Goodness, what if there's an air-raid whilst they're here? Having all of us, plus the land girls and then three strange men and another girl in the shelter in the cellars won't be fun.'

Liza did a rapid mental calculation. 'That's fourteen girls, Ma, four adult women, one boy and three men. If it's during the day, add another three women as Aggie, Doris and Edith will be here as well. We can't fit so many in that cellar.'

'Silly girl,' Elizabeth said. 'During the day our American visitors will be elsewhere.'

'Course they will, Grandma, they're hardly going to hang around here when they've come to see Manston and the other bases.'

'When and where will they eat, Joanna? Do I have to do something special for them or do they eat whatever we're having?' Jean had her notebook and pencil at the ready.

'The amount the War Office is paying, they will expect a three-course dinner. They can eat in the breakfast room, we'll eat in the kitchen after the girls have finished.'

'I have no wish to dine in the kitchen, Joanna,' Elizabeth said firmly.

'It's only for three nights, Elizabeth. There's a war on, we all have to make sacrifices.'

'At least it's warm in there,' Jean said.

'Thank goodness there's ample wine in the cellar. After half a bottle each, I'm sure they won't really mind what they get. I wonder if Rose would mind going up to the dairy and getting cream, butter and milk,' Joanna said hurriedly, relieved her mother-in-law had given in so easily.

'As she's living here free, Ma, she can't complain. I'll go and tell her, shall I?'

'No, darling, I'll do it. I have to get some of the other girls to prepare the rooms. If the driver's a man, then he'll have to be in a room adjacent to the Americans. Let's hope they don't complain.'

Instead of asking for volunteers as she usually did, Joanna selected two girls to do the cleaning and make up the beds. Sandra and Joyce worked at Whitehouse Farm and were lazy, so these were her choice.

'You're living here free of charge at the moment, and I've noticed that neither of you has been pulling your weight. I suggest that you do so, otherwise I can assure you that you will both be leaving here at the end of next week.'

The girls didn't look at her but were on their feet and heading for the butler's pantry where the cleaning materials were stored before she'd finished speaking. That was one problem solved.

'Jill, I wish you to have a supervisory role. If you would be kind enough to take the necessary bed linens and towels, check exactly what needs doing to make the rooms immaculate and tell the other two what's expected.'

'Yes, my lady, I'll be happy to. It's about time Sandra and Joyce did their share. I'll fill up as many hot water bottles as I can find and put them in their beds once they're made. Shall I light the fires?'

'Yes, the rooms have been unoccupied for several weeks and will be cold and damp.'

Joe returned with good news. 'Aggie and Doris will be here tomorrow morning and Edith will do the afternoon and early evening shift.'

'That's excellent news. You appear to be unscathed – I take it you didn't fall off your bicycle.'

He grinned. 'No, Ma, all tickety-boo. It's perishing out there but there've been enough buses back and forth to flatten the snow and I just stuck to the tyre tracks.'

Yet another squadron of fighters screamed over the house, making conversation impossible. There was a lot of activity on the base today and the relative peace of the past few weeks had come to an end. Manston had been so badly damaged last year it had been all but abandoned.

Joanna still hadn't solved the conundrum of how to fit so many people into the shelter in the event of an air-raid. Perhaps the men could sit outside the door – it would be a lot colder – but just as safe as being inside the converted cellar.

In the evening, she inspected the three rooms and was delighted with their appearance. Sandra and Joyce had done a splendid job. The rosewood and walnut furniture was polished to a high shine, a fire burned merrily in each grate, the best monogrammed sheets had been put on the beds and the towels were hanging neatly on the rail by the sink. The only thing that was missing was a fresh bar of soap for each of them.

She just had to hope they brought their own with them as there wasn't any available in the shops even for her. It wouldn't be right if her rank and wealth gave her things ordinary people couldn't access. Going to church tomorrow morning wasn't something she was looking forward to, but walking with all the girls, as well as Jean and her children, would make the journey slightly more enjoyable. Elizabeth remained at home with Biggins, and Mr Evans, the vicar, visited when he could to conduct an informal service for the two of them.

Liza and Joe had been spending their evenings in the kitchen with the land girls but now fires had been lit in some of the bedrooms, the girls retired upstairs after supper. Elizabeth also went up early as she too had warmth in her room.

This meant the twins were with her listening to ITMA – *It's That Man Again* – and she loved having them close. They were growing up too fast and Joe was constantly talking about joining the RAF and Liza about becoming a nurse, even though they still had another two years before being able to do either. She was dreading the day when they were old enough to leave home and do their bit for the war effort.

'Ma,' Liza said, 'Charlie's having lunch at the doc's house tomorrow after church. I think there might be something going on between them after all.'

* * *

Charlie had been looking forward to Sunday all week. But now she and the rest of the girls were crunching their way down the road to the church, she was having second thoughts. She was almost sure she had feelings for James and that he felt the same way about her, but she wasn't sure she was ready to begin a relationship with any man, even one as charming and attractive as James.

Five years ago, she'd been relatively happy, helping to run a prosperous and efficient farm for her uncle. She had two cousins, one, Nigel, two years younger than her and away at university, and the other a year older, William, who would be taking over the farm when Uncle Richard eventually retired.

She'd trusted William implicitly – they worked well together, and she hadn't thought twice when he'd asked her to help him with some paperwork in the farm office one summer afternoon. Even when he'd locked the door, she'd not realised his intentions. She'd screamed, kicked, done everything she could to hold him off, but he was twice her weight and was able to force himself on her.

Instead of taking her side, acting against the monster who'd raped her, her family had sent her away in disgrace. Since then, she'd avoided any sort of contact with men, which was why she was so happy working with just girls. Now she'd agreed to have Sunday lunch with James at his house – they would sit side by side in church this morning and leave together – making it clear to the entire village that they were more than just friends.

She stumbled and only Sal's quick reaction stopped her from falling. 'Blimey, that were a close one. You okay? Not having second thoughts about this lunch?'

'I am, but I can't let what happened ruin my life. I'm going to tell him today and depending on his reaction, things will either end or we'll...' She wasn't exactly sure what would happen and a small part of her almost wished he would reject her and then she'd not have to make such a difficult decision.

'Don't worry about it, Charlie, look what happened with Bob. I thought I didn't love him but realised that I did. I think it'll be the same for you. Thinking about it too much will only make things harder for you.' Daphne slipped her arm through hers and Sal linked up on the other side so they were walking three abreast.

'Thank you, both of you, I don't know what I'd do without my friends.' They were now approaching the churchyard and there was a steady stream of people, young, old, and also children, as the younger ones had returned from their evacuation in Norfolk.

'It doesn't seem right not having the church bell ringing to welcome us. I hope the next time we hear it, it isn't to announce that Hitler's invading,' Daphne said.

'That won't happen now our boys in blue have driven the Luftwaffe away,' Charlie said. 'Prime Minister Churchill called it the Battle of Britain and said that the RAF had saved us. But what a dreadful loss of lives. I know that Lady Harcourt was very upset a few weeks ago when she heard one of the WAAF who had lived here had lost her husband and another one's husband was missing.'

'Shocking, I'm so glad that Bob's ground crew,' Daphne said as they reached the church. The two friends walked in ahead of Charlie as James was waiting in the porch for her.

'Good morning, Charlie, shall we go in? I can't feel my extremities.'

'Sorry, I didn't realise I was late.'

His smile was warm. 'You aren't, I was early.'

She felt everybody was looking at her with the doctor and making possibly incorrect assumptions. They slipped into a pew at the rear of the church, the closest he could get to the exit, and she smiled her thanks.

'We can make a rapid retreat, avoid the cross-examination.' He spoke softly so only she could hear him. 'I've been avoiding predatory mothers and their daughters ever since I arrived here five years ago.'

'Shush, James, someone might hear you. We've come here to

pay our respects to the Almighty, so shall we leave that sort of conversation until afterwards?' She regretted her words as she sounded like someone twice her age. She glanced nervously at him, expecting him to be cross with her.

'Point taken. However, I shall hold you to your word and we shall have that conversation.'

The familiarity of the morning service, the repetition of the words she knew by heart calmed Charlie and when he put his arm gently around her waist to guide her out, she didn't flinch away as she usually did.

The vicar thanked them for coming but made no further comment. James's house was on the outskirts of Stodham, in the same direction the entire party from Goodwill House would be going. She really didn't want to be sniggered and smiled at by any of them.

'Shall we hurry? That mackintosh doesn't look nearly warm enough and I don't want you to get cold. I intend to drive you back home. Lady Harcourt has now given me access to her petrol, so I'm able to use my car as often as I want.'

He kept his arm firmly around her waist and increased his speed. She didn't quite have to run to keep pace with him but without his support she would probably have gone flying on her backside more than once.

When they arrived at his house, Charlie was breathless, but lovely and warm. He opened the door and stood aside to let her go in first. She knew the house well, having stayed there for two weeks when she'd been concussed last summer.

James took her mac, gloves, scarf and hideous hat and put them in the closet. 'It's wonderfully warm in here. The problem with living in a stately home is that more than half of it is as cold as it is outside. I doubt that I'll want to go home.'

'I'm hoping, my dear, that one day I can persuade you to make *this* your home.'

* * *

James had just blurted out the one thing he'd intended to keep to himself until after lunch. He waited for her to snatch back her coat and make a run for it.

'Is that an offer to take me in as a paying guest or a roundabout way of proposing marriage?' She stood in front of him, her face still rosy from the cold. She'd never looked lovelier. She raised an eyebrow and was obviously enjoying his discomfort.

'I'd happily drop down on one knee and make the proposal official if I thought you would accept me. I'm sorry, Charlie, I didn't mean to put you in such a difficult position before you'd eaten your lunch.'

'So, it'll be perfectly acceptable to embarrass me after lunch? That's fine by me. I can smell something delicious and I'm absolutely ravenous.' This was a side of her he'd not seen before – he was intrigued and somewhat surprised by her reaction but not downhearted.

'Then we shall eat. Mary insisted that we eat in the dining room, although I'd much prefer to do so in the kitchen – such a waste of fuel.' He'd only agreed to this extravagance because he'd moved two armchairs from the sitting room so they could remain in there, therefore two rooms didn't have to be heated.

Her delightful laugh echoed in the passageway. 'How incredibly unromantic of you, James. I've come here not only for an excellent Sunday lunch but also to be possibly swept off my feet and persuaded to do something I really don't want to do.' Hopefully he'd know she was joking, as he understood her so well.

The dining room door was open. The table was resplendent

with a snowy white tablecloth, silver cutlery, and there was an impressive silver candelabra at one end which he didn't even know he owned. It was also considerably warmer than the corridor.

'This looks quite wonderful. Mary has certainly gone to town with the table.'

'If you take the seat closest to the fire then I'll sit opposite.'

They were scarcely settled when Dolly staggered in with an assortment of matching terrines and dishes. His instinct was to stand up and assist her, but he refrained as the girl hated to be helped as if somehow this made her less efficient. She was from a poor home and terrified of being sent back there. The maid slid the tray onto the sideboard and then began to bring over each item.

'There's roast potatoes in this one, carrots and sprouts in this, mash in that dish, and these are the Yorkshire puddings.'

'Thank you, it all looks and smells absolutely wonderful,' Charlie said and the girl beamed as if she was actually responsible for the cooking.

A piping hot dinner plate was placed in front of them and then the girl dashed off to fetch the pièce de resistance – whatever roasted meat was being served today. Presumably if there were Yorkshire puddings then it should be beef, but meat rationing meant it was almost impossible to get a joint of any size.

To James's astonishment, Mary came in triumphantly bearing a silver salver upon which a splendid joint of topside sat.

'I thought you'd want to carve yourself, sir, so have brought it in for you to do.'

'I don't know how you managed this miracle, Mary, but thank you. I've done more than enough carving in the past few days so if you'd be so kind, would you do it for us?'

Mary just nodded but Charlie looked a little shocked at his

casual reference to his surgeries as being similar to cutting meat. He must be more careful in future.

When his housekeeper was about to leave the joint, he shook his head. 'You and Dolly eat now whilst it's still hot.'

The beef was succulent, slightly rare, which was how he liked it, and with extra gravy, the pair of them emptied every receptacle on the table. He loved to see a girl with a healthy appetite.

'We've been very greedy, James, I do hope I can manage to eat whatever dessert Mary has prepared for us.'

'Don't worry, I'll go and speak to her. Whatever it is, it will be just as good eaten at tea as for lunch. However, I do have a rare treat for you.'

'Chocolate or coffee?'

'Both. I was at the base last week doing a bit of minor repairs to some RAF chaps and obviously I make no charge. The wing commander insisted on paying me in kind.'

'My two favourite things – as I think I've told you several times before – and a perfect ending to an absolutely spiffing luncheon.'

The two comfortable upholstered armchairs were placed on either side of the fire and he gestured towards them.

'Pity to waste all this lovely warmth, so we're staying in here. Ignore the debris on the table.'

'I'll do no such thing. I don't like being waited on as if I'm someone special. Let's pile everything back on the tray and then you can return it to the kitchen and collect the coffee.' She looked around the room and spotted the box of Mackintosh's Quality Street he'd put on a side table.

'Goody, my absolute favourites. I know sweets aren't rationed yet, but the local shops never have anything apart from small bars of chocolate and I much prefer something with a filling.'

Whilst she was speaking, she'd got up and had already stacked half the empty dishes on the tray. She might not like being waited on, but she certainly enjoyed giving instructions. He intended to find out everything there was to know about her background, and he would tell her anything she cared to know about his.

'Coffee – an entire jug full. I also have sugar and cream but I'm not sure if you take either.'

'Cream but no sugar, thank you. I can't tell you how much I am enjoying today. I've been looking forward to it ever since you were kind enough to invite me.'

He was about to respond but saw she had something else to say so waited.

'I need to get this out of the way,' Charlie said. 'Please would you sit down and promise not to interrupt until I've finished.'

'You don't have to tell me anything you don't want to, sweetheart, I really don't care about your past – it's your future I'm interested in.'

He listened, unsurprised by her horrific revelation. His overriding feeling was that it was fortunate the rapist was already behind bars for life, or he'd have gone in search of him. He'd suspected this to be the case and was glad she'd had the courage to tell him something so painful.

'That was so brave of you, darling, and I'd more or less guessed this was why you're nervous around me. I'm a medical man, I understand that sort of thing. I love you and want to marry you, but I won't pressure you into doing anything you're not comfortable with. I'm prepared to wait as long as it takes.'

'I love you, too, and I promise that one day I will be ready but not just yet.' She swallowed and rummaged for her hanky.

He wanted to snatch her up, hold her close, wipe away her tears, but they had the rest of their lives for that. Now he would be happy just to know that eventually Charlie would marry him and become his true wife.

4

Joanna had expected a telephone call from the War Office giving her the names of her VIP guests and the officer who would be escorting them. It would also have been helpful to know exactly when they were expected to arrive. The weather was still most unpleasant, but as the fog lifted mid-morning, it would make it somewhat easier for whoever was driving them from London to Stodham.

Elizabeth had made a particular effort with her appearance this morning – or it would be more accurate to say that Biggins had done so.

'You look very smart, Elizabeth, every inch the lady of the manor. I think midcalf is the perfect length for you. Is that ensemble silk?'

'Naturally, my dear, what else would it be? Surely you're not going to welcome our prestigious visitors in slacks and a twinset?'

'I certainly am. This house is perishing and it's far warmer in slacks than it is in a skirt and stockings. Comfort comes first in my opinion. Anyway, I didn't invite them and I don't need to impress them.'

Joe burst into the sitting room, beaming. 'A load of coal has just arrived. The coal cellar's chock-a-block and I had to get the coalmen to put the rest in the Dutch barn. We can have fires everywhere now.'

'How splendid – I knew this was a good idea, Joanna. Joe, would you organise fires in the ballroom and the grand hall?'

He looked at Joanna and she nodded. After all, the fuel was for the benefit of the visitors and it would be mean-spirited of her not to make the house more pleasant.

'I'll get some of the other girls involved. That misery, Sandra, and her shadow, Joyce, have been falling over themselves to offer help. Wonder why that is?' He grinned – knowing full well the two of them had been threatened with eviction.

'It's eleven o'clock. It will take several hours to get the house really warm but with any luck they won't arrive until mid-afternoon. Have you no lessons today, Joe?' asked Joanna.

'Mr Kent rang from the village to say he was under the weather and not to come until the end of the week. We've got plenty to get on with, but lighting fires is more important.'

'I expect a lorry will turn up any day now with the glass for the drawing room, Joanna. We could then use it again.'

Joanna was about to point out how cold the drawing room was even with both fires lit when her mother-in-law continued.

'But I prefer the sitting room in this sort of weather. Why don't you see if you can get the boiler fixed and then we can have the radiators working? I can't tell you how pleasant it was having the entire house habitable in the winter.'

'There's a shortage of spare parts for any boilers or machines and our central heating must come very low on the list of priorities. However, I will speak to the charming Wing Commander Butterfield at the base and see if he's got any suggestions.'

Joanna had no intention of contacting anyone about the central heating. Others were living with almost nothing and they would be considered to be living in the lap of luxury. To ask for anything extra would be unpatriotic.

* * *

The Bentley arrived just as it was getting dark. The house was now perfectly pleasant everywhere including the grand hall. The girls were overjoyed to have their recreation space back and the sound of music being played on the record player, laughter and loud voices made the house seem happier somehow.

Edith had agreed to live in whilst the visitors were here so that she could answer the door, fetch and carry as necessary. It's what Americans would expect of an English stately home, after all.

The breakfast room was ready, suitably accoutred, and her guests would be offered afternoon tea now and a splendid three-course dinner at seven o'clock. Claret had already been decanted and would be perfect by then.

Joanna had arranged with Edith that the visitors would be escorted to the sitting room and announced formally. This would make it easier as then she and Elizabeth would actually know their names.

All three women from the village had agreed to wear the black dresses, white aprons and frilly hats that had been the official uniform for staff in David's time. Joanna wasn't comfortable with it, but the ladies had been happy to join in the pretence as they knew they would be back in their wraparound pinnies and turbans as soon as the Americans departed.

Joanna realised something was wrong when Edith arrived at the door looking flustered. She was already standing, as was Elizabeth, to greet the visitors formally.

'My lady, Mr Ronald Lynch, Mr Larry Randall and Lieutenant Colonel Harcourt.'

Joanna's fists clenched. It had been almost three months since she'd seen Peter Harcourt and having him under her roof again was the most hideous of coincidences. She straightened, pinned on a polite smile and greeted her unwelcome guests.

'Gentlemen, I hope your journey wasn't too tiresome. Allow me to present my mother-in-law, Lady Elizabeth Harcourt. I'll have someone conduct you to your rooms immediately and then tea will be served in the breakfast room.'

She didn't offer her hand and this might seem impolite to the Americans but she had no wish to have any physical contact at all with Peter.

'Thank you for allowing us into your magnificent home, my lady, we appreciate it,' Mr Lynch said. She expected him to say *gee* or *sure thing*, or to have a very distinctive drawl, but he sounded just like an Englishman. He was a little older than herself, immaculately dressed in a cashmere coat if she wasn't mistaken, and looked very wealthy indeed. Even his cufflinks were solid gold. Did he know what she'd been thinking? His companion looked less impressed and said nothing at all.

She ignored Peter and he made no attempt to speak to her. The three gentlemen would be dining without her and Elizabeth for company – this had been a decision she'd made earlier and was now glad that she had. Being obliged to spend an evening with a man she detested would have been excruciating.

* * *

Charlie had decided to cycle to Fiddler's Farm in order to discover if she and her friends were wanted, but Joe suggested she rode Star as the mare would find it easier picking her way through the frozen snow. After the wonderful day she'd spent with James yesterday, she was bristling with energy and wanted to burn some of it off by working.

'As I'm already wearing jodhs, I don't even have to change. Thank you, Joe, I'll take up your offer. I've not ridden for a few years but I'm sure I'll have no difficulty.'

'I'll get her ready, Charlie, if you like.'

'Shall we do it together? Have you met the American gentlemen yet?'

'They seem all right. I think Ma isn't happy that Lord Harcourt has accompanied them. They fell out last year and he's not been mentioned since. I've no idea what it was all about but if my mother doesn't like him then neither do I.'

'I can't tell you how thrilled we girls are that Lady Harcourt agreed to do this. If she hadn't, we'd all be freezing and now we've got lovely warm bedrooms, can walk about the place without our coats on and have our ballroom back for the evenings.'

'I think if she'd known that Lord Harcourt would be coming, she'd have refused to do it even for the extra fuel.'

'I wonder what happened to cause the rift? Sorry, it's absolutely none of my business.'

Joe nodded. 'Better not to ask.'

Charlie enjoyed the ride to the farm and the pretty grey mare didn't put a foot wrong. She was somewhat disconcerted to find that the farmyard still needed the deep snow to be cleared and there was only a narrow path leading from the house to the buildings where the livestock were housed.

She dismounted from Star and led her into an empty stall next to the huge shire horses. They were old friends so greeted each other enthusiastically. She didn't bother to untack, just loosened the girth and left her mount to pick at the hay in the manger.

It was a relief to see the horses were content, fresh water in their buckets and plenty of sweet-smelling hay for them to eat. They'd obviously been mucked out that morning.

She walked across to the farmhouse and saw a curtain twitch and the back door opened before she got there.

'Just the girl I want to see! Wait there, I'll get my boots and coat on and come out and join you, Charlie,' Mr Pickering said with a broad smile.

'I'll be in the barn. I rode over.'

'Good show, I'll not be a tick.'

He was true to his word and arrived a few minutes later.

'I know you said not to come until the weather improved, but I think there's a lot we can still do for you.'

'The missus wanted to save the wages and said she'd help out but it's too much for her. She's in the family way again. We're expecting another little one in the summer.'

'Oh, congratulations to you both. We'll be here first thing tomorrow. Shall we start on clearing the yard?'

'You do that, I'll take care of the cows and pigs and you three can do the chickens and horses. Can you take the deliveries to the village before doing the yard?'

'We'll have to clear a path to get the tractor through before we do anything else. I suppose there haven't been any deliveries. I wonder how they've managed in the village.'

'Brook Farm supply the village – people just buy from me because I'm cheaper,' Mr Pickering said. 'I've been making butter with the milk and feeding the whey to the livestock. Nothing gets wasted.'

'What about the eggs?'

'There aren't that many this time of the year, so we've been eating them ourselves. Don't suppose the Ministry of Agriculture would approve but too late for them to poke their noses in.'

'We'll be here as usual at first light. Congratulations again on your forthcoming event.'

Charlie collected the mare from the stall, tightened the girth, and swung into the saddle. She risked a brisk jog down the drive but thought it would be safer to remain at an extended walk on the hard surface of the country road.

When she got back to Goodwill House, Joe was messing about in the barn and insisted on seeing to the horse himself. 'The Yanks have gone to visit Manston. Ma said they'll probably come back for lunch and that wasn't included in the arrangement. She's not too pleased.'

'They can have soup and spam and piccalilli sandwiches like us. We're back to work tomorrow and I can't wait – I'm not sure Sal and Daphne will be as pleased as I am, but I just hate being idle.' For the first time, possibly in her entire life, she was feeling optimistic about the future, despite that fact that they were in the middle of a terrible war. Becoming closer to James was the reason and not even icy weather could take that happiness away.

'I'll check your bikes, Charlie, they've not been used for a bit.'

* * *

The following morning, the three of them pedalled cautiously down the slippery drive and out onto the less perilous road. They arrived without mishap, but they were horribly cold. The inadequate mac had done nothing to keep out the icy air and even with two scarves, one wrapped around her head, and gloves on, Charlie's teeth were chattering.

'Let's hope clearing snow will warm us up, girls, as otherwise by the end of today, we're all going to be suffering from hypothermia. I've got on a vest, liberty bodice, both my shirts and my jumper under these dungarees and I'm still chilled to the marrow.'

'We're getting soft, that's the trouble,' Sal said cheerfully as she propped her bike against the wall in the barn. 'We've been living in luxury with all them fires everywhere, not that I'm complaining, mind, but it makes being out blooming hard. I reckon we'll all have chilblains.'

'The manual we were given says we've got to exercise our toes and fingers whenever possible,' Daphne said. 'Surely our toes and fingers are being exercised continually when we're at work. The remedy's menthol mixed with olive oil – I don't suppose either of those things are available.'

'Clearing the snow so we can get the tractor and trailer out of the barn should warm us up a bit. I hope you all put your spare socks on inside your gumboots.' Charlie was relieved they'd done the same as her.

Mr Pickering didn't come out to see if they were following his instructions, but she supposed he was inside getting breakfast after having milked the cows and done everything necessary in the dairy earlier.

After an hour of backbreaking work, the three of them leaned on their shovels and admired the pathway they'd made.

'Just the ticket – I ain't driving that blooming tractor after what happened last time,' Sal said.

'I should think not, I don't think that poor postman will ever recover from having his van towed backwards down the High Street,' Daphne said, laughing.

'Are all three of us going into the village?'

'No, if you and Sal go, Charlie, I'll get on with the horses,' Daphne said.

'If you don't mind, Daphne, that sounds like a good idea. I doubt that Mr Pickering has done more than let out the chickens and scattered a bit of grain for them. I'll see if there are any eggs and get them washed and put them in the trays if you like.'

'I ain't messing around with that tractor, even to attach the trailer or fill up the tank. I'll do the hens and you go with Charlie,' Sal said, and this made sense.

The original pigs had been butchered and the sty was now occupied by piglets. Charlie thought the succulent ham they'd had for supper a few times might well be from one of them. This didn't bother her, she'd grown up on a farm, but Sal didn't need reminding as she'd loved those pigs.

Half an hour later, Daphne was perched in the trailer surrounded by two small churns of milk, two decent slabs of butter wrapped in greaseproof paper on a tin tray and, clutched on her lap, three dozen eggs, pointy side down, and all spotlessly clean.

Charlie didn't dare to look over her shoulder to see how her friend was managing as the road was absolutely beastly. When they approached the outskirts of the village proper, the snow had been cleared, as had the pavements, which made things so much easier.

Mr Pickering had said to take everything to Mr Raven at his general stores and the road was empty of both pedestrians and vehicles, so she decided to pull up outside. She was pretty sure there wasn't a bus in either direction for at least another half an hour.

The shop owner came out in his usual grubby apron, his grey hair slicked back with Brylcreem but with a broad smile of welcome instead of his usual surly expression.

'Thank God you've come, girls, I'm that desperate for dairy produce. My customers don't like having to pay extra at the other shops or when the milk round comes from Brook's.'

'We've got two churns of milk, five pounds of butter but only three dozen eggs. Do you want everything today?'

'I certainly do, Charlie. You stop there with your tractor and trailer – you're in nobody's way and Daphne and I can get this in quick enough.'

Whilst they got on with it, Charlie looked up and down the street, wondering why there were no shoppers on the pavements. Maybe it was just too cold for them to come out. She rather liked the emptiness of it all.

Then the peace was shattered as the local lunatic, the religious maniac known as Holy Joe, started yelling from just outside his own little shop on the opposite side of the road. He sold paraffin, kindling and other bits and pieces, but nobody ventured into his premises unless they were desperate as they wouldn't escape without being harangued about their lack of godliness.

'God sees all. Your sins have been found out. You will go to the fiery furnace for your immorality.'

She looked around, wondering who he was railing at this time, but there was nobody else visible but herself. Daphne and Mr Raven had heard the racket and burst out of the shop.

'Put a sock in it, Joe, we don't want your nonsense this morning,' Mr Raven yelled back but his intervention made Holy Joe even more vocal.

'That girl is a harlot, a seducer of men. She will go to the fiery pit for her sins.'

Charlie was mortified, her cheeks scarlet, wishing the ground would open up and swallow her as by now there were several interested spectators watching the show.

Daphne ran across and grabbed the nasty little man by the elbows, bundled him back inside his shop and then slammed the door. Charlie could still hear him shouting but at least he didn't come out and continue her public humiliation.

5

James was leaving the house of a young couple after a successful delivery of twins. The first baby had arrived easily enough but the unexpected second had been breech and James had been called in by the local midwife to assist. As the baby was slightly smaller than her brother, a healthy six pounds, she'd arrived easily enough and he'd left the family shellshocked but delighted with their new arrivals.

Their cottage was off the small market square, adjacent to the post office and he'd parked his car in front of the village hall, as this was the closest he could get without blocking access to the other cottages.

He could hear Holy Joe shouting at some unfortunate villager as he approached the High Street. As he turned into the road, he saw the tractor from Fiddler's Farm and that Charlie was driving it. He didn't know she could drive – there was a lot he didn't know about her, but there was plenty of time to find out.

He had heard the religious maniac yelling but hadn't really registered what he was saying and to whom he was saying it but then two things became apparent. The woman he loved was leaning forward, almost resting her face on the steering wheel, and the few people who'd come out to listen were staring at her.

Daphne suddenly raced across the road and bundled the vile man back into his shop. James could think of only one reason why Holy Joe had been attacking Charlie – somehow he'd heard about her spending Sunday with him. He dropped his bag by the front wheel of the tractor and moved in close so that what he said couldn't be overheard by those watching developments with interest.

'Sweetheart, I don't know what he said, but it's obviously upset you. The man's a lunatic – nobody takes any notice of him.'

She didn't look at him but spoke with her head still lowered. 'He said I was immoral. How could he know about what happened to me?'

He laughed, which certainly got her attention. She sat up and glared at him. 'He doesn't know anything about anything, my love, he shouts that sort of thing at all the young women.' He reached up, put his hands around her waist and before she could protest swung her to the ground. 'Shall we give them all something to gossip about?'

Her eyes widened. He waited. He wasn't going to kiss her unless she gave him permission. Then she slid her arms around his neck and leaned towards him. He pulled her closer and kissed her. Nothing passionate, just a gentle pressure of his lips on hers.

He raised his head and saw she was radiant. 'Goodness me – that's the very first time I've been kissed and I must say I rather enjoyed it.' She peeped around his shoulder and then hid her face against his coat. 'Everybody's staring at us.'

'I know, that was the general idea, darling. I wanted people to know that we're involved. This wasn't quite how I intended to announce it, but it's done now.'

'I think most people would have guessed after we sat together in church and then ran off hand in hand afterwards.'

'Bloody freezing out here and I think I can hear a car coming. You're going to have to move the tractor and trailer.'

She smiled. 'Don't use such bad language, James, it's not appropriate for a doctor.'

'I'm not going to apologise. The occasional curse is good for releasing tension. Here, you'd better climb back. If I don't get called out this evening, then I'll come and see you.'

The tractor had been grumbling and rocking back and forth as Daphne climbed back in it, the engine still just about running. 'See you later, James.'

She had to drive in the wrong direction as there was nowhere to turn safely until she reached the other side of the village. With his bag swinging in one hand, James strode back to his car, ignoring the knowing looks and smiles. It was nobody's business but his and Charlie's and he didn't need their approval for his choice.

The waiting room was already half-full, he was late, but only ten minutes after surgery should have started. It was going to be a busy day. The final patient departed at dusk. Miss Turnbull took care of the accounts, wrote up his records, and did everything else that was necessary to keep James's practice running smoothly. She wasn't given to chitchat – in fact, she rarely said anything on any subject unrelated to work or the war. This afternoon was an exception.

'You have caused quite a stir, Dr Willoughby, by kissing Miss Somiton in public.'

'Have I? My fiancée didn't object and it's nobody else's business how we behave in public or anywhere else.'

'Congratulations, Dr Willoughby. It's high time you got

married and had a family of your own. I shall be finished here in half an hour. I'll post the letters on my way home.'

'Thank you, Miss Turnbull. I'll see you next week.'

What in God's name had made him blurt out that he and Charlie were engaged? They were involved but nothing official had been said on either side. Then he smiled. Kissing a young woman in full view of the villagers was a public statement of intent. He was old-fashioned enough to believe a gentleman shouldn't do this unless he was engaged to the girl in question.

It was a good thing he was going to see her later. His redoubtable receptionist was no gossip, but he was quite sure that the information would be all over the village by tomorrow night as Mary would have heard the conversation.

Mary was an excellent housekeeper, a better cook and her only flaw was that she was the hub of Stodham gossip. He was an easy-going sort of employer, had absolutely no objection to her having visitors during her working day as long as they didn't impinge on him. Therefore, salacious, mysterious or interesting titbits of news arrived and departed from his kitchen at regular intervals.

This was the first time the gossip would be about him, though. Trying to prevent Mary from tittle-tattling was as impossible as turning back the clock. Often the land girls who worked on the other side of Stodham called in at one of the shops on their way home so it was just feasible news of her engagement might reach Charlie before she was aware of it herself!

Not bothering to do more than wash his hands and face, James shrugged into his thick tweed coat, wrapped a scarf around his neck and pulled on his less than flattering tweed cap. He was a bit low on fuel but could fill up at Goodwill House. He wasn't sure how long this secret stash of petrol would last but whilst it did, he was going to take advantage of it. Having to travel to the hospital by bus would be a damned nuisance and make his long days even

longer. Using his bicycle to make house calls would be even more tedious.

'Mary,' he yelled as he was about to depart. 'I'm going out – I'll be back for supper.'

Blackouts were already down, his headlights reduced to a pinprick, driving anything but slowly was impossible. But it wasn't quite dark yet and his meagre lights reflected on the snow, making visibility reasonable.

There was no need for him to brake as he approached the entrance to the drive as he was already creeping along at around fifteen miles an hour. He took the turn sedately – thank God he did, as a large black car was stationary a few yards past the turning.

Braking would just have exacerbated the situation so he let the car drift slowly forward and collide with the vehicle. The impact jarred his teeth; he absorbed it through his braced arms, but he was pretty sure the collision would have done no lasting damage to his car or the one parked so inconveniently in his way.

He pulled on the brake and scrambled out, praying his medical knowledge wouldn't be needed. 'Hello there, are you all right? Why the hell are you parked in the middle of the drive?'

By this time, he'd reached the rear of the car and pulled open the door. The vehicle was empty, but the interior was still warm, so the occupants hadn't been gone long. That was one worry removed.

The Bentley must have run out of petrol or broken down and the passengers and driver must have walked to the house. Charlie had said some important Yanks were staying and James assumed this was the car they'd been travelling in.

He shone his torch onto the rear bumper of the Bentley and the front bumper of his Rover – as he'd suspected, no damage done to either. He walked around to the driver's door, leaned in, released the handbrake, and put the car in first gear.

Even without anyone behind the wheel, he thought he could gently push the stranded car up to the house by driving his own vehicle without too much difficulty. He checked its front wheels were securely in the ruts made by previous vehicles – this would mean the car should slide forward without veering into the field. There wasn't room for him to turn round where he was so this would be beneficial to him as well.

Everything was progressing smoothly; he was within fifty yards of the turning circle, when two figures ran towards him flashing torches and shouting loudly – not that he could hear what they were saying above the noise of the engine and the crunch of the wheels on the frozen snow. Neither of them seemed at all impressed by his ingenuity or the fact that he was being of assistance to them.

James decided to ignore the approaching figures and complete the task in hand. Abandoning both cars in order to deal with the men made no sense. Presumably these were the Yanks, but why they were so incensed was a mystery and not one he cared to solve until the vehicles were safely parked at the side of the house.

As he was moving at a snail's pace and they were running, it was inevitable that they arrived before he did. Well, it should have been a foregone conclusion that one, or both, would start banging on his window demanding that he stop. They obviously thought it might be hazardous being directly beside the cars when one was travelling without a driver or brakes so had left the relative safety of the drive and were on the ploughed field that ran alongside it. What happened next was predictable and to James, very funny.

Both lost their footing and vanished from his view, arms waving frantically as they fell. This wouldn't improve their tempers. He was now close enough to see them stagger onto their feet. They were dressed inappropriately for the inclement conditions and their expensive suits and shoes wouldn't be improved by their nose-diving into the snow.

There was little point in attempting to stop and offer assistance, so he trundled past them and braked slowly as soon as the Bentley was in the parking area. He then steered past it and parked safely next to it.

He was still smiling as he checked his torch was working, pushed open his door and ducked out into the night. That was the last thing he knew as something hard and painful cracked across the back of his head and everything went black.

* * *

Joanna's fear that the trio would return to Goodwill House for lunch was unfounded. Instead, they came back late in the afternoon. She was happily filling in the household ledgers when Liza burst in, laughing.

'You'll never guess what happened, Ma. That posh Bentley has broken down at the end of the drive and they've all had to walk to the house. Edith let them in and they weren't happy, I can tell you. Their ATS driver's hiding in the kitchen.'

'That sounds like a sensible move on her part. I suppose I'd better speak to our American visitors.'

'I shouldn't, leave Lord Harcourt to sort it out. He's on the telephone barking orders at someone. I expect a new car will arrive by the morning and this one will be towed away.'

'They can use ours. I know it works perfectly well. If the Bentley has broken down at the end of the drive, it's going to cause problems as nobody will be able to see it in the dark.'

Elizabeth, now her bedroom was warm, had resumed her habit of taking an afternoon nap upstairs. Biggins would have her downstairs in plenty of time for dinner. This meant that Joanna had the luxury of the sitting room to herself in the afternoon.

As she emerged from the end of the passageway into the grand hall, the two Americans were talking quietly by the door. She ignored them and walked over to Peter.

'Lord Harcourt, I believe that your vehicle is out of action. You're welcome to use my Bentley whilst you're here. Joe drives it around the barn a couple of times a week so I know it's fully functioning.'

For a horrible moment, she thought he was going to ignore her. His eyes were hard, his lips thin and his hands were clenched.

'That would be helpful, my lady, thank you for the offer.' He turned his back on her and walked across to the Americans, leaving her standing rather foolishly in the middle of the hall.

Her instinct was to retreat but this was her house, she could stand where she liked even if it was an inconvenience for the other three. She couldn't help but overhear what they were talking about.

'I'm sure your briefcases and personal items are perfectly safe in the car. However, I wonder why you didn't think to bring them with you and then this wouldn't be an issue.' Peter was looking at the Americans with equal disapproval, which made her feel a little better. Perhaps he was as uncomfortable being here as she was having him.

'Do you have a torch, Lieutenant Colonel?'

'I do, but I think it might be best if you let me fetch your belongings. I'm familiar with the road and less likely to come to grief in the darkness.'

In order to go out and not let even a glimmer of light into the night, one had to sidle around the heavy material that had been hung in front of the door and only then attempt to open it.

'We'll collect our own things. We just need your torch,' the previously silent American said. He sounded annoyed and he also seemed to be in charge.

Whatever did they have in the car that was so important they had to fetch it themselves and wouldn't let Peter go for it? Joanna was now intrigued by what was happening and slid unobtrusively across the hall to stand in front of the log fire that had taken the chill from the air but done little else. She turned her back on them as if warming herself when she was, in fact, listening to the conversation.

Peter reluctantly handed over his torch and there was an icy blast as the front door was opened. She almost tipped headfirst into the fire when one of the men started shouting as soon as they got outside.

She dropped the pretence of being an uninterested bystander and rushed to the door, arriving at the same time as Peter.

'What's going on? Why are they in such a flap?'

'Listen, I can hear another car. I think someone's pushing the abandoned Bentley up to the house.'

'I would have thought that this was a good thing and not something to shout about. Surely, they don't think whoever's driving is going to steal their belongings?'

'It sounds as if that's exactly what they think. God knows what they've got in those briefcases but I'm beginning to think there's a lot more to this visit than I thought.'

In the excitement, they'd reverted to their old manner of talking, their animosity temporarily forgotten.

Joanna shivered as she stood in the open doorway, watching the Americans run towards their vehicle. They were just discernible in the faint light of the other car's headlights. She blinked and squinted. The silent man was running, the other trying to restrain him.

'Go inside, Joanna, it's too cold out here for you.' His abrupt tone reignited her dislike.

'What I do is none of your concern, Lord Harcourt. If I wish to freeze, that's my business.'

He said something extremely rude under his breath but didn't reply directly. Things were far too interesting out here to go in even if she was unpleasantly cold. Then both men fell headlong into the ploughed field.

'I'll leave you to it, Lord Harcourt, I think a hot toddy and warm blankets are going to be needed and I'd better get that organised.'

As she turned to go, the cars were close enough for her to recognise the one pushing the Bentley. It was the owned by Dr Willoughby – he must be coming to see Charlie. She thought the three girls from Fiddler's Farm were probably in the kitchen and returned to the relative warmth of the hall to find them, closing the door behind her.

Charlie was helping lay the table in the dining room and Joanna explained what was going on outside.

'James said he would come and see me later, but I really didn't expect him until after supper. Thank you for telling me, my lady, but I think I'd better stay inside until whatever's going on has been settled.'

Joanna asked two of the girls to find some blankets and fill hot water bottles. They willingly went in search of the required items whilst she put on her outdoor boots, found a warm coat from the rack in the boot room, and grabbed a working torch.

Whatever was going on, she wanted to be part of it. It irritated her that Peter had taken charge as if he had the right to dictate what happened in *her* house. When she appeared under the portico, she shone the thready beam towards the sound of an altercation.

She watched in horror as Peter smashed his fist into the nose of one of the Americans. The man staggered back and collapsed onto his backside on the gravel. Was that another body on the ground? What was going on here?

The floored American was attempting to stem the flow of blood from his nose but remained on the ground. Then she realised there were not one but two injured men and one was Dr Willoughby! She turned and ran back inside, calling for assistance. The other American was on his knees next to his friend.

'Quickly, Joe, Liza, Charlie, I need you here right now.'

The three of them arrived, closely followed by the rest of the land girls, including those who had gone in search of blankets and hot water bottles.

'What's going on, my lady?' Charlie asked.

'Something has happened outside. Dr Willoughby appears to be unconscious on the ground and Lord Harcourt has just attacked one of the Americans. I'm not sure if I should call the police.'

Joanna was talking to empty space as Charlie had hurtled across the hall and out through the front door.

6

Charlie took the front steps in one jump and dropped to her knees beside James. Lord Harcourt spoke from behind her.

'We need to get him indoors. One of these bastards attacked him, but I've dealt with that for the moment.'

'Why would they want to hurt him? I don't understand.'

'I'm not sure that I do – but I intend to find out. Good – reinforcements are arriving.'

Liza was first and checked James's pulse. 'He's not deeply unconscious and although there's a large contusion on the back of his head, there's no blood.'

The girl stood up – she was normally quiet, self-effacing, but when it came to first aid, she took charge.

'Lord Harcourt, if we roll him onto this blanket then we can carry him in on that. Do you want me to look at the other one?' Liza asked.

'Absolutely not.'

Whilst they manoeuvred James onto the blanket, his lordship told Joe to remove the briefcases from the rear seat of the car. Was this what all the fuss was about?

Ignoring all the blackout rules, Lady Harcourt had opened the front door wide so light flooded out, making it so much easier to carry James inside. Charlie hoped no vigilant ARP warden had seen the breach and would come to investigate.

'I've put some blankets and a cushion down by the fire so you can put him there. I've put the first-aid kit out for you, Liza,' Lady Harcourt said.

Even with eight of them clutching a handful of blanket each, it had still been difficult getting James inside. Charlie stood aside to let Liza do a more thorough check. She was somewhat reassured by Liza's assessment of his condition but seeing him prostrate like this made her blink back tears.

'Shall I call the police? An ambulance perhaps?' Lady Harcourt enquired.

'No, not for me. I'm absolutely fine.'

To Charlie's surprise and delight, James sat up, a bit dishevelled but apart from that looking undamaged.

'Actually, Dr Willoughby, I was rather thinking about the man outside. One of them looked as if he had a broken nose.'

'Serves him right. But – Hippocratic Oath and all that – I'd better take a look at them both. My medical bag's in my car.' He touched the back of his head and winced and then grinned at Lord Harcourt. 'We can't very well leave them out there to freeze, even though they attacked me.'

'Good heavens – how very exciting,' the older Lady Harcourt trilled from the staircase. 'What have I missed whilst having my siesta?'

'Elizabeth, you've come down at an inopportune time. Joe, please escort your grandmother to the small sitting room where she will be safe.'

All present knew that what was meant was to somewhere that

the redoubtable old lady could be kept out of the way so as not to interfere.

'Charlie, I need to speak to you, but it will have to wait until I've finished outside.' James flashed his charming smile and rushed off as if ten minutes ago he hadn't been flat out on the floor, dead to the world.

Lord Harcourt followed him, and a shiver of apprehension ran down Charlie's spine when she saw that he had his gun in his hand. Despite the fact she'd been shot in the leg by a German plane and endured several bombing raids, seeing this made the war seem so close.

Joe had returned from the sitting room and pointed to the briefcases abandoned on the floor. 'Shall we have a dekko? There has to be something in here that made them attack the doc.'

'I don't think we should even attempt to open them, but I don't see why we shouldn't examine the outside before we put them somewhere safe.'

Liza, unfazed by the prospect of being confronted by two angry Americans, had followed the two men into the darkness, carrying blankets. Lady Harcourt had hurried off to placate her mother-in-law and the other girls had drifted back into the ballroom to discuss what they'd seen and what might be going to happen next, leaving Charlie and Joe temporarily alone.

He handed her one of the heavy black leather cases and whilst she turned hers over, he did the same with the one he had. At first, she thought there was nothing untoward about either of them then noticed something suspicious.

'Look, this could be the lens of a camera – it's very small – but I can't think what else it is. I wonder if there's a button on the handle to press in order to take a picture.'

They both pressed, prodded and poked to no avail but Joe

agreed with her, the briefcase she had in her hand definitely had a camera in it.

'Joe, I think we'd better lock these briefcases in the gun cupboard. We don't know what those Americans might do to recover them.'

'I was thinking that myself, Charlie. I'll take them and keep the key in my pocket. I'll tell Ma what we've discovered.'

Joe hurried off, leaving her to worry about James. He'd said he was perfectly well, but if he'd been knocked out, he probably wasn't tickety-boo and was just doing his duty.

It was nail biting hanging about, not knowing what was going on outside. She was expecting at any moment to hear gunfire and was terrified it might be James who got shot. After all, one of the horrible Americans had already knocked him out once.

Charlie heard the girls go in for their evening meal but didn't join them. She decided to run upstairs for the overcoat she'd managed to find in the village rummage sale a few months ago. No one was supposed to wear anything but the uniform provided by the Land Army but, as the months had gone by, the girls were gradually supplementing their inadequate winter clothing with civilian items of one sort or another.

She realised if she left the lights off in her bedroom, she could stand in front of the blackout curtain and be able to see what was going on outside. It took a few moments for her eyes to adjust but once they had, everything was clearer.

James was just getting off his knees, wiping his hands on his handkerchief, obviously having finished his ministrations. Lord Harcourt was standing in front of the two men who were propped up against the Bentley. He had his gun pointed firmly at them. It was difficult to see everything, but Charlie was pretty sure the men had their hands tied in front of them.

Without opening the window, she couldn't hear what was

being said but she saw the two men, with some difficulty, slither their backs up the icy car and manage to regain their feet. Lord Harcourt gestured with his gun and James stood at his side with his medical bag in one hand.

The Americans were obviously now prisoners – what an extraordinary thing to have happened. It didn't seem credible that the War Office had sent two spies to visit crucial RAF bases believing that they were American diplomats. She was sure Lady Harcourt had said Lord Harcourt was something high up in the intelligence service – this made what was happening even more extraordinary.

There was no need for her to go outside, as James would obviously be coming in once he and Lord Harcourt had found somewhere safe to lock the villains. In the months she'd been living at Goodwill House, they'd had more than their fair share of excitement.

Last year, two German pilots had hidden in the cellars, someone called Bert Smith had inadvertently set fire to the disused Victorian wing – since demolished – and Goodwill House had been used as a convalescent home for a couple of RAF ground crew. No one could say her life wasn't interesting.

Jean came looking for her. 'I've put your supper in the slow oven, Charlie. What a palaver! Do you know if I'm expected to serve a three-course dinner to the visitors?'

'I shouldn't think so, Jean, as they're being locked in a shed somewhere. I expect Lord Harcourt will want feeding, though – the prisoners can just have bread and water.'

Jean looked shocked and then smiled. 'Goodness, for a moment I thought you were being serious. He'll have to eat with us – I don't think Joanna will like it, but I can hardly put him on his own in the breakfast room.'

The housekeeper hurried off to relay the bad news. The family had been eating in the kitchen – the table laid with a white cloth and the correct cutlery and crockery used – and the breakfast room had been given over to the guests. No doubt the Harcourts and Jean would use the breakfast room and Lady Harcourt would smile and pretend she was happy with the situation. That's what ladies did.

* * *

James had been uncomfortable about locking the injured American into an outbuilding, but his protests were ignored by his lordship.

'I'm sorry, old man, I can hardly have these two wandering about unfettered in the house. The cameras in the briefcases that Joe and the land girl found makes it likely that they're fascists, supporters of Hitler, and therefore to be on the safe side they must be incarcerated until my men get here and arrest them.'

'Then they will quite likely find two corpses if you leave them with no food or protection against the sub-zero temperatures,' James said. 'What if you're wrong? There might be another explanation for them attacking me.'

'What? Tell me – I'd like to hear it.' His tone was abrupt, patronising even, and James lost his temper.

'You don't give the orders around here and certainly not to me. One of them is my patient and I decide how he'll be treated. I'm letting them out and taking them in and you'll have to shoot me or lock me up in order to stop me.'

He shoved past Harcourt, ignoring the gun, and unlocked the outhouse door. He shone his torch inside.

'Right, you two, on your feet. You're coming inside. Lord Harcourt will shoot without question if you try any nonsense.'

They were on their feet and at the door without argument.

They looked as guilty as hell – resigned to their fate – bang to rights was a phrase he'd heard and he thought it suited this occasion perfectly.

It was odd they didn't protest at this harsh treatment and he was determined to ask them some questions once they were indoors even if Harcourt didn't.

He went ahead and the two men followed him closely, looking nervously at the stony-faced soldier with the gun in his hand. There were numerous unused rooms in this vast establishment and James was pretty sure there was an anteroom tucked away under the stairs which would be ideal.

Joe met them in the passageway and had grasped what was going on. 'I've lit a fire in there, Doc, and put in some blankets and so on. I thought I'd get a bucket with a lid – they might need the bog during the night.'

'Good plan. Does your mother know what's going on?'

'She does.'

The small room wasn't warm, but it wasn't dangerously cold either. The young man had provided blankets and pillows, a jug of cold water and wash basin and two towels, and there was a plate of sandwiches and a pot of tea waiting for them. More than they deserved, considering their behaviour, but after the luxury they'd been enjoying here, it certainly made a point.

Lord Harcourt stared around the room. Something was bothering him. He pointed to the makeshift beds and the men slunk across and sat down. They could hardly eat or pee with their hands tied, so the restraints would have to come off.

'Joe, Dr Willoughby, there are things we need to remove from this room if it's to function safely as a cell.'

James looked around and saw there were a couple of brass candlesticks, the fire irons and several alabaster ornaments.

'What about the books, sir?' Joe asked as he scooped up everything apart from the ornaments.

'Leave the books.' Lord Harcourt looked every inch a senior officer, one used to being in charge and a chap who knew how to deal with the situation. James didn't mind how terse the man was, at least he'd got his way. He wouldn't have been able to sleep tonight knowing these two could have died from hypothermia. They might not be who they purported to be, but they didn't deserve to perish without a fair trial, even if there was a war on.

Fortunately, the door opened outwards so even without a lock it was a simple matter to barricade the door, and the window in the room was too small for even Joe to climb out of.

'Aren't you going to question them, Harcourt?'

'No, they've got diplomatic immunity so better to leave it to someone higher up the food chain than me.'

James had helped move the heavy furniture, which was a mistake. Despite claiming he was perfectly well, he was suddenly aware that he wasn't. He was suffering from a mild concussion and should really be resting in a darkened room, not heaving furniture about the place.

He leaned against the oak sideboard until he regained his balance and was sure he wasn't going to vomit.

'James, you look absolutely ghastly. Lady Harcourt says you're to stay here tonight. Someone has changed the sheets in one of the guest rooms and it's waiting for you. I'll not take any argument. You're to come with me.' Charlie took his arm; she was looking up at him anxiously.

'I've got a mild concussion, sweetheart, nothing terminal. However, I do need to lie down, so lead the way.'

* * *

He felt considerably better by the time he got to the room and almost refused to go in. Charlie sensed his hesitation and gently pushed him through the door. 'No, if you don't go to bed, then I'm going to call an ambulance.'

'Good God – don't do that. I'd be the laughingstock of the hospital.' He looked around and was relieved to see a basin by the bed in case he vomited – quite likely, the way he felt at the moment.

'Could you ring Mary and tell her what's happening? She'll contact my receptionist who in turn will let the hospital know I'm out of action tomorrow.'

'I've already done that. I'm afraid you're going to have to wear a pair of pyjamas that belonged to the spy who was sleeping in here. They are clean – in fact, they look brand-new.'

Charlie turned to go but he took her hand. 'Just a minute, darling, I came here to tell you something. I inadvertently referred to you as my fiancée and Mary overheard. I'm afraid the entire village will think we're engaged.'

'That's all right – we were sort of engaged already and you've just made it official. I'll leave you to get into bed and then check that you don't need anything. The bathroom's at the end of the corridor but there's a pot under the bed.'

He was feeling decidedly seedy but managed to pull himself together sufficiently to remove the ring box from his jacket pocket. 'This belonged to my grandmother and I hope it fits.'

'I love it and I'm almost sure that I'm in love with you.'

To his delight, she held out her left hand and he pushed the ring over her knuckle. The square-cut diamond caught the light and the emeralds that surrounded it were perfect – so was the fit.

'I love you, Charlie, I know you don't want to rush into anything but I'm prepared to wait as long as it takes. Our engagement can be for months or years – I'd prefer the former but there'll be no pressure from me.'

'I love you too. Now go to bed before you collapse in a heap on the carpet.'

'Can you turn out the central light as you go? I'll be better in the dark.'

From the light of the fire, he undressed, then, breaking a habit of a lifetime, dropped his clothes in a heap. He pulled on the pyjama bottoms but ignored the top and with some difficulty got between the sheets.

He was a medical man – he knew he was going to have a very unpleasant twenty-four hours and he had no wish for Charlie to be his nurse.

* * *

Joanna was reeling from the dramatic events of the evening. Joe revelled in the excitement and had volunteered to stand guard outside the room in which the Americans were incarcerated with his shotgun.

'His lordship and I will take shifts. They can't move the furniture, we've made very sure of that, but just in case someone needs to be on guard.'

There was little point telling her son that he was only fifteen, still a boy as far as she was concerned, because tonight he'd shown her he'd become a young man and this was a genie she couldn't put back in the bottle. Liza was already a young woman, confident and competent in her chosen field, so it was inevitable that her twin would follow suit.

'If Lord Harcourt is happy for you to do so, then I won't cavil. Jean's about to serve dinner and I'm quite sure those men will be safe without supervision for the brief time it takes either you or Lord Harcourt to eat.'

'Dr Willoughby's concussed but he insists he doesn't need medical attention.' Joe laughed and she joined in.

'It is all very confusing,' Elizabeth said, sounding anything but. 'The two Americans we made such a fuss of, Joanna, are in fact spying for Hitler. The local doctor is now upstairs injured and the two of them are imprisoned in an anteroom. This is even more exciting than having Luftwaffe pilots in the cellar.'

Peter was making free with the telephone, presumably talking to someone at the War Office. They wouldn't want this debacle to become common knowledge as those who had arranged this so-called tour would be made to look incompetent.

'Jean's taking food through on the trolley. Shall we go in? I'm sure Lord Harcourt will join us when he's finished making his important calls.'

The land girls had eaten and those whose turn it was had cleared the table and done the washing-up. Charlie, Sal and Daphne were now exempt from domestic chores as they were, like the three at Brook Farm, working again.

The five of them were halfway through their vegetable soup when Peter arrived. 'I apologise for being late. I'm glad you started without me.'

Jean started to get up in order to serve him, but he shook his head.

'No, stay where you are. I'll help myself.'

He was obviously ravenous as they all finished at roughly the same time. Whilst Jean and Liza cleared the table and went to fetch the main course, Peter explained what was going to happen next.

'Joe spotted that one of the briefcases has a camera in it. As far as I'm concerned, I don't need any further evidence that these two are Nazi sympathisers.'

'Lord Harcourt, explain to me how someone in the intelligence department is escorting two possible German spies about the place. How did they come to be considered as diplomats?'

He looked at Elizabeth as if deciding whether he should explain to a civilian. 'You're right to question my powers of deduction, my lady, but I was already suspicious. This is why I was accompanying them. God knows what made them behave so stupidly tonight because, if they hadn't, they might well have got away with it for a day or two longer.'

'Are they Germans and not Americans?' Joanna asked.

'Definitely Yanks. And they are here with diplomatic protection, but in reality are businessmen, very, very wealthy, and we were informed that the purpose of this visit was for them to decide if they were going to invest in our war effort. We need all the financial help we can get, as the American government so far hasn't been very forthcoming.'

7

Charlie was on her way to check on James when Liza stopped her in the passageway. 'Leave him, Charlie, he won't want you seeing him being ill. Not very romantic when you've just got engaged.'

'I don't care about that. I know how horrible concussion is. He and his housekeeper took care of me last year when I stayed at his house.'

'Yes, but he's a doctor and you're not. I'll do what's needed. I'm a qualified first aider and will be a student nurse in a couple of years.'

'All right. But I have to be at work at seven-thirty tomorrow so won't be able to see him when he gets up.'

Liza smiled. 'He's not going to be up until tomorrow night at the earliest. He'll still be here when you get home.'

'What about his patients?'

'I'm sure they'll cope without him for a couple of days.'

Charlie didn't want to rejoin the girls in the ballroom and be congratulated on her new status. It wouldn't be right without James standing beside her. Therefore, she wandered to the kitchen to make her nightly cocoa. Jean had warned them all that this too would vanish from the menu when the last two tins were finished.

She was pleased to find her roommates in the kitchen waiting for her. They all hugged her when she told them the news.

'So happy for you both, Charlie, now Sal has to find a fellow of her own and we'll all be spoken for,' Daphne said.

'I ain't looking for no man in me life, ta very much. Den put me off that sort of thing for life. No, I'm staying single.'

Charlie nodded. 'So are we for the moment. I'm in no hurry to tie the knot and neither is Daphne.'

'That's good. We're a team and I like working and living with you.'

The milk rose in the saucepan and Sal, who was nearest, grabbed it before it spilled onto the range. With their hot drinks and hot water bottles, they retreated to the privacy and quiet of their bedroom.

'The others are noisy tonight,' Charlie said as a shrill laugh echoed across the grand hall.

'Sandra and Joyce *found* some sherry,' Daphne told her disapprovingly. 'Sherry doesn't get lost – they stole it from the wine cellar.'

'Those two are a bad influence,' Charlie said. 'Lady Harcourt has let us live here for almost nothing since before Christmas when the weather closed in, now they're abusing her generosity by stealing from her. I'm sure she's aware of what's going on. I doubt those involved will be here for much longer.'

'I reckon she'd have to be deaf not to hear them. Things ain't right here now. Maybe we could find somewhere to live on our own. Rent something like.'

They reached the warmth of their own room and Charlie closed the door behind them. The hall was a bit warmer with fires lit but the passageways were still arctic.

'A bit of all right, ain't it, having a fire in here now? I reckon they won't be having any more posh visitors after this last lot turned out to be spies.'

'I suppose we shouldn't jump to conclusions,' Charlie said. 'There might be a perfectly reasonable explanation...'

Both girls laughed. Daphne shook her head. 'Golly, do you really think that Lord Harcourt would have them locked up and a guard outside if he wasn't absolutely certain they're villains?'

'Joe with a shotgun is hardly an armed guard, but I get what you mean. If they were innocent then they'd be making a fuss, shouting the odds, but we've not heard a peep from them. They hit James because they thought he was going to take their briefcase and that makes them criminals as far as I'm concerned.'

* * *

Charlie was woken by the loud voices, giggles and heavy footsteps as the inebriated girls eventually came up to bed. The other two remained asleep but she was now wide awake. There was sufficient light from the dying fire for her to get out of bed without stubbing a toe on anything. She pulled on her woolly dressing gown, pushed her bare feet in her slippers and sat on the end of her bed waiting for the passageway to fall silent again, meaning the bathroom was available.

Having decided that she needed the loo, waiting became uncomfortable. She would slip down to the one near the boot room as she had a nasty suspicion it wouldn't be very pleasant in the bathroom the twelve of them shared in this corridor.

Joe was slouched in a chair but wide awake as he looked at her when she walked past. 'Shall I make you a cuppa?'

'Thanks, that would be kind. I'm not sure his lordship would approve of my drinking on duty.'

'He'll never know. I'll put the kettle on as I go past.'

Charlie recalled that in-between her bouts of nausea when she'd had concussion, she'd welcomed a cup of tea. Liza wasn't there to interfere, so she'd take a mug of tea up to James too. He might well need something emptying or cleaning and she was quite prepared to do that for him. In sickness and health, after all.

As she didn't require a hot drink, she only had one to carry upstairs. There were no fires in the passageways and her torch was essential. She wasn't at all happy about him being left on his own as he'd told her, when she'd recovered enough to take notice of anything that was said to her, that a concussed patient needed to be checked on frequently. She wasn't exactly sure why, but that didn't matter.

She knocked quietly on the door – not because she wasn't going to go in if she got no answer but because it was the polite thing to do. There was a slight sound and the door opened. James was standing there looking absolutely fine but with nothing on his top half at all. He was very attractive.

The hot tea slopped onto her fingers. He reached out and removed the mug.

'How did you know I was gasping for this? Sorry about my state of undress – you'd better come in, it's perishing out here.'

She really shouldn't go into his bedroom but didn't hesitate. He drank the tea down in three swallows. She was fascinated, watching the strong column of his neck convulse. She'd never seen a man unclothed – when she'd been assaulted, the only garments removed had been her knickers.

Without saying a word, she turned and fled. She shouldn't have come. Seeing him like that reminded her of her ordeal and she wasn't ready to be intimate with James even though she loved him.

* * *

James heard her go and threw the empty mug across the room. It smashed, which helped his temper but not the mug. What in God's name had prompted him to open the door half-naked when he'd guessed it was Charlie? He was a doctor, for God's sake, he knew that seeing him might well trigger a negative reaction but he'd done it anyway.

He needed the WC so went in search of it and then returned to his room, frustrated by his crass behaviour. He loved her, wanted to *make* love to her, and had thought seeing him might cause her to feel some of the physical attraction that he did. He was in good shape, lean and muscled, but his arrogance had possibly done irreversible damage to their relationship, and it was his fault.

Tomorrow he would be up in time to speak to her before she left, make a grovelling apology, and promise not to frighten her like that again. He'd meant what he'd said about waiting as long as it took. If tonight had set things back even further then he would have to buckle down, take a lot of cold showers and early-morning runs, and pray eventually she could overcome her fear of intimacy.

After a restless night, he was downstairs before even the housekeeper was in the kitchen. He riddled the range, put the kettle on to boil and got out the makings for tea. Apart from a slight headache and a large lump on the back of his head, he was absolutely fine. His next task was to ring the hospital and let them know he would be there as planned today and be able to complete his list.

He could already hear Harcourt on the telephone – there must be pandemonium at the War Office after what had happened. It still seemed unbelievable these two had been sent to visit all the bases in Kent without being properly checked.

He headed for the hall. 'I'm making tea. Have you looked in on the occupants of that room? Do I need to go in?'

Harcourt walked over. He seemed remarkably relaxed considering what he was dealing with. 'Tea would be splendid. I went round and peered in the window and they're perfectly well. Not happy – but not dead, if that's what you were worried about.'

'Excellent. If you've finished with the telephone, I need to make a call.'

'Go ahead. I'm expecting someone to ring me back but not for a bit.'

Despite the hour, he was quickly connected to the theatre sister, who was delighted to hear that he would be working.

'I was keeping my fingers crossed, sir, that you'd make a miraculous recovery so hadn't actually cancelled anything. Your patients will be prepped and ready as always.'

Harcourt had been listening. 'Good God, you were on your knees last night and yet you're going to operate all day.'

'I'm more or less fighting fit now. Are you coming into the kitchen for your tea?' What he meant was he wasn't bringing it out, so if Harcourt wanted tea, he needed to fetch it for himself. The message was received and understood.

James made toast and they sat on either side of the long scrubbed-pine table, munching happily. He felt a lot better with a full stomach as he'd missed dinner last night.

'Tell me, how can two spies have been given carte blanche to wander about the place taking photographs?'

Rather than being offended by this direct question, his companion laughed. 'They are, in fact, exactly who they said they were – very wealthy American businessman interested in investing in the UK. What they failed to mention was that they were also Nazi sympathisers. They obviously haven't said this but there's no other explanation for them taking photographs of RAF bases.'

'Well, that was remiss of them. They should have put that at the top of their letter of intent. What will happen to them now?'

'They will be deported post-haste. We can't detain them, much as we'd like to, but we'll hang onto their briefcases. They'll return to the US later today. A car's coming to collect them and will deliver them to an airfield where an American plane will be waiting.'

'I shouldn't think Lady Harcourt will want to take any further foreign guests after this debacle.'

'The whole scheme has been shelved. At least the house is now warm and I'll make sure a second delivery of coal is made as compensation for the inconvenience.'

The housekeeper came in and wasn't at all put out by there being two strange gentlemen in her kitchen.

'Good morning, my lord, Dr Willoughby, I see you've made yourselves comfortable, but could I ask you to please give me room to work? Joe's already made up the fires everywhere so would you be kind enough to go to the breakfast room?'

James finished his tea in two swallows but took the remains of his toast with him. The telephone rang noisily and Harcourt hurried off to answer it. James checked his watch and saw it was a little after six o'clock.

Speaking to Charlie was going to be impossible as she'd be with her friends now and he'd no intention of embarrassing her and making things worse. He'd leave – that would give him time to get home, shave, wash and put on a clean shirt before he headed for Ramsgate.

'Hang on, Willoughby, we need to talk before you go.'

James was tempted to refuse – there was something about Lord Harcourt that grated – but it was probably relating to state security, confidentiality, and needed to be said officially.

'I don't have long, so make this quick.'

Harcourt gestured that they step into the freezing dark drawing room and close the door behind them. 'Do I need to tell you that this episode must remain out of the public eye?'

'I'm not going to talk about what happened here. Is that all?'

'Unfortunately, the entire house is talking about American spies and this won't improve the relationship between our countries. We need their help if we're going to win this war and if we accuse some of their fellow citizens of espionage, you can imagine what the reaction of the government will be. President Roosevelt doesn't want to drag his country into a war that doesn't appear to have anything to do with them.'

'Rather short-sighted of him, don't you think?' James said. 'If Hitler controls Europe, he'll start looking in their direction. Things aren't great in the Pacific at the moment from what I've been reading in the papers.'

'Which is why it's imperative the narrative's changed. I need your help to do this, I'd look rather foolish if the truth came out. I want you to start telling people these were Germans, not Yanks, and that they will be disposed of.'

James nodded and flinched as his collar caught the contusion on the back of his head. 'I'd be happy to do that. It actually makes more sense that they are German spies. I take it that you'll make sure the land girls and everyone else here believe the same story.'

'I've already done so. Thank you for your assistance and I'm sorry that you got caught up in this.' Harcourt offered his hand and James shook it.

'I really do have to get off.'

'Before you go, I was wondering if you'd considered taking a commission? We're desperate for surgeons in the army.'

'I'm needed here and I'm in a reserved occupation – so no, I've no intention of joining the military.'

This was something he'd considered many times, but good doctors were needed at home as well as on the battle front.

* * *

Joanna didn't believe for one minute that the two prisoners who'd just been escorted from the premises by armed guards were Germans. But what she said to Peter was the opposite.

'That makes more sense, Lord Harcourt, although it begs the question as to how a senior officer in the intelligence service failed to identify them.' This was unfair of her, but he was an objectionable man – arrogant and patronising – and deserved every criticism he received.

'*Mea culpa*, my lady, I admit that I'm at fault. I'll be lucky to keep my position after this.' For the first time since he'd arrived, she looked directly at him and he was trying hard not to smile.

'As long as I'm not expected to take in any more spies *or* genuine visitors then I'll say no more about it. We both know your story is a complete fabrication, but I'll go along with it. I assume there'll be no necessity for you to visit again without invitation?'

The amusement in his eyes vanished, to be replaced by something rather more dangerous. They were standing under the portico watching the Americans depart in ignominy. A mechanic had come from the village and repaired his car, so he would leave in that.

'Why did you tell me about having an affair if it wasn't to indicate that you'd be interested in doing the same with me?'

'I wanted you to know that I was in love with somebody else and could only offer you friendship. I didn't expect to be treated like... like a woman who would consider becoming your mistress.'

'I see. Well, to be perfectly frank, I don't understand any of it. I had absolutely no intention of offending you so grievously, I just misunderstood the signals you were giving me.'

'Signals? There were no signals,' Joanna said. 'What offended me the most was that my having had an affair with a man I fell in love with and still love, somehow made me a suitable person to be your kept woman. You have the same name as me and my children but that's all we have in common. I've no wish to have any further contact with you. Do I make myself quite clear?'

He nodded. 'Absolutely crystal, my lady, and I have as little wish to continue this... whatever it is. Goodbye and thank you for your hospitality and understanding about the situation.'

He marched down the steps. His driver was waiting to open the door of the car and saluted him in. Joanna turned her back, deciding that as far as she was concerned, Lord Harcourt was a *persona non grata* at Goodwill House.

In some ways, this aborted visit had been beneficial. They had enough fuel to see them through the rest of the winter, even with all the fires being lit. They still had the two large hampers of luxury food items sent down from Fortnum and Mason. He hadn't asked for them to be returned and she would have refused if he had. Joe had said they'd been promised one more fuel delivery to compensate for the upset to the household.

All this was good news but even better was that she'd no longer have to see or speak to the arrogant Lord Peter Harcourt. His low opinion of her morals had made her reconsider her decision to send John away. If she was already beyond the pale, then why not have what she wanted and be happy? She would never fall in love again, John had captured her heart during their brief affair last year. Didn't they have the right, like everyone else, to be happy?

She was going to find out where he was and try to re-establish the connection. Even if they couldn't be together whilst there was a war on, if he still wanted to be a permanent part of her life, then she'd do everything she could to make that happen.

She would write to Sarah, tell her about John, and ask her fiancé, Angus, who was a squadron leader, how to find John without causing any unnecessary fuss.

First, she had the unpleasant duty of informing Mrs Ramsbottom that two of her girls, Sandra and Joyce, had been stealing alcohol and although she didn't intend to press charges, she was evicting them from the house immediately.

The area organiser for the Land Army was absolutely horrified. 'I cannot tell you how sorry I am that two of our girls have let the side down so badly. They will be dismissed from the service. It's up to the farmer where they work if he wishes to continue to employ them, but they'll have to find their own accommodation and their uniform must be returned.'

'I'm going to speak to them now. Although it might be preferable for you to tell them. Shall I fetch them to the telephone?'

'Yes, my lady, that would be the perfect solution.'

An hour after this conversation, the two very crestfallen girls had left the house, carrying a small suitcase each. Joanna had had stern words with the other four and told them they were treading on very thin ice indeed. She was certain there would be no more pilfering.

'Let me be perfectly clear, girls, from now on, I require your full sixteen shillings a week, therefore, you need to get back to work today.'

They rushed off to put on their gumboots and macs. If the girls at Fiddler's Farm were working, then so should the others be. Only the dairy farm had a telephone, so she'd have to send Joe up to inform the farm where Sandra and Joyce had been placed that they were no longer available as land girls.

8

Charlie hadn't told her friends what had happened the previous night with James and pushed the worry that she would never be ready to marry him aside and concentrated on clearing the ditch. Physical work was exhausting but therapeutic and by the time she was cycling home with her friends, she was less fraught.

'Blimey, I ain't half glad to be home,' Sal said as the three of them propped their bikes up in the barn. 'It's taters and I can't feel me blooming toes. I reckon we'll all have chilblains.'

'Don't be so pessimistic. We've managed to avoid them so far, haven't we?' Daphne said cheerfully.

'The other car's gone, so a mechanic must have repaired it. Imagine having had actual German spies living here? I'm glad they've been arrested and that no important information was sent to Hitler.' Charlie was first at the boot scraper and carefully removed the worst of the mud and ice from her gumboots before stepping out of them, taking them in with her. If they left them outside, as they did in the summer, they would be frozen solid by the morning.

They hung their macs on the pegs in the boot room and put

their boots underneath. Then, in their socks, they padded inside for a much-needed hot drink. Working outside all day with just a couple of sandwiches and a single flask of tea between them wasn't really adequate, but there was a war on and Charlie wasn't going to complain.

After washing the worst of the mud from their faces and hands in the downstairs cloakroom, they headed for the kitchen. Jean had their tea waiting.

'You look absolutely perished, girls, take your tea into the ballroom – it's lovely and warm in there and... well, there's something you need to know but it's better it comes from your friends.'

'Thanks, Jean. I hope that's your delicious vegetable soup simmering on the stove. It's exactly what we need to thaw us out,' Charlie said as she picked up her tea and curled her fingers around the mug with a sigh of pleasure.

They were usually the last to arrive each evening as they had the furthest to travel. Tonight there were two girls missing and she knew at once what had happened.

'Have Sandra and Joyce been given the sack?'

'They have,' Jill, one of the dairy girls, said sadly. 'I didn't really like either of them, but one can't help feeling sorry for them. Freezing cold, and they've no home and no job.'

Sal was less sympathetic. 'Serves them right. You don't nick nothing from where you live – stands to reason they were going to get thrown out. I never thought Sandra was that stupid.'

'They had to hand in every scrap of their uniform. The ladies from the village have laundered it and when it's dry, it'll be pressed and parcelled up. Mrs Ramsbottom will call in to collect it when the weather improves,' Jill said.

'Do you think we'll get replacements? The farmer will need someone – he and his son can't do everything. But I suppose they can manage until spring,' Daphne added.

That was the last time Sandra or Joyce were mentioned. It was as though they'd never been there at all. The conversation turned at once to the excitement of the previous day and this continued until they were called through to eat.

'Shall we go up now, girls, it's a bit gloomy down here tonight?' Charlie suggested.

'It's my turn to make the cocoa, I do hope there's enough milk as it doesn't taste nearly as nice done with half and half,' Daphne said.

'We'll get the fire going so it'll be toasty-warm when you come up.' Charlie wanted to tell them about the embarrassing incident. She was relieved James hadn't been in touch as she wanted to get things straight in her head before she spoke to him.

* * *

The girls' routine was to change into their pyjamas and dressing gowns and then sit on the rug in front of the fire to drink their cocoa with a blanket around them. There were three plain bentwood chairs, but these weren't as comfortable as the floor.

Once they were settled, Charlie told them what had happened. Sal's reaction made her smile.

'You'd never think it to look at him, would you? He's always bundled up in tweed coats and that, ain't he?'

'He's a medical man and can hardly walk around displaying his manly chest to all and sundry, can he?'

Daphne understood. 'Seeing him frightened you, made you think about what happened, didn't it?'

'Yes. I know James is attractive, I know he loves me, but I don't think I'll ever be able to be intimate with him. I just don't know what to do. It's not fair to keep him hanging on when I'm pretty sure I'll never be able to marry him because of what I'll have to do afterwards.'

'Marriage ain't all about a bit of the other, Charlie. It's about love, friendship, building a life together. I reckon there's loads of couples what don't do it very often, or even at all and they're perfectly happy.'

'Thank you for saying that, Sal, but James is a young man and I can't expect him to live like a monk. We haven't talked about it, obviously, but I expect he'll want a family one day and I couldn't give him that either.' She smiled sadly. 'I would love to have a baby but just can't imagine being able to do what you have to do in order to have one.'

'Are you going to break off your engagement? It'll be the shortest one ever if you do,' Daphne pointed out.

'I don't know what else I can do. I realise now I've been permanently damaged by what happened. I'll never be able to enjoy the physical side of a marriage, never have children of my own. I can't expect any man to agree to that.'

'Don't make a hasty decision, Charlie, wait until you see him again. He must know how you feel – after all, you ran away, didn't you? If anybody's going to be able to help you get through this, it's a doctor. Imagine your good fortune that the man you're engaged to is one of those.'

* * *

James's final operation of the day was an emergency admission. A child had bitten off the end of a thermometer and swallowed the piece containing the mercury. Normally this might have passed through his digestive system safely but unfortunately it had lodged in his appendix so it had to come out.

The anaesthetist today was a retired general practitioner – not a chap that he knew well – but he'd done sterling work and he had no complaints.

'Thank you, sir, we got through those ops in record time. Are you my anaesthetist tomorrow?'

'No, young man, the occasional day is as much as I can do. They've asked me to attend to a room full of malingerers but I'm going home. I'm afraid you'll have to do it.'

James wasn't exactly sure about whom the testy old doctor was talking. They had indeed finished two hours earlier than expected, so he was officially still on call. A stout matron, immaculate in navy blue, was waiting for him as he emerged into the main corridor.

'There you are, Dr Willoughby, there was supposed to be an army medic here but he's failed to appear, so you will have to fill in. There are a dozen home guard men seeking medical treatment. It's free for those in uniform so they wait until there's a clinic and don't see their own doctors as they have to pay them.'

'I'd be happy to help out. I assume they're in the outpatients' waiting room?'

She sniffed but didn't bother to answer, obviously thinking the question rhetorical. She marched off, her crisply starched white apron rustling as she bustled down the corridor, leaving him to go in search of these home guard chaps.

He might as well start at outpatients and was greeted with delight by a staff nurse and a student nurse. 'Everything's ready for you in the examination room, Dr Willoughby. The usual coughs, colds and aches and pains. I shouldn't think it'll take you long to get through them.'

The staff nurse was correct, and he doled out cough mixture, aspirin and kaolin and morphine for diarrhoea for an hour and then the final patient was ushered in.

This old boy apologised for being a nuisance. 'I don't like to bother you, Dr Willoughby, but I've had a bit of pain in my chest since yesterday. Probably indigestion. Or it could be muscle strain working on my allotment. I grow lovely vegetables, you know.'

'That's splendid. If you put your gas mask on the chair and undo your battledress then I'll give you a quick once-over.' James listened to the old boy's heart and lungs with a stethoscope and found nothing untoward. His pulse was steady and his blood pressure normal.

'Nothing to worry about. You can get dressed again now.'

The old chap buttoned himself up, put his gas mask over his shoulder, put his cap on at a jaunty angle and saluted. Then he collapsed. For a second, James was immobile.

He did everything he could to revive the old chap, but he'd clearly had a massive heart attack. Vague pains in the chest very rarely led to such a catastrophic event but he still felt guilty. Not that he could have done anything to prevent it.

The corpse was lifted onto a trolley, covered with a white sheet and taken to the morgue. James had to fill in several forms but was eventually free to leave. He didn't do ward rounds – he left that to those permanently employed here – but tonight he checked in on the little boy who'd swallowed the end of his thermometer. The child was awake and chatting happily to his parents.

If he'd had an early start the next day he would have bunked down in doctors' accommodation, but his first surgery wasn't until lunchtime. He turned the collar of his coat up, turned on his torch, and stepped out into the darkness. It was raining. Whilst he'd been busy all day, the temperature had risen and already most of the snow had melted.

He had mixed feelings about the change in the weather. Snow, ice and freezing fog wasn't good for old folk or farmers, but the Luftwaffe hadn't been coming over in such large numbers to bomb London. Visibility was poor but night flying using instruments was commonplace now. He'd better get back before the siren went as there was bound to be a raid tonight.

Rain on ice wasn't a pleasant surface to drive on and twice he almost lost control of the car. If there'd been any other traffic, he might well have come to grief. As always, he reversed the car into the garage so it was facing forwards and he could leave in a hurry if necessary.

Mary had written down his messages and he quickly scanned the sheet, thinking there might be one from Charlie; he wasn't surprised that she hadn't contacted him. They had to talk – after all, they were engaged – and he was dreading that conversation. He knew her well enough to guess she might ask to be released from the engagement as she believed she'd never be able to consummate the marriage. Certain that would be what she was feeling if her reaction to seeing him bare-chested was anything to go by.

After much thought, he decided he would pre-empt her actions by writing a letter. So much easier for her to discuss intimate matters on paper rather than in person. He'd bought himself a Parker Vacumatic fountain pen a year ago and didn't regret the extravagant purchase. The gold nib made even his scrawly handwriting look good and so far it had lived up to its reputation and didn't blot or leak when in use.

'I've a letter to write, Mary, I'll come in for my supper as soon as it's done.' He sat at his desk, got out the ink bottle and dipped the nib into the liquid, then pulled out the little gold handle on the side of the barrel. Satisfied the pen was full, he put out three pieces of Basildon Bond plus a matching envelope and was ready to write.

My dear Charlie,

I know I upset you last night and I apologise. I didn't want to bring back unpleasant memories and know that was what happened.

I can guess that at the moment you've decided you wish to break off the engagement as you can't see yourself ever being in the position to marry me.

Please don't do that. I give you my word that I'll make no demands on you. I love you and am sure that you reciprocate my feelings. Why throw away something so precious? One day, I promise you, you will feel differently. It might take a long time, but we've got the rest of our lives.

Don't come to any hasty decisions I beg you, we will both regret it if you do.

I love you,

He scrawled his signature across the bottom of the page and blotted it. He read it through and was satisfied with what he had written and relieved he hadn't had to start again. He dabbed the stamp on the wet sponge in the little pot on his desk and stuck it down. He'd post it on his way to the hospital tomorrow morning.

* * *

Joanna wrote to Sarah and asked her to pass on her request for John's whereabouts to Angus. She smiled as she remembered hearing the name for the first time. Sergeant John Sergeant – a spectacularly attractive young man with curly black hair, mismatched eyes – one brown, one green – and about a decade younger than her. He'd got a scholarship to Oxford, a first-class degree, but had refused a commission and had been happy to be ground crew and not one of the elite in the RAF.

But that wasn't the only thing that made the continuance of the relationship impossible – he was a socialist and abhorred all that someone from her class stood for. He'd made it clear he wouldn't be comfortable living in her world and she couldn't live in his. She had responsibilities to the Harcourt name, her ancient mother-in-law, her estates and family, and for this reason they had sadly parted.

John had already held a pilot's licence which he'd gained when he was at Oxford, as had many of his friends. Even so, his dislike of the 'chinless wonders' as he called them who had been selected for pilot training because of their background had made him decide not to become aircrew. Things were different now and there were hundreds of non-commissioned pilots, as over half of the original cohort had perished or been injured during Dunkirk and the Battle of Britain. Therefore, John would be aircrew of some sort, although not an officer. Joanna prayed he was still alive, as the life expectancy of aircrew was terrifyingly short.

What had changed her mind about John was simple. If Harcourt thought her a fallen woman, not someone he respected, then it was quite possible he'd mentioned this to someone in the Officers' Mess. David's friends had never accepted her into their rarefied circle as she came from a middle-class family. Even a whiff of immorality on her part and what little standing she'd gained in the neighbourhood would vanish. So why deny them both a possibility of happiness?

She was jolted from her reverie by Joe bursting in. 'Ma, another load of coal has come. Where shall I tell them to tip it?'

'I've no idea, darling, you know more about that sort of thing than I do. It was worth the upset of having two spies here just for the extra coal. Could you bear to cycle to the village and post my letter to Sarah?'

'Be happy to. It seems a bit quiet here now all the girls are back at work. Shall I call in and see how Mr Briggs is managing without the two land girls?'

'It's in the wrong direction, Joe, so don't do that today. Is it my imagination or is it warmer today?'

'Thawing, definitely. I'll ride Star to the farm tomorrow if it's not freezing, as she could do with the exercise.'

'I expect Mrs Ramsbottom will call soon for the uniforms. I'm wondering if she'll allocate two girls to replace the ones that have gone.'

'I wouldn't want to be the girls who get second-hand uniforms. The Land Army is called an army but doesn't get the same respect or perks that the other services get. I bet a WAAF recruit doesn't get old clothes.'

'I do know they have to hand everything in – even their underwear – when they leave. If they don't give it out again, then what happens to it?'

A strange conversation to be having when her heart was thudding, half in excitement, half in dread, at the thought of what Angus might discover about John. Perhaps it would be better not to find out if John had been shot down, hideously injured or taken prisoner. Ignorance was bliss – that's what people said, didn't they?

* * *

The following morning, Joanna woke to a very different view from her bedroom. The snow had gone, there was a watery winter sun shining on the fields. She stood watching the seagulls swooping and diving, their distinctive call audible from where she was standing.

The siren went on the base – hardly surprising, as the Luftwaffe would be in action now the skies were clear – followed almost immediately by the one in the village. The house shook as one after another, squadrons of fighters roared overhead.

Biggins, Elizabeth's personal dresser, would get her mother-in-law down to the cellar in good time. The girls would already have left for work and no doubt would have to hide in a ditch or under a hedge until the all-clear was sounded.

Aggie, one of the ladies from the village who worked in the house, was here this morning, but the other two wouldn't come until after lunch. This meant there would only be seven of them going down to the shelter. No one really enjoyed being there, especially since two German pilots had taken refuge for several nights last year. Even though every item and every surface had been disinfected, the place no longer seemed theirs.

'The paraffin heater's on, blankets and cushions are down there and Jean's just filling hot water bottles. I've already taken down the Thermos flasks,' Liza said cheerfully.

'Good girl, has your grandmother gone down yet?'

The girl grinned. 'She wasn't too happy, but Miss Biggins is very good with her and promised to play cards – I think poker was mentioned. I didn't know Grandma could play that.'

'There's a lot you don't know about your grandmother, my dear, you must ask her to tell you about her time in the south of France. I think you're old enough to hear that story now.'

The back door banged and Joanna heard Joe pushing across the bolts. It was his task to check the windows and doors were secure. He must have been outside preparing to cycle to the village.

Thank goodness he hadn't set off. He was much safer and warmer in the cellar with everybody else.

9

Charlie was halfway to the village with Sal doing the daily delivery when the siren started to yowl.

'We're a blooming great target with this tractor and trailer. I don't reckon it'll matter if we leave it in the road and take shelter in that wood over there,' Sal yelled from her seat in the trailer.

'Right – I'll have to turn the engine off and you know how hard it is to start. It almost snapped my fingers off this morning.'

'I'll do it – I'm a dab hand at it.'

Charlie steered the little Ferguson onto the verge and prayed it wouldn't get stuck as everywhere was impossibly muddy now the snow had melted. The siren continued to wail, Spitfires and Hurricanes raced into the sky to try and stop whatever bombers were heading this way. She had no wish to be shot a second time so jumped down from the metal seat of the tractor and made a mad dash for the wooded area just ahead. Sal was close behind.

'Good job it ain't hot or the milk would turn,' she said as the two of them took shelter under the meagre protection of the bare winter branches.

'There's a clump of holly trees over there, I think we'd be safer amongst them,' Charlie said.

'Our boys in blue will stop them German buggers coming. I don't reckon none of them will get as far as this.'

Charlie wasn't going to remind her friend that she'd been shot by a German fighter bomber – who might have mistaken her khaki overalls for the uniform of a soldier – and a German plane had crashed and exploded, blowing out all the windows at the front of Goodwill House.

They huddled under the prickly protection of the holly and watched the sky for German planes. None were seen and half an hour later, the all-clear sounded at the same time as there was a furious honking in the road.

'Quick, the bus is waiting. Let's hope the tractor starts first time or there'll be a lot of very cross passengers,' Charlie said as she ran towards the abandoned tractor.

The ticket collector was standing by the tractor as if expecting it to miraculously burst into life and move itself out of the way.

'Sorry, we had no choice but to leave it when the siren went. As soon as we get it going, we'll be on our way.'

Charlie expected to be greeted with grumbles but to her surprise, he grinned. 'Them things are absolute buggers to start. You hop on, love, and I'll do it for you.'

Sal handed him the handle whilst she clambered back onto the seat. Charlie was about to warn him about getting his knuckles rapped but he seemed to know what he was doing. With two heaves, the engine stuttered into life. She heard an ironic cheer coming from the passengers in the waiting bus.

'Ta ever so, you're a gent,' Sal said as she retrieved the starting handle and raced around to dive headfirst onto the trailer.

Charlie had never driven the tractor at full speed but thought today called for such a daring move. 'Hang on, Sal, it might be a bit bumpy.'

With more luck than judgement, they arrived safely but, as the bus would want to get past and continue on its way to Ramsgate, she couldn't wait outside Raven's shop as she usually did. She kept going until she reached the grassy clearing just outside the village where she could swing round in a wide circle and then go back in the opposite direction.

The bus chugged past a few minutes later and the driver waved, no longer cross with the delay. 'Mr Raven will think we've taken his goods elsewhere. The snow's gone but I'm chilled to the marrow. To be honest, I'd rather be clearing ditches than driving this tractor when it's so cold.'

The shopkeeper was waiting anxiously outside and the three of them unloaded the trailer in double quick time. On their return to the farm, a horse and cart and an old man on a bicycle passed them travelling in the opposite direction but nothing was held up behind them. Charlie was relieved to turn into the lane that led to the farm.

The girls finished clearing the ditch that had been flooding into the field by the time it got dark. They were used to cycling back, barely able to see where they were going, so it didn't bother any of them.

Mr Pickering came out as they were about to leave. 'I heard that those two girls got the boot. Reggie Foster has asked if you'd work there tomorrow as his two girls were here for a week last year.'

'All three of us?' Daphne asked.

'No, just Charlie and Sal – you stop here. I need someone to do the chickens and feed the pigs now my missus can't help.'

'I'll do that, I'm better with the porkers than what the others are,' Sal said, and he agreed.

They pedalled furiously as soon as they got onto the Tarmac in the vain hope that by doing so they'd be a bit warmer when they got home. They washed and went into the kitchen to grab a mug of tea to keep them going until supper.

'A letter came for you, Charlie, Aggie put it in your room,' Jean said.

'Thank you, I'll read it when I go to bed. I doubt it's anything important.' The last letter Charlie had received had been months ago and hadn't been good news, so she was in no hurry to read this one.

When she saw the envelope on the dressing table, her heart lurched. It had a local postmark. The only person it could be from was James. Her fingers trembled as she pulled the envelope open. Her eyes were blurred by the time she'd finished.

How could she have contemplated breaking the engagement to this wonderful, kind, sensitive, understanding man? Thank goodness he'd written before she'd gone ahead. Knowing he was prepared to let her decide when to set a date meant she could forget her fears for the moment and just enjoy his company.

She had to speak to him immediately. Lady Harcourt wouldn't mind her using the telephone as it was a sort of emergency. The operator connected the call and Mary answered.

'Hello, Mary, it's Charlie. Is James there?'

'Good heavens, it's very late to be making a social call. I thought it was an emergency.'

'It's nine o'clock, Mary, not late at all. Please fetch James to the phone. He will be cross if you don't.'

The housekeeper snorted but did as she asked. The sound of someone running made her smile. He was as eager to speak to her as she was to him.

'Darling, I can't tell you what a relief it is to have you call me.'

'Thank you for your lovely letter, James. I was considering

ending the engagement but am now not going to. Have you had a horrid day?'

'Not really. When I'm in theatre, I can't think about anything else. I was beginning to assume you weren't going to call as you would have got my letter hours ago.'

'If I'd realised it was from you then I'd have read it earlier. I'm sorry to have left you in suspense. When do you have a Saturday free?'

'All my Saturdays are supposedly my own. Emergencies only. What do you have in mind?'

'We could go to the cinema. There's bound to be something good showing.'

'The Picture House closed last year. However, Mary said there's a matinée of *His Girl Friday* with Cary Grant and Rosalind Russell being shown in the village hall. What about going to that?'

'Oh, yes, please. Could we have a fish and chip tea afterwards?'

He chuckled. 'I think I can manage that, sweetheart. We could bring our fish and chips back here and give Mary the evening off. She'll be thrilled to eat something she hasn't had to cook.'

'I'll catch the bus in but would be glad of a lift home if you don't mind.'

'Charlie, you don't have to ask. We're engaged, it's my absolute pleasure to do anything that will make you happy.'

She skipped back to bed, beginning to believe that against all the odds they might be able to make this work.

* * *

James was aware that Mary had been eavesdropping – one of her few flaws – but on this occasion, her doing so annoyed him. She was putting tomorrow's bread on the back of the range to pretend she'd been there all the time.

'Mary, if you want to continue your employment here then you will desist from listening to conversations that are none of your business. I hope you understand.'

She nodded, not at all bothered by his reprimand. 'If I didn't listen, I'd never know what's going on. You don't tell me.'

'For God's sake, Mary! My private life is exactly that. I'm well aware that you gossip—'

'No, sir, I don't tittle-tattle about medical matters. You can trust me on that.'

'I do, if I thought you were breaking medical confidences then I'd have dismissed you long ago. But I don't want you spreading what you hear around the village about my personal life. Charlie and I will be getting married and it's quite possible she won't want anyone living in. Think about that next time you're tempted to listen to my calls.'

Now he had her attention. 'I'll mind my Ps and Qs from now on. I'll close the door when you're on the telephone in future.'

'Good. As you already know, there's no need for me to tell you we'll be having fish and chips for supper on Saturday, is there?' She flushed and fussed with her apron. 'I don't want any cocoa tonight. I've papers to read for tomorrow. Goodnight.'

* * *

The atmosphere at home was bit subdued for the next few days but by Saturday good relations were restored. It was cold and dry, a pleasant change from the freezing rain that had been falling the last few days. It must have been appalling working outside and James hoped that when eventually he persuaded Charlie to marry him she'd be prepared to give up her employment as a land girl.

He was waiting at the bus stop when it rattled to a halt across the road from his house. She stepped out looking radiant and it took all his control not to snatch her up and kiss her.

'You look lovely as always. This is the first time I've seen you in anything but your uniform. I didn't know you had civilian clothes with you at Goodwill House.'

'We've all got a couple of outfits. This is sadly out of date, as the hem is too—'

'I really don't care about fashion. Blue suits you and you look stunning.'

'And you look very warm – I can't see what you're wearing under that big overcoat, thick scarf and flat cap. I would have thought that a trilby would be more in keeping with your station than a working man's hat.'

'This keeps my head warm. Come on, it's too cold to be hanging about out here having a conversation. Let's head for the village hall and get ourselves decent seats. Do you prefer to be at the front or the back?'

She'd slipped her arm through his and was walking so close he could feel her hip through the many thicknesses of material.

'As I've only been to the cinema once in my life, I can't really answer that question. I think I would rather be towards the rear of the hall, although that means we'll have the projector whirring away behind us.'

'I imagine it'll be centre back so if we sit on the side, we should be fine. Mary tells me they're serving tea and biscuits and it's included in the price.'

'Jolly good – a nice cup of tea will warm me up. The bus was absolutely freezing – there was ice on the inside of the window.'

They were almost the first to arrive and had the pick of the room. 'If we put our coats on two chairs, not only will it make them more comfortable, it will also save places for us whilst we have our tea.'

'Are you sure? Wouldn't it be better to put them in the cloakroom?'

'I don't think so but as you're an important person, I suppose you must know best.' She peeped at him from under her eyelashes and he laughed, turning several heads.

'Whatever I say, you'll do as you like. I'm putting my outdoor stuff in the cloakroom like a good boy and you must do as you please.' James tried to look stern but failed miserably. Charlie giggled.

'You put yours elsewhere and I'll put mine on the chairs. I'll have no sympathy when you complain of being uncomfortable in the interval. By the way, is there a second film after the main event?'

'I think it's a Disney cartoon of some sort.' One of the ladies taking their one and sixpences overheard his answer.

'*Snow White and the Seven Dwarfs*, Dr Willoughby. Actually, that will be shown first so the children can go home in the interval as the second film isn't really suitable for little ones.'

He was waiting for her to congratulate them on their engagement, as Mary must have told all her cronies, but nothing was said and he began to wonder if he'd misjudged his housekeeper.

The hall was filling up and he saw several villagers eyeing Charlie's coat, which had secured the best two seats in the house. He nodded and smiled and took his place, wondering where she was. She certainly wasn't in the hall so must have gone to the WC. Cold weather could have that effect on a person's bladder.

'Here, Doc, you'll be in trouble moving that. That posh land girl who works at Fiddler's Farm put it there,' a rather disgruntled old chap said.

'As we're now engaged to be married, this seat is for me.' James smiled to himself, knowing that this information would travel like wildfire around the room. He owed his housekeeper an apology as obviously she'd not passed on what she'd heard.

Charlie joined him and raised an eyebrow. He grinned. 'Sorry, thought it time we made it public.'

'I was pounced on by all and sundry and told I was a lucky girl, I wasn't up to the task of being a doctor's wife, oh,' she smiled in a way that made him a little uneasy, 'and that my marrying you would be breaking several young ladies' hearts.'

'Good God! I'm so sorry. I can assure you, darling, that I've not been involved with anyone in the five years I've been here.'

It was her turn to look surprised. 'What, not even gone out with someone?'

He shook his head. 'Didn't even miss having a woman in my life until I met you last year.' They were more or less whispering and as they were on the far end of the back row, there was no danger of being overheard. 'I notice it was the broken-hearted comments that you wanted to query.'

Her delightful laugh rang out and again several heads turned. How he loved this girl. It was he that was the lucky one and not Charlie.

* * *

Joanna tried to calculate how long it would take for her letter to reach Sarah, then how soon her daughter could pass on the request to Angus. He was no longer flying as he'd done more than sixty sorties and was now doing something important at Hornchurch.

Would Angus have either the time or the inclination to pursue her request? Obviously, she'd given Sarah permission to explain her reasons for wanting to find John. Maybe Angus would be so shocked, as Harcourt had been, that he'd not want to help her.

A week later, Angus rang, asking to speak to her. Her heart was hammering as she gripped the receiver. Was it the worst possible news?

'Joanna, how are you? I will have to be brief. There's a flap on and I'm needed at a meeting in five minutes.'

'Angus, how good of you to ring. What have you found out?'

'Serjeant is now a warrant officer and flying a Spitfire. He's well, already an ace, but unfortunately is now with his squadron in Malta. Do you have a pen handy? I'll give you his number and then you can write to him.'

She had a pen in her handbag, which was on the console next to the telephone. She scrabbled about and was ready to write on the back of an envelope. She repeated the numbers back.

'Yes, that's right. Before I go, thanks for your advice to Sarah. Everything's splendid between us now.'

'So happy it is. Goodbye and thank you.'

She hung up, smiling. She'd needn't have worried about whether Angus would help her.

Mrs Ramsbottom was arriving at any moment, otherwise she'd write the all-important letter now. The area organiser of the Land Army turned up on time and Joanna thought she would take her into the sitting room. Elizabeth would also be in there, but that couldn't be helped. Although they now had sufficient coal to light all the fires, this wouldn't be patriotic, so the one in the grand hall was unlit, as were the ones in the breakfast room and the library. The girls were allowed one hod full of coal a night for their rooms.

'Did you have a good journey, Mrs Ramsbottom? It must be so much easier driving about the county now the weather has improved a bit.'

'No problems at all, my lady, thank you. Ah, I see the uniforms are ready. We've decided that in future, second-hand clothes will be offered to serving girls as spares. Do you think any of your girls could find a use for these?'

'Absolutely. Spare items will be very popular. Please, follow me to the sitting room. It's warm in there.'

'I'm afraid I can't stop, much as I'd like to. I have two more visits to make today. I wanted to let you know that two new girls will be arriving at the weekend. They are transferring from somewhere in Yorkshire. They found the weather and primitive conditions too much for them. They're originally from London.'

'Have you let the farm know?'

'I called in on the way past. Goodbye, my lady, don't hesitate to contact me if there are any further problems.'

Mrs Ramsbottom was a charming lady, but Joanna was glad that she could return to her letter.

10

Charlie had thoroughly enjoyed the outing with James, but they had come to a mutual decision to only meet on a Saturday afternoon in future. Of course, they would see each other at church if he attended, but she wasn't going back to his house again for lunch as that had seemed too intimate.

She wasn't exactly sure why he'd agreed so readily to restricting the amount of time they would spend together but was relieved that he'd done so. She loved being in his company and no longer flinched if he brushed against her or put his arm around her waist to steady her when they were walking. Anything else would be too difficult for her at the moment.

All week, she'd been with Daphne on the other farm and they'd been picking sprouts, which was a horrible job. The farmer dealt with the livestock, and he had an incredibly ancient labourer who did his best, but the bulk of the work was done by Charlie and Daphne.

'I'll be blooming glad when the new girls come and we can return to Fiddler's Farm. It doesn't seem the same working here.'

'We've been getting a hot drink at lunchtime which is more

than we get normally,' Charlie said. 'I don't think Sal's enjoying being the only one there either.' She straightened and rubbed her aching back. 'It'll be dark in half an hour. By the time we get the trailer back to the barn, I'll be more than ready to go home.'

Manston was now almost as busy as it had been last year, with aircraft landing and taking off at all times of the day and night. One only became aware just how noisy it had been when blessed silence resumed.

Sal was waiting for them at the end of the lane that led to Fiddler's Farm so they could pedal home together.

'When do you see your fiancé again? He only lives a couple of miles away – if it was my Bob living so close, we'd see each other every night,' Daphne said.

'We've decided just to go out on a Saturday afternoon – he works so hard and does such long hours at the hospital, I don't want him wasting his time coming to see me in the evenings.'

'Crikey, I bet he don't think it a waste of time. You still having second thoughts, Charlie?' Sal asked sympathetically.

They'd now reached the barn and it was easier to talk when they were stationary. 'No, the reverse is true. I had a wonderful time last Saturday. I do love him very much, but I'm just not ready to get married at the moment.'

'I told Bob I didn't want to get married but I've changed my mind,' Daphne said. 'I've only seen him twice since we got engaged last year. I know there's a war on and that some women don't see their men at all, but he's ground crew at Folkestone and that's only a few miles away. I want to be with him all the time we have free.'

'Are you saying that if he gets permission to marry, is allowed to live off base, that you'll be getting married soon?' Charlie asked.

'I suggested that in my last letter, but I've not had a reply yet. We did say that if he got posted back to Manston – which hasn't happened yet – then we would be married but I really don't want to wait that long.'

Sal wasn't interested in men but was happy to share in their conversations about their respective loves. After the horrible experience she'd had when she was living with an East End villain, she'd vowed never to get involved with anyone again. It had been nine months and so far, she'd stuck to her word.

'Why don't you have a double wedding? I know you ain't ready yet, Charlie, but I reckon by the spring you'll have changed your mind. You could get married in the village and then ask Lady Harcourt if you could have the reception here in the ballroom. I'd be a lot cheaper doing it together.'

Charlie was horrified at the thought of getting married so soon, but Daphne shrieked and threw her arms around her.

'That would be absolutely spiffing. I'll go and ask Lady Harcourt right now.' She'd gone before Charlie could call her back.

'Sal, this is a disaster. I don't even want to get married this year, let alone in the spring.'

'Don't worry, Daphne's getting ahead of herself, ain't she? She's not spoken to Bob, he's not spoken to his CO, so I don't think you've got anything to worry about.'

'I hope you're right. It will be embarrassing to have to explain to Lady Harcourt that I don't want to get married that soon.'

Her ladyship was busy, so Daphne had been unable to speak to her and there was no opportunity to talk about it again until they retired to their cosy bedroom after supper. None of them wished to mingle with the remaining girls, as they'd all been involved in the illegal drinking spree. It seemed unfair that only Sandra and Joyce had been punished.

* * *

Once they were curled up in their blankets in front of the fire, Charlie tried to explain to Daphne how she felt.

'Daphne, please don't mention a double or any sort of wedding that involves me. It would be lovely for you and Bob to get married here, but not me.'

'I'm sorry, I was so excited at the thought of sharing my special day with one of my best friends I didn't stop to check if you were happy with this.'

'I do want to marry James, but not this year. Maybe next summer...'

'Blimey, Charlie, we could all be blown up or moved away by then. If you ain't ready to marry your man in a couple of months, then I don't reckon you'll ever want to.'

This remark struck home. Would she ever be ready to marry him? 'I fear you might be right, Sal. I'm not going to make any hasty decisions, but if by the end of next month I've not changed my mind, then I'll break the engagement. It's not fair to keep James dangling.' As she said this, Charlie swallowed, the thought of not having James in her life didn't appeal. Was it possible that she'd finally recovered from her horrible experience?

'End of February it is. Would you agree to a double wedding in April if you have decided to go ahead?'

Charlie didn't hesitate. 'Yes, definitely. But promise me you won't mention it to anyone until then? I don't want to talk about it either.'

'Okay, weddings are taboo until then,' Daphne said. 'It would give us two months to arrange things. Good Friday is the 11th, so it has to be after that. Shall we pencil in Saturday the 26th?'

Charlie didn't want to 'pencil in' any date at all but agreeing to a hypothetical wedding wasn't the same as actually agreeing to a real one, was it? It was Saturday tomorrow and Mr Pickering had given them the whole day off as they'd worked hard all week and his neighbour was pleased with them.

She didn't sleep, despite being so tired, as her head was whirling with thoughts of seeing James and how she was going to be able to know when or if she was ready to be intimate with him.

* * *

James was more than ready to put aside his gruelling medical schedule for a couple of days and spend time with Charlie. He'd agreed readily to her suggesting they only met at weekends because being with her for longer would be hard as he had to be so careful not to express his love in any way but verbally.

He wouldn't have expected her to sleep with him even without her difficulties but, under normal circumstances, as her fiancé he'd be able to hold her hand, put his arm around her shoulders and kiss her. He wasn't a regular churchgoer but if by so doing this meant he could sit next to her and perhaps persuade her, when the weather was clement, to take a stroll with him before she returned to Goodwill House, then he'd be there every week unless he was on an emergency call.

At least the weather was dry, none of the filthy freezing rain they'd had the past few days. God knows what the land girls had been doing during this time, but he wouldn't have wanted to be out pulling turnips or clearing ditches. These girls were tough, doing everything on a farm that their male counterparts had done and for half the remuneration.

'Dr Willoughby, your young lady has just turned onto the path. You asked me to tell you so you could be ready when she knocked.'

'Thank you, Mary, I'm not sure when I'll be back. I won't be needing supper tonight. Feel free to take the evening off, invite friends round, whatever you want.'

He'd been making a particular effort to let her know how much he appreciated her since his faux pas about her gossiping. He really didn't want to have to find another housekeeper and he was pretty sure he wouldn't find anybody as good as her.

Charlie didn't need to knock on the door as he opened it as she stepped under the porch. 'Good afternoon, my love, you look quite enchanting. I don't believe I've seen you in any headgear apart from your hideous uniform hat.'

She smiled and patted the pretty felt cloche with a gloved hand. 'Believe it or not, this is Sal's. Jean made her a new wardrobe last summer when she was going to leave and she's the best dressed girl in the house – apart from Liza, of course.'

'I thought blue was the perfect colour for you but burgundy looks just as good. I expect you noticed my car is waiting on the drive. We're going to The Royal Hotel in Ramsgate for afternoon tea.'

Her smile rocked him back on his heels. He wanted to snatch her up and kiss her breathless but instead gestured towards the car and she dashed off in front of him. He followed, steadying his breathing before he was obliged to sit close to her in the confined interior of his car.

'I do so love an afternoon tea, James, and haven't had a real one for years. Do you think there'll be scones, cakes and dainty sandwiches?'

'They assured me there would. I've asked for a table overlooking the sea, but it won't be the view it used to be. The beach is covered with concrete barriers and barbed wire now.'

'I really don't care. It'll be absolutely spiffing just being with you all afternoon.'

He smiled at her enthusiasm. The prospect of cake and scones tended to have this effect on ladies. He couldn't see the point in afternoon tea – he'd rather have an actual meal at the proper time

– but if it made her happy then afternoon tea was his new favourite.

She was bubbling with inconsequential chatter about her week and by the time he'd negotiated the steep hill that led down to the promenade where the hotel was situated and turned into the car park on the beach side of the hotel, he was beginning to think things might have changed between them. Surely just the prospect of tea couldn't be causing her to be so happy in his company?

The interior of this splendid hotel was pristine, the head waiter who greeted them politely was resplendent in black tails and the waitresses, in frilly white caps and aprons over smart black uniforms, were equally gracious.

'Good afternoon, sir, miss, allow me to show you to your table.'

The waiter marched off, not waiting for a reply, and they followed. The table was, as promised, positioned by the window. James had deliberately booked early as the blackouts would be drawn by three o'clock and he wanted her to be able to watch the waves for an hour.

Once seated, they were left alone whilst their tea was fetched. Charlie gazed out of the window at the grey English Channel and the fortifications, with obvious enjoyment. He thought the scene depressing but if it pleased her, that was more than enough.

'Thank you for bringing me here. I know it's not a jolly view today, but I can imagine what it was like before the war and in the summer.' She turned and beamed. 'Goodness, that was quick. Our tea's already on its way.'

James wasn't a big fan of cucumber finger sandwiches, but the scones were warm and light, the cakes delicious. There was even a small dish of cream to pile on top of the strawberry jam.

Even when the heavy curtains were drawn and the view obscured, the merry mood continued. 'That was scrumptious,

James, thank you so much for arranging this. The girls will be so jealous when they hear where I've been this afternoon.'

'I'm glad you've enjoyed it, sweetheart, I certainly have.' He smiled wryly. 'Although, to be frank, it's your company, not the tea, that has made this a delightful occasion for me.'

'For a gentleman who professes not to have enjoyed his tea, I notice there's not a crumb left on your plate.'

'I was hungry. I can even eat the hospital food when I'm hungry.'

She pursed her lips and pretended to look cross. He caved before she could admonish him, even in jest.

'It was all surprisingly delicious, apart from the sandwiches. As crusts have to be eaten, I wonder what happened to the ones cut from our sandwiches.'

She laughed. 'I can answer that. Jean told me crusts are made into crumbs to use on fish and in pies.'

'Thank you for that information. I should have been worrying about it for months.' He winked at her and she giggled. He waved a hand at the lurking head waiter and mimed writing. The man bowed and vanished. The bill would arrive promptly, of that he had no doubt.

It was eye-blinkingly expensive but worth every penny. Charlie slipped her arm through his without being asked and he felt as though he was walking on air. He was prepared to spend every penny he had if it brought her closer to him. They stepped out into the dark, but worse than that, it was also foggy. Driving home wasn't going to be fun.

'Thank you, dear James, for bringing me here. Imagine how lovely it will be coming in the summer.'

'My absolute pleasure, my love. Shall we make this a monthly treat?' He tried to keep the excitement from his voice. If she was talking about a summer visit, then perhaps she wasn't going to break off their engagement as he kept fearing that she would.

* * *

Joanna blotted the letter to John that had taken her several days to complete to her satisfaction. This was her fourth and final version. She read the three pages one more time to be sure it was what she wanted to say.

Dear John,

I know we agreed that we would never contact each other again but as the months have passed, the war intensifies, our decision seems less and less sensible.

I still love you, believe I always will, and that kind of love is a once in lifetime sort of thing. Obviously if one's partner dies then one has to move on. However, that is not the case for us.

We parted because I convinced you we couldn't be together, that our worlds were too far apart for either of us to successfully make the necessary adjustments.

I no longer care about protocol, etiquette, and other antiquated notions. I want to be happy and know I can never really be so apart from you.

I intend to give Goodwill House to whoever might want it for war work and move somewhere more manageable. If you could bear to be involved with a titled lady, to accept that we have differing views, then come back to me when you can. I do not think our politics are so diverse that we can't meet amicably in the middle.

I know I told you to find a young woman who can give you children, not oblige you to compromise your socialist principles, and I will understand if you have moved on. I have not.

If by some miracle you are still in love with me, want to spend the rest of your life with me and my family, then write back when you can.

If you do not, then ignore this letter. If I hear nothing by the summer then I'll understand and put all thought of being with you aside.

Please take care and do not take unnecessary risks. Even if we are not together, I shall always care about your safety and want you to survive this dreadful war and live a happy and fulfilled life after it is eventually over.

All my love,

Joanna

She carefully folded the flimsy air mail paper and placed it in the matching pale blue envelope. This was one letter she would post herself and not in the village post office. A trip to Ramsgate was called for, where she was more or less anonymous.

Joanna smiled as she recalled the incident that had taken place when Elizabeth had first arrived. Her mother-in-law had handed over a thick white envelope and expected Joanna to post it to France at her own expense. How different things were between them now. She loved her and believed that once the old lady had recovered from the shock, she would accept John into the family. If a choice had to be made, then Joanna had no doubt it would be John she chose.

She'd been convinced that the confusion Elizabeth had shown occasionally was the precursor to something permanent but for some reason, there had been no further bouts of bewilderment and Joanna didn't think that senile dementia fluctuated in this way. Next time she saw Dr Willoughby, she'd ask him his opinion.

She put the precious envelope into her handbag – although

she was eager to post it, there was really no rush. It might take weeks to reach him, so what did a few more days matter?

The two new land girls would be arriving sometime today and she thought she ought to be there to greet them, as she was their landlady. If the girls were living in a hostel run by the Land Army, then there would be a matron or someone similar keeping an eye on the girls, so this role had fallen to her at Goodwill House.

She shrugged; she hadn't been doing a very good job if two of the girls had been dismissed for stealing and four others had joined in, even if they hadn't actually gone into the wine cellar and taken the alcohol themselves. Next time Mrs Ramsbottom called in, hopefully for more than a few moments, she would mention that she was thinking of moving from Goodwill House and that other arrangements needed to be made for the girls – not immediately but by the autumn of this year.

Liza was becoming restless, wanted something more useful to do than just help Jean in the kitchen and spend her mornings with the tutor. Of course, she had her weekly St John's meetings and also came to the monthly WVS and WI ones – but she was legally old enough to be working full-time and Joanna feared Liza might insist that she found employment in Ramsgate until she was old enough to enrol as a student nurse. Her daughter poked her head around the sitting room door.

'Ma, the new recruits have just turned onto the drive. I thought you'd like to know.'

'Thank you, my dear, I certainly do. Before we go out to greet them, I've a suggestion to make. Mrs Evans has asked me several times if you would like to be the nanny for their children and I said you weren't old enough, but I think you are now. Is that something you'd be interested in doing?'

Liza pushed the door so hard it knocked plaster off the wall as she hurtled in and hugged Joanna. 'That's exactly what I'd like to do and it'll be good training for when I become a nurse. I want to work with children when I'm qualified. Thank you so much.' She stepped back and her smile slipped a little. 'I don't have to live in, do I? I really don't want to.'

'No, when you go off to train will be soon enough for you to leave home. You'll work weekdays only and Mrs Evans wants you there at eight o'clock and you'll finish at five. We didn't discuss remuneration, that's up to you to negotiate. If you're old enough to work, then you're quite capable of arranging the financial details too.'

'I'll pop down now and sort things out. I thought you'd keep me with my nose in a book until next year.'

'I've spoken to Mr Kent and your tutor's confident that as long as you spend an hour or so every evening on your studies, you'll pass the school certificate next summer with flying colours.'

How her life had changed since David had left at the start of the war. She was no longer a timid, subservient wife but a confident and efficient widow. She looked around with a happy smile. All she needed to make her life wonderful was to hear from John.

11

Charlie clung onto James's arm as they ventured out into the darkness and fog. 'Will you be able to drive home safely in this? We can't see more than a few feet in front of us.'

'I'll do my best, sweetheart. You could walk in front holding a red lantern if you like.'

She laughed. 'I'd be happy to if you provide the lantern. I do have a torch, wait a minute whilst I get it out. I assume that you have one too.'

'A fat lot of good they are in this fog, but better than nothing, I suppose.'

They were still laughing when they walked into a wall. His quick reactions kept them both from falling. His language wasn't at all polite.

'Are you hurt, Charlie? God, I'm so sorry, there shouldn't be a wall in the middle of the pavement.'

Despite her shock, she giggled. 'We're obviously not on the pavement. Have you any idea where we are?'

'Not in the foggiest, sweetheart.' Then he laughed the sound somewhat muffled in the salt-smelling fog that surrounded them.

'No pun intended. Let me think, try and visualise the street outside the hotel. We have to find our way back there and wait it out. It's coming from the sea so should blow over in an hour or so.'

Charlie wasn't worried as she had every confidence James would get them both back safely. She stood waiting for him to decide exactly where they were. Then a man shouted into the darkness.

'Anyone out there? Follow my voice. I'm standing on the steps of the hotel.'

'Just the ticket, be much easier to find the place this way. Hold my hand, Charlie, it'll be safer travelling single file. I want to go first so if I bump into anything, you won't.'

Now wasn't the time for hesitation and squeamishness. She willingly put her hand in his, finding it by touch as now they couldn't even see a foot in front of them. Even through his glove, she was aware of his strength.

'Do you think there's anyone else wandering about out here, James?'

'Possibly. What the hell was that? Careful, here's something solid in front of us.'

'I know where we are. We're across the road. I think we walked into a garden wall and now have bumped into a parked car.'

'Good God! How could I have been so stupid? I'm so sorry, sweetheart, this debacle is my fault.'

The voice from the hotel steps boomed out again.

'Shouldn't you call back so he knows we're coming? He might go in otherwise, thinking he's shouting to himself.'

He squeezed her hand. 'Good thing one of us is thinking clearly. I think we have to cross the road diagonally and then should be roughly in front of the hotel. If there wasn't a blackout, it might be easier.'

'For heaven's sake, James, I'm beginning to think all the excitement has gone to your head. Don't worry – I'll shout for you.' She took a deep breath and yelled at the top of her voice. 'We can hear you – keep calling, please.'

There was a strange noise coming from him and for a moment, she couldn't work out what it was. 'This is no laughing matter, Dr Willoughby, I can't think why you're finding it so amusing.'

He gulped but seemed incapable of speech. Whoever was guiding them back had stopped calling out, which was a worry. Then, ignoring all the blackout rules, a beam of light was pointed in their direction.

There was no danger that the light would be seen by any marauding Luftwaffe, as nothing would be in the air tonight. Then someone in the hotel must have come to the same conclusion as not only was there the torchlight, there was suddenly light flooding from open doors.

'Come on, darling, let's make a run for it.'

'No running, James, we might be able to see the light but we can't see any obstacles between us and it.'

'What could there possibly be in the middle of the road?' He set off at a brisk pace, towing her along behind him, and immediately discovered exactly why travelling at speed had been a very poor decision on his part. He walked into a lamp post.

His language was so appalling, Charlie was tempted to cover her ears. Then, floating about in the ghostly fog, she could see the outline of a man waving a torch and behind him the open doors of the hotel.

'Stop swearing, James, and let's get inside. Is your nose broken? I do hope not.'

He laughed. 'It's my pride that's bruised, not my person. Look, we're not the only ones returning here.'

Suddenly another couple was beside them – it was hard to tell whether they were old or young, male or female, but they were equally relieved to be out of the suffocating fog.

Charlie was stunned to find the person who'd been guiding them back, yelling with such gusto, was the rather stern and unfriendly head waiter.

'I didn't realise it was so bad, sir, miss, or I wouldn't have let you go out. Thank God the four of you have come to no serious harm. Our telephone is at your disposal if you wish to make a call to explain your tardiness.'

'I'm Dr Willoughby, I must let my housekeeper know and my fiancée will wish to ring Lady Harcourt as she lives at Goodwill House.'

The other couple were about James's age and Charlie introduced herself. The woman responded.

'I'm Valerie Sanderson and the chap heading for the telephone with Dr Willoughby is my husband, Thomas. We only live a ten-minute walk from here but it's quite impossible to get home at the moment.'

'We bumped into several things and I've laddered my last pair of stockings. I'm going to find the ladies' room and see if I can repair some of the damage.'

'I'll come with you. I put my hands in something quite unspeakable and really must wash them.'

By the time they left the ladies' room, they were on first-name terms. Mr Sanderson was a bank manager and deaf in one ear so hadn't been able to enlist in any of the services.

James and Thomas had also established a rapport and the foursome retreated to a small sitting room, where a welcome pot of tea was waiting.

'Lady Harcourt is aware of the circumstances, as is Mary. As neither of us have to work tomorrow, I've arranged for us to stay here. I hope that's all right, sweetheart?' James said. 'The hotel's more or less empty so there are plenty of rooms available.'

Valerie smiled. 'I'm hoping we won't have to stay but will do so if necessary. I don't suppose either of you play bridge?'

'I do,' Charlie said eagerly, 'but I don't know about James as it's not something we've ever discussed. We've only been engaged a couple of weeks.'

'I should think I do, how else do you think junior doctors fill their time on night duty?'

'I thought you'd probably be sleeping like a sensible person,' she said and squeezed his hand. This was the first time she'd initiated any physical contact. The small gesture made his eyes blaze and his happiness, his love, was plain to see.

Valerie nodded. 'Gosh, you two take me back to when we were first engaged. Enjoy these weeks before you get married – it's a wonderful time. Every day you learn something new about the person you love and planning a life together is so exciting.'

The fog had been a blessing, as spending more time with James was exactly what she needed to confirm her decision to marry him. He was the perfect choice for her.

* * *

James enjoyed every minute of their enforced stay at Ramsgate. They played bridge and he and Charlie won every rubber.

'I'm going to check on the fog,' Valerie said, 'it might have cleared enough for us to go home.'

James looked at Charlie. 'Do you want to return tonight if it has?'

'Heavens, no. It's too late to drive back as the house will be locked up for the night. If you don't mind, I'd rather stay here.'

He tried not to look delighted at her decision, but Thomas

winked. This had the same effect as having a bucket of sea water tipped over his head. This idiot thought he was pleased because he intended to creep into Charlie's room during the night.

Valerie returned and shook her head. 'Still too thick to venture out, even for us. Not to worry, shall we order some supper and listen to the radio? There might be something on we could dance to.'

'That's the ticket, Valerie, I'll attack the wireless and you take care of the food. I want something a bit stronger than tea to accompany it.'

James nodded. 'I'll have a beer, if they've got any, what about you, sweetheart?'

'I'd really like coffee but that might not be possible.'

The girls rushed off to find someone who could arrange things for them and Thomas switched on the handsome wireless that stood on the mantelpiece. The wooden case wasn't veneered but the genuine article. It hissed and clicked as the valves warmed up and then when the light came on, Thomas twiddled the knobs. After a lot of crackling, he found the Home Service. He continued to turn a knob and eventually dance music flooded the room. The Light Service had entertainment, the Home Service the news and propaganda.

'Shall we ask permission to move the chairs and make room for us to dance?' James didn't want to upset the management.

'I think there are only two other rooms occupied, so it will be a skeleton staff. They'll be glad we've taken matters into our own hands.'

When the two girls returned, the half a dozen armchairs had been pushed to either end and the two coffee tables put to one side. Whatever supper appeared could be placed on these. This left ample room for two couples to enjoy themselves. But James was still concerned that Thomas had the wrong idea.

As soon as he saw Charlie's expression, he realised Valerie must have said something similar to her. 'Excuse me, you two, I need to talk to my fiancée in private.' He didn't give her the opportunity to refuse but put his arm around her waist and guided her out.

'I can guess what Valerie said to you. Ignore it, sweetheart, I gave you my word as a gentleman and wouldn't dream of reneging on it.'

'I know that, I'm not upset with you but with them. Of course there are girls who don't want to wait until their wedding night but I'm not in that number. I was offended that Valerie thought I was.' She smiled and the band around his chest slackened. 'I put her straight and she had the grace to apologise.'

'Then I expect she's explaining our feelings to Thomas and we can return without fear of embarrassment on either side.'

'We can – the kitchen's closed so no hot food. The night manager promised we'll get whatever's available. I expect it will be the leftovers from our afternoon tea.'

'I don't give a damn about the food or drink. I'm just relieved you're not upset by what happened.'

The sound of Glenn Miller and his band drifted across the foyer and without being asked, Charlie grabbed his hand and almost pulled him back into the small sitting room. An elderly waiter appeared with their food and drink and grinned as he saw them whirling around the small dance floor.

'I'll put your supper on the table. Mr Jones is bringing your beer and coffee.'

'Thank you, we appreciate being looked after so well,' James said as he manoeuvred Charlie out of the way. They continued to dance until the number ended and then Valerie turned the volume down on the wireless.

He thoroughly enjoyed the miscellany of items provided but he wasn't sure the others were quite so enthusiastic. As a junior doctor, he'd learned to grab whatever was available and stuff it down so was far less fussy than the others.

Valerie pointed to something unrecognisable on one of the serving platters. 'What do you think that is? It looks like a squashed meat pasty but why would that be on the same plate as slices of fruit pie?'

'It's pastry, Valerie, that's how they've arranged things,' he said with a smile. 'Bread-related items on the other plate regardless of whether they're savoury or sweet.' He reached down and removed the offending item. 'I'm happy to eat this.' He took an exploratory bite and nodded. 'Definitely meat and surprisingly tasty.'

They were too full to resume dancing so restored the room to its former arrangement and sat and chatted about nothing much until eleven o'clock.

'Time to turn in. I hope there's someone to give us our room keys,' Valerie said. 'We should have collected them earlier.'

The night manager was waiting and handed them over. All three rooms were on the first floor facing the sea, so no complicated directions were necessary.

The other two grabbed their key and rushed off, leaving James and Charlie alone.

'I've had an absolutely spiffing evening, James, thank you so much.'

'I'm glad you've enjoyed it – I certainly have. I'm going to look like a pirate tomorrow morning.' He ran his palm over his already bristly chin. 'Being dark, I need to shave every day.'

She tilted her head and looked at him. 'Actually, I think looking slightly disreputable suits you. I hate not being able to clean my teeth, but I expect we'll both survive the experience.'

'We certainly can't attend church tomorrow morning, as it would be the scandal of the village.'

'I'm sure God won't mind this once. If that's the case, then we don't need to rush off tomorrow but can enjoy a leisurely breakfast.'

He handed her the key to the first room and stepped back, not wanting to crowd her or make her uncomfortable. To his surprise and delight, she stepped in, stood on tiptoe and pressed a light kiss on his lips. It took all his strength of will not to pull her closer.

'Goodnight, my darling girl, I love you.'

She turned as she pushed opened the door to her room. 'And I love you too and think one day we might be like Valerie and Thomas. I'm not sure when but I do know now that I *am* going to marry you, James.'

He wanted to turn a cartwheel down the corridor, to punch the air, on hearing this. Things were moving more smoothly and far quicker than he'd ever dared hope. Not quite at the stage of planning a wedding, but at least marriage was now definitely on the cards.

* * *

Joanna was impressed with the two new arrivals – both East End girls like Sal, and equally competent and forthright. She rather thought that the three of them might become good friends as Daphne and Charlie now had other things to think about.

The fog had lifted a little the next day but was still too dense to even consider attending church service that morning. None of the girls worked at the weekends at the moment and not all of them walked down to the church in the village now it wasn't a way of avoiding labouring on Sunday morning.

Elizabeth, now she had personal attendant, took her breakfast on a tray in her bedroom. This meant that Joanna could eat in the kitchen without being made to feel guilty for lowering standards.

'Good morning, Jean, I don't suppose the ladies from the village will come today. If you need any help, just let me know.' They both knew help wouldn't be asked for and if any was needed then her children and the girls making so much noise in the dining room would be the ones to provide it.

'Morning, Joanna, Joe's taking care of the animals and the dog's with him. Liza's finishing an essay she wants to hand into Mr Kent tomorrow before she starts work at the vicarage.'

'Good, I don't want her to let her studies slip. There are things we need to discuss.' She was almost tempted to tell her friend – not just a housekeeper – about the letter burning a hole in her handbag but resisted. 'Jean, I've decided that I want to move somewhere smaller, somewhere more manageable, by the end of the year. I'm going to ask Mrs Ramsbottom to start looking for alternative accommodation for our girls. Obviously, they need to stay in the neighbourhood as they work here but I won't be able to host them once we move.'

'I'm shocked as I never thought you'd want to leave the family home, but I think it's the right decision. I know Lady Harcourt will kick up a fuss but once we're settled somewhere warmer, she'll be glad we've moved.' Jean smiled. 'I'm assuming that I'm coming with you as somebody needs to run the house. It won't be a little cottage, will it?'

'Good heavens, no. When I was at the last WI meeting, I heard someone say that The Manse will be empty. Mrs Peabody is moving to Dorset to live with her sister. I don't blame her – she wouldn't want to continue to rattle around in the house on her own after her husband died last year.'

Jean put a rack of toast in front of Joanna and then sat down opposite. 'I know where you mean. I think it would be perfect. Somewhere to keep chickens and grow vegetables but nowhere for the horse.'

'Sarah told me I can sell Star if I have to as long as she goes to a good home. She's a useful mare as she goes well in harness. We wouldn't have a winter's store of logs if Joe hadn't used her to fetch them from the wood.'

'The Manse is the other side of Stodham, several miles from the base and no nearer to Ramsgate. It'll be a lot safer and a lot quieter there. It's also a lot closer to the village and the bus,' Jean said.

'That's exactly what I thought. The only drawback is that it does need a lot of work doing before it'll be ready for us to move into. This is why I don't think we'll be moving until the end of the year. I want indoor plumbing on all floors, central heating and the kitchen needs to be updated too.'

'I don't want one of those newfangled gas cookers – I like my Aga – I hope I can have another one. Miss Biggins might be a bit happier in a smaller house, too. I know she doesn't like it on the nursery floor with me.'

'Joe and Liza will be gone in two years and I want what time we have left together to be simpler, more relaxed,' Joanna said. 'All this formality isn't what they're used to, and I know they'll be much happier somewhere smaller.'

As she spoke, Joanna was thinking about John. If he did agree to resume their relationship, then where would they meet? She could hardly ask him to stay overnight wherever she was living as for Elizabeth to find out about the affair would be unconscionable.

She pushed these unwanted worries aside. The letter wasn't even posted yet, and she might never hear from him again. Time enough to worry about the details if he actually replied. She prayed he'd stayed in one piece, was able to answer her letter, and hadn't been shot down or injured whilst flying sortie after sortie in Malta.

12

Charlie eventually returned home just in time for Sunday lunch. The fog had cleared sufficiently for James to drive back slowly but safely from Ramsgate. She barely had time to rush upstairs, wash and change from yesterday's clothes into her uniform before the dinner gong sounded.

She was rather dreading being questioned about her overnight stay but apart from Daphne, no one seemed to have noticed she'd been missing.

'Did you have a good time?' Daphne asked.

'I don't think I've ever had a better one.' Charlie then went on to explain in exhaustive detail what had happened and only when she saw her friend's eyes were glazing did she pause for breath. 'I'm so sorry, I've been rattling on and not asked a single thing about what's been happening here. Has Sal deserted us for the newcomers?'

'I think she might have, and I must say I don't really blame her. We talk about nothing but our fiancés and she must be heartily sick of it. Also, the new girls are from Poplar too. They've got so much in common. I've a feeling she's going to ask if we mind if she moves in with them.'

'Golly, she's only known them a few hours. If she really wants to be with them and not us, then it makes sense for her to remain put and for us to move. Our room's set up for three and the other one isn't.'

'We'll speak to her after lunch. Do you think we need to ask Lady Harcourt before we start shifting about?'

Daphne was right – they were guests here, paying guests, and it would be impolite to change things without her ladyship's approval. After eating such a substantial breakfast only a few hours ago, she didn't really do justice to the roast dinner. Joe had killed a large cockerel in honour of the new arrivals and it was certainly appreciated by everyone else.

The girls on domestic duty cheerily cleared the table after dessert was finished and Charlie and Daphne went to speak to Lady Harcourt, who was quite amenable to them moving rooms.

'I'm surprised that Sal's so ready to abandon you two. I thought you were the best of friends.'

'We are, my lady, but Daphne and I might well be getting married sometime this year and Sal must be heartily fed up with us discussing our future plans.'

Until she'd said this, Charlie hadn't realised she'd made up her mind, but a surge of joy flooded through her. She thanked God that she and James had been trapped by the fog last night. Without having spent so much time with him, seeing just how kind and sensitive he was, she might never have come to this exciting decision.

Daphne hugged her and then turned to Lady Harcourt. 'We were wondering, my lady, if it might be possible to hold a reception here? We thought we would have a double wedding as that will keep the cost down and the ballroom would be absolutely perfect.'

'A wedding at Goodwill House? What a wonderful idea – do you have a date in mind?'

'I've not spoken to Bob yet, but now Charlie's made up her mind and we've got your permission, I'll write to him.'

'Good show. Were you thinking of a spring or summer wedding?'

'After Easter we thought, so any time after 14 April. Of course, it depends when Bob can get a pass. I'm sure that James will fit in with whatever dates are suitable for Daphne and Bob.'

They went in search of Sal and didn't have to go far as she was looking for them. She was relieved when they offered to exchange rooms with her new friends.

'I'm ever so pleased that you two are tying the knot but I ain't keen on listening to you going on about receptions and that. Lil and Flo are like me, they've had their fill of men and just want to get on with doing their bit. They knew Den but never knew me.'

'Shall we do it now? I think it's very likely both Daphne and I will leave the Land Army once we're married, so why don't we ask Mrs Ramsbottom if the three of you can work at Fiddler's Farm and then we can replace Sandra and Joyce as they only need two girls on that farm?'

'I never thought of that. Come on, I'll introduce you to me new mates. You'll always be me best friends too, though.'

It didn't take long to move things with five of them involved. Charlie left Daphne to finish organising things in their new, smaller, but equally pleasant room, and made her way downstairs. She asked permission to use the telephone and waited, her heart hammering, for the operator to connect her. Mary answered and immediately fetched James to speak to her.

'What's wrong? I nearly choked on my tea when Mary said it was you calling.'

'There's nothing wrong, my love, I've come to a decision and would like to get married the week after Easter this year. I just wanted to check that's acceptable to you. Lady Harcourt says we can have a double reception in the ballroom.' This was the first time she'd used any form of endearment and it felt rather racy and daring.

He didn't answer for a moment and her heart plummeted to her boots. Had she misjudged his feelings? Perhaps he wouldn't want to get married so quickly after all?

'I'm sorry, my darling, not to have answered immediately. I was too overcome to speak. I'll marry you anytime, anywhere and with as many others there as you want. Are you quite sure, though?'

His voice cracked; he'd not been able to speak because he loved her so much and was overjoyed at her agreeing to marry him.

'It depends on when Bob can get leave. He's ground crew, but they're the men who keep the aircraft flying, so getting time off might be a bit tricky.'

He cleared his throat. 'Would you agree to marry me in April even if Daphne and Bob can't do so at the same time?'

She didn't hesitate. 'Yes. In fact, if I'm being absolutely honest, I'd prefer it to be just our day and not to share it even with my dearest friend. I think the padre on the base could marry them without banns being called so she could go there if necessary. He just needs his commanding officer's permission.'

'We need to talk. I know we said we wouldn't meet apart from Saturday, but can I come and see you now?'

'If it's safe to drive, then come. We've got so much to discuss. I love you, James, and I want to spend the rest of my life with you.'

* * *

James was prepared to walk to Goodwill House if necessary, but the fog had cleared and visibility was reasonable. The temperature had dropped alarmingly and he thought they could be in for more snow.

'I'll be back for supper, Mary, and any emergencies, ring Goodwill House.'

'Yes, sir, I'll do that. Take care, it's a mite slippery out there. Nearly went on my backside when I fetched in the coal.'

His trusty car started first time and he drove smoothly out of the drive into the road. Not surprising it was cold as it was still winter. He had to be at the hospital by seven tomorrow morning as he had a full day of surgeries. Routine stuff, as the exciting things were handled by the chief surgeon and his registrar.

His mouth curved when he saw Charlie waiting in the turning circle. She must have seen him turn onto the drive.

He almost fell out of the car and she threw herself into his arms. He lost his footing and they fell backwards. The bulk of the car prevented a catastrophe and he regained his balance.

'That was a close call, darling, but I'm equally delighted to see you.' Should he risk kissing her or would that be pushing it? She solved his dilemma by tilting her head. He kissed her more thoroughly than he'd ever done before but still kept it gentle – too soon to bring passion into things.

She sighed and relaxed into his embrace. He closed his arms and held her tight, scarcely able to believe his good fortune.

'We can't hang about out here, it's far too cold. Is there somewhere inside we can talk privately?'

'Everybody – that's to say all the land girls – are in the ballroom so the dining room is empty.'

'Excellent.'

She led him to the rear of the house and they entered through the boot room door.

James kept his arm firmly around her waist past the kitchen, along the passageway and into the huge dining room. 'Jean said I can make you a cup of tea...'

'Dammit, Charlie, I don't want any tea, I want to talk to you. Shall we take a couple of chairs near the fire?'

'I wish you wouldn't swear but I suppose I'll just have to get used it.'

'I'll try and moderate my language, but I can't promise I'll succeed.'

He hadn't offered to carry a chair for her as she was capable of doing this for herself and would probably be offended by the suggestion. She was a very independent young woman.

'I'm a lot older than you—'

It was her turn to interrupt him. 'I know that, silly, and it makes no difference to me. How old are you exactly?'

'I'll be thirty-six in June – and you?'

'I'll be twenty-four in May. See, James, the difference is less than twelve years.'

'If you're happy about it...'

'It wouldn't make any difference if I wasn't as there's nothing we can do about it. I love you and you love me and we're here to talk about far more interesting things than our ages.'

'I agree. April 19th is the first Saturday after Easter – do we ask Mr Evans if he can marry us then or do you want to wait until Daphne has been able to speak to her chap?'

'I want to go ahead – if she can join us then so be it, if she can't then that's all right too. I don't have any family who I want to invite. Do you?'

'I'm an only child and unfortunately both my parents are deceased. My father was twenty-five years older than my mother and was in his fifties when I was born. He died when I was a medical student.'

'And your mother?'

'She couldn't manage without him and took her own life.'

Charlie rushed over to put her arms around him before he'd finished speaking. 'I'm so sorry. What a dreadful thing to happen. We share deep unhappiness in our past but now we can look forward to a blissfully happy future together, can't we?'

Without thinking, he pulled her down onto his lap and she didn't resist. He held her close for a few moments, enjoying the weight of her across his thighs, and then the inevitable happened and he hastily stood up, hoping she'd not noticed.

'Actually, having rejected your kind offer of tea, I now think we're going to need it as we've still got so much to talk about.'

'I'll get it, you stay here.'

She whisked away and his breath hissed through his teeth. He was going to have to be more careful over the next few weeks if he didn't want to reawaken her fear of intimacy. When she returned, he was fully recovered and had moved a table between them so she could put the tray down.

'If we've got no family then who exactly do we invite to our wedding?'

'Good point, sweetheart. I've got half a dozen London friends, chaps that I trained with, and the same number who I work with now. I'd like to invite them. Presumably all the land girls will come, as well as the Harcourt family.'

'Golly, that makes at least forty. That's more than enough. If Daphne and Bob join us, it could be double that number.'

'Then let's hope they decide to get married somewhere else. I'm afraid I won't be able to take any time off for a honeymoon.' He'd considered this point carefully on the way over and believed forcing her to spend time alone with him when she'd know it was customary for them to spend most of their time in bed together wouldn't be helpful.

'You couldn't even squeeze in a night or two? We don't have to go far – I'll be perfectly happy staying at The Royal in Ramsgate. I really don't want to spend my wedding night at your house with Mary watching our every move.'

'I can take Monday off, that would give us two nights. I'd suggest that we went to London but it's just not safe there with the bombs dropping every night.'

'Do you want me to give up work when we're married?'

'If you want my honest answer, darling, then I would much rather you worked with me. I'm desperate for secretarial help and am so far behind with my paperwork I daren't even look in my desk. However, it's entirely up to you.'

'Then I'll leave the Land Army. I'd love to be your secretary – it's what I did when I was in London before I joined up. I can also join the Women's Institute and Women's Voluntary Service.' Charlie smiled as she poured him a second cup of tea. 'What I'd really like to do is join the Observer Corps, but women aren't allowed in at the moment.'

'If women can do everything else, including collecting and delivering aircraft for the RAF, driving trams and buses, ambulances and tractors then I can't see why they won't put you in charge of a pair of binoculars.'

She laughed. 'It's absolutely vital work, James. There are a couple of men, too old to be called up, who are members and they identify incoming German planes and send the information to RAF headquarters.'

'I don't know a lot about the Observer Corps but if and when women are invited to join then you'd have my full support.'

Now wasn't the time to say that possibly in a few months' time she might be carrying his child and working anywhere would be out of the question. James smiled ruefully. He might be jumping the gun a bit here as it might be months before she was ready to make love. As long as she was his wife, he'd be a happy man.

* * *

Joanna was excited about having at least one wedding reception at Goodwill House and planning with Jean how this was to be accomplished took her mind off the letter yet to be posted. Dr Willoughby was paying for everything even if Daphne and Bob did manage to arrange their wedding for the same day.

'We have a bit less than two months to collect the luxury items we need,' Jean said as she licked her pencil and prepared to write a list.

'Don't forget we still have those hampers. There must be things in there that will be ideal.'

'I was thinking about the cake – no icing allowed – and no dried fruit to be had even with enough points to buy some.' Jean frowned. 'At least we have eggs, butter and cream, so I can make a two-tier sponge or madeira cake.'

'There should still be daffodils and forsythia in the garden so that solves the problem of flowers,' Joanna said. 'Joe had a good look in the wine cellar, and we have plenty of sherry and red wine but only a dozen bottles of white.'

'Folk won't care what they drink. Tea will do just fine. Didn't the doc say he can organise some light ale for the men? I can make a fruit punch similar to the one we did for the twins last year and add a bottle of sherry to liven it up.'

'Splendid. Scones and jam, sandwiches, cake, with punch, beer and tea to drink.' Joanna shook her head. 'That doesn't sound very celebratory, does it? I wish we still had Champagne in the cellar.'

'I can make an apple pie and game pâté with toast triangles and do something with the tins of peaches from the hamper.'

'Much better, Jean, I want to make this a memorable occasion. It will be the only wedding reception held here as we'll not be living in Goodwill House for much longer.'

'Have you told Lady Harcourt about the move?'

'No, but the twins are delighted. Mrs Ramsbottom was very understanding and is already looking into new accommodation for our girls. She said she's hoping to keep them together and thinks there might be a suitable place on the road that goes to Dover.'

'When will you tell them?'

'Heavens, not for a while. When Mrs Ramsbottom has somewhere organised will be soon enough. I explained to her that the house I'm purchasing won't be fit for habitation for months so there's no immediate rush.'

'Well, before then, I'm sure whatever we do will be appreciated by the bride and groom,' Jean said.

'I'm sure it will. Dr Willoughby gave Sarah a lot of advice and tuition and I feel I owe it to him to make his wedding special.'

'I have to go into Ramsgate tomorrow. Is there anything you need?'

'There are a few things that I can't get in the village – I'll make you a list. Let's hope there's no more snow or freezing fog.'

'It's definitely cold enough for snow but that doesn't seem to be stopping our boys in blue from coming and going at Manston.'

Joanna left the kitchen and her thoughts turned to Liza who'd started her new job at the vicarage, taking care of the children, this morning. She needed to speak to Joe, tell him the arrangements she intended to make for him.

She pulled on her warmest coat, added hat, scarf and gloves and then went in search of her son. Even with fires lit in many of the rooms, walking about in house slippers just wasn't feasible so she always had on outdoor shoes.

She heard Lazzy barking in the vegetable garden and headed

in that direction. Where her dog was so would be her son. She arrived at the gate and stopped.

'Good heavens, what's going on here?'

'Hello, Ma, the chickens shouldn't be in here and Lazzy and I are doing our best to herd them out.'

'I'll give you a hand. Thank goodness there's not a lot growing. As long as they don't get into the greenhouse or orangery where the winter salads are and everything else is stored.'

She spent an enjoyable twenty minutes flapping her arms and running up and down at the appropriate moment until every last hen and cockerel was out. She wiped the perspiration from her forehead and laughed.

'Well, that was fun. I wonder who left the gate open?'

Joe looked sheepish. 'It was me, but I won't do it again. Were you looking for me, Ma?'

'I was. I want to make your work here official, like the ladies from the village, Miss Biggins and Jean. The fact that you're a Harcourt doesn't mean you should work for nothing. Your sister now has employment and will be earning her own money and I'm sure you'd like to do the same.'

'You don't have to pay me for what I do, I'm your son, this is my home.'

'I know I don't have to, but I want to. When we move, hopefully at the end of the year, things will be different. You'll be buried in your books getting ready to take the Higher School Certificate so you can apply to join the RAF as an officer. You won't have time for anything else.'

'Then okay. I'll put the money aside for later. Liza's gone to the village to meet her friends. They're having lunch at the café.'

'I'm going to catch the next bus into town. Do you need anything?'

'No, thanks, Ma. It's going to snow again. Can't you leave it until Monday?'

'No, I've urgent business to attend to. It has to be today.' For some reason, posting this letter immediately gave her hope that one day she and John would be together again.

13

Charlie and Daphne left Fiddler's Farm with regret because they'd been happy working for Mr Pickering, but it made more sense for Sal and the new girls to transfer there.

'It's blooming cold today,' Daphne said as she attempted to prise up a stalk of sprouts. 'Like chipping away at concrete.'

Charlie looked up and a flake of snow fell on her face. 'It's only a few more hours and then it's the weekend and we're free.'

'I don't like February or November, the weather's always grey and miserable and nothing to look forward to during either month.'

'We've got our weddings to look forward to. It's a shame you can't have yours with me. If James and I had a big family, then we'd probably have wanted to marry somewhere else as well. I can see why your families want it to be in your local church. I don't suppose your father will be giving you away.'

'No, he's left the neighbourhood, thank goodness. My brother will walk me down the aisle.' Daphne leaned on her fork and smiled dreamily as if already listening to the organ playing the wedding march. 'Bob's got four days and he's also been promoted to sergeant.'

'That's good news. Mrs R has been very helpful, hasn't she? I bet you're pleased you can continue to be a land girl and still live with Bob.'

'I wouldn't have agreed to marry him otherwise. I didn't want to share or work with anyone else after you, so it's good I'm starting again somewhere fresh.'

'You'll be able to come to my wedding and I hope James and I get an invite to yours.'

'Goes without saying,' Daphne said. 'You'll be a lady of leisure then so don't have to get permission from anyone to do anything.'

'James is very accommodating, and we'll be a partnership, not him as an authority figure like happens in so many marriages.'

They continued to pick the sprouts and whilst doing so it gave Charlie time to think. There were no horses on this farm and she missed them. There were dozens of pigs, a hundred chickens and a couple of house cows but the old boy and the farmer took care of the livestock. The rest of farm was arable, hence the need for them to dig up the remaining sprouts. She was going to miss being a land girl but being married to James would be even better.

'It's getting too dark to see what we're doing. Shall we take what we've got in the trailer back to the farm?' Daphne asked.

'They'll come to no harm until Monday. Look, that was another snowflake. I hope we're not in for more nasty weather.'

'There's barely been an hour of sunshine a day since December. I'm not coming in on Monday if it's snowing,' Daphne said firmly.

Tomorrow Charlie and James were going to start reorganising his study and sorting out his long-ignored paperwork. As she didn't have to work weekends at the moment, she'd suggested this chore would be best started immediately.

He'd not taken much persuading as he hated doing it himself. His able receptionist, Miss Turnbull, dealt with the surgery patients – it was those he visited that weren't being billed. Having a responsible job to do suited her perfectly as she wanted to be involved with his life. She smiled. She wouldn't miss being out in the cold picking sprouts, that was for sure.

* * *

'Lunch is ready, darling, and I've made the tea,' James called from the kitchen.

She'd been so engrossed in her secretarial duties that she'd not heard him come in. Her stomach rumbled and her mouth watered as the delicious aroma of the newspaper-wrapped fish and chip parcels drifted through to her.

'I'm coming. I'm absolutely starving.' Charlie rushed into the kitchen and skidded to a halt. 'Goodness me, you look like a snowman.'

He'd put the fish and chips on the closed lids of the Aga and was in the process of removing his snow-covered outer garments. 'It's already several inches deep. I think you're going to have to stay here tonight.'

He said this almost nervously as if expecting her to refuse. Things were different between them now and she trusted him not to do anything to unsettle her.

'Actually, I brought my toothbrush and necessities just in case. Has Mary gone far? Will she be able to get back?'

'She's gone into Ramsgate where her sister lives. I told her not to worry about coming back until the buses are running again.'

'I'm sure your pantry's well stocked and I'm an excellent cook. That's something you didn't know about me.'

He ran his fingers through his dark hair to dislodge the remaining snow. He really was a handsome man and her pulse skipped a beat. Despite wearing a working man's cap, his head had been covered with the white stuff. 'I'd prefer not to have anyone living in when we're married. Mary told me that she's ready to retire and move to Ramsgate to be with her sister if we could manage without her.'

'The heavy work's something I'd rather not do, which sounds dreadful considering how many women have to do everything,' Charlie said.

'Mary said there's somebody in the village who would be happy to come in as often as we want to do the cleaning and laundry. If you're prepared to cook for us, then that's perfect. We can't ask Dolly to do that as she's only fourteen.'

She laughed. 'Wait until you've tasted what I cook before you sound so enthusiastic. Let's eat those fish and chips before it gets cold.'

She was just licking the last of the vinegar and salt from her fingers when the siren started to howl.

'I don't have an Anderson shelter. It's either under the Morrison in here or in the basement.'

'Under the table. It'll be hideously cold in the cellar.'

A Morrison shelter was a large metal table which, so the information said, was guaranteed to protect you from anything that might fall on the house. They'd been sitting at it but as it was covered with a large floral tablecloth, she hadn't actually seen what it looked like.

He flicked the cloth over the debris they'd left from their lunch and she ducked down to see there were blankets and pillows neatly folded waiting for such an eventuality.

'Quickly, darling, sounds as if it might be a big one.'

The windows had rattled several times as the fighters based at Manston had screamed into the air and the big guns were already firing. She didn't need telling twice and dived under the table. Between them, they spread out the blankets, making a comfortable surface to lie on and leaving two more blankets to cover them.

The noise of approaching bombers filled her with dread. She rolled towards him and he gathered her into his arms, offering his warmth and protection. If she was going to die, then in his arms was the place she wanted to be.

* * *

James could feel Charlie trembling and held her close, murmuring words of love and encouragement until she relaxed. 'I don't see how the blighters are here when there's so much snow about.'

'Daphne told me that Bob told her when it's this cold, ice forms on the wings of the planes so they can't fly. That's obviously incorrect.' She laughed against his shoulder and a surge of heat travelled though him. How he loved this wonderful girl.

Talking about the RAF was ridiculous in the circumstances. He wanted to tell her how much he adored her, that he'd keep her safe, that nobody would ever hurt her again but he couldn't do that as it wouldn't be true. He could protect her from most things but not from a bomb dropped by the Nazis.

'It's very cosy under here but I don't think it would be quite so enjoyable if Mary was in here too.'

He laughed and she joined in. 'Good God – I'd not thought of that. I've usually been at the hospital when the sirens went before.'

'I hope we don't have to stay here very long as I had three cups of tea.'

'Keep your legs crossed, sweetheart.'

She poked him in the ribs. 'That's hardly helpful, Dr

Willoughby. You keep telling me you're a medical man and I expected better from you.'

He kissed the top of her head. 'A chamber pot wasn't something either Mary or I considered when this Morrison shelter was set up.'

'I'm sorry, just talking about needing the loo has made it worse. I won't be a minute.'

She wriggled free of his arms and was gone before he could restrain her. He certainly wasn't going to remain in safety whilst his beloved girl was in possible danger. He rolled out and hurried after her.

'Don't stand outside the door – it's most impolite and inconvenient,' she called.

He chuckled and then retreated to the kitchen. He could hear the ominous drone of German bombers and wanted them both back in the relative safety of the shelter. As soon as she was finished, he grabbed her arm.

'Under, now, that sounds very close.'

She didn't need telling twice and together they rolled into the shelter again. This time, he pulled down the tablecloth – it wasn't just there for decoration. The top layer was an actual cloth, but underneath was a thick felt-like substance which would offer some protection from bomb blast and fire. He didn't know how effective this was as nobody he knew had been under a Morrison shelter when a bomb had dropped on their house.

'Gosh, it's very dark and stuffy now you've pulled that down. It would be ironic if we suffocated taking shelter from a bomb.'

This was a side to his future wife that he hadn't seen enough of. 'Talking uses up oxygen, so I suggest you pipe down.'

She giggled but did as he suggested and snuggled against him. Having her so close was a heady experience. He began to run through the operations performed yesterday, hoping that would dampen his desire.

Then the house shook. He heard the windows implode and instinctively rolled so his bulk was protecting her. He held his breath, waiting for the sound of falling masonry, but after the explosion it was eerily quiet.

He raised himself on his hands and shuffled sideways so she was unencumbered. 'I'm sorry about that, darling, it was instinctive.'

'I understand. I'm a bit squashed but otherwise unharmed. You're much heavier than you look.'

'I'm not sure how to take that. Stay put for a moment and I'll see what was hit. The windows in here blew in that's for sure.'

'I heard them. What a good thing we had the sides down. Hurry up and look, I'm feeling a bit claustrophobic under here.'

He pushed the material up carefully from the inside. Good thing he had as there were lethal shards of glass embedded in the other side. 'I'll hold this up on my shoulders, you creep out but don't put your hands down. Can you do that whilst remaining on your feet?'

'I was always good at bunny-hops. I think that's what's called for here.'

He thought she was joking but she wasn't. She hopped past him and rose smoothly to her feet as soon as she was clear of the table. He followed.

'Bloody hell! What a mess. Be careful where you step, there's glass everywhere. I've got to grab my bag and see if I'm needed out there. Something had a direct hit and I think it might have been next door.'

'The all-clear hasn't gone. It's not safe to go out yet.'

'I'm a doctor. Those rules don't apply to me.'

The front of the house was relatively unscathed; James grabbed his damp coat and medical bag and exited at a run. The snow had stopped, thank God, but visibility was poor because of the dust flying around.

It wasn't a bomb that had caused the explosion but the tail end of a German bomber which had crashed into the rear of Mr and Mrs Miller's house. If they'd been in the kitchen, then there would be nothing he could do for them.

They didn't lock the front door, he opened it and called out, 'Anyone here? It's the doctor.'

A surprisingly strong voice answered. 'I'm unhurt, Dr Willoughby, just a bit shaken. The kitchen's a goner, though.' Mr Miller, a tall, spare man in his fifties, greeted him cheerfully enough.

'What about your wife?'

'Beth's gone to Ramsgate. She'd have been in there otherwise.'

'I can't smell burning. Shall we go around to the back and see just how bad it is?'

'I was in the cellar. We've made it snug and the paraffin stove keeps us warm.'

As they emerged from the house, several locals arrived with offers of help. James was just about to slip away, glad his services weren't required this time, when an old man waylaid him.

'Here, Doc, you'd best be getting to Ramsgate. They'll be needing you at the hospital. Them German buggers dropped a load on the town just now.'

* * *

Joanna posted the letter and then trudged through the snow to purchase the various items Jean had asked for. She'd caught the midday bus and didn't intend to stay long in Ramsgate but return on the next one which left at two.

It was cold and a few flakes of snow brushed her cheeks. Thank goodness she'd finished her errands and could make her way to the bus. She was at the bus stop when the sirens howled.

A woman with a bulging shopping bag grabbed her arm. 'This way, down the tunnels. We'll be safe down there.'

Joanna knew about these underground shelters, knew that hundreds of people left homeless after the bombing last August were now living permanently in them, but she'd not visited herself.

There was now a stream of people heading for the nearest entrance. The steps were steep, seemed to go down for ever, and she was glad to have the metal banister to hold on to. There was no need to dig out her torch from her handbag as these tunnels were lit by electricity. No one seemed unduly flustered and all appeared to know where to go.

'This way, love, there's a caf, a bog and everything down here. Safe as houses it is,' the kind woman who'd directed her to the tunnel, said.

Houses above ground were certainly not anywhere one would want to be right now, but Joanna smiled and thanked her temporary companion.

There were benches on one side of the tunnel and she decided to sit on one not wishing to venture any deeper into this maze of passageways. There were signposts, street names and so on as if this was indeed a genuine village. Being deep underground, although safe, wasn't something she enjoyed. The walls and ceiling seemed to be pressing in on her.

'Lady Harcourt, I never expected to meet you in these tunnels.'

The woman who had sat next to her was the doctor's housekeeper, Mary Brown.

'Mrs Brown, good afternoon. Were you heading for the bus as I was when the sirens went off?'

'No, I'm visiting my sister. I was just fetching a few bits the doc needs and was on my way back to Sylvie's. She'll be down here somewhere but it's a rabbit warren and I'll not find her.' She smiled. 'It's ever so clever what they've done down here, isn't it? Not that I'd want to live underground all the time like some folk, but better than nothing, I suppose.'

Something small landed on Joanna's gloved hands. She looked down and then up. It was a flake of plaster from the tunnel roof. Did this mean a bomb had dropped directly above them?

She stared nervously at the ceiling, watching for further flakes to fall. The bench shook. They were showered with plaster again.

'Blimey O'Riley, that was a big one,' Mary said. For a second or two, the tunnel was quiet, as if all present were holding their breath. There was a further vibration that ran along the wall behind her.

Then nothing else. Everyone started talking at once, a rush of nervous chatter to cover up the fact that they'd all been terrified.

The loudspeaker at the end of the tunnel crackled into life. A distorted and tinny voice started to speak.

'There's nothing to be alarmed about, ladies and gents. There have been a few bombs dropped up there but no serious damage as they've fallen on the already bombed buildings. It's the incendiaries that are a problem. Best stay put until the firemen have put out the fires.'

'Bleeding Nazis,' an old man said. 'I'd have their guts for garters if I got my hands on them.'

This sentiment was echoed down the tunnel and shortly after the announcement there was the welcome rattle of a tea trolley. Two WVS ladies wheeled it around the corner and handed out buns and tea.

'Good heavens, Lady Harcourt, we didn't expect to find you down here,' one of the WVS women said loudly. Heads turned and Joanna flushed. She hated being the centre of attention.

She smiled and then buried her nose in her teacup in the hope the conversation would move on. She smiled wryly to herself, thinking about the letter she'd just posted to John. If he still loved her as she did him and agreed to resume their relationship, then she'd have to get used to being gossiped about. It would be the scandal of the century, but she no longer cared about such things. Why should people be unhappy just to placate those who disagreed with their choices?

Eventually they were told the all-clear was sounding and it was safe to return to the outside world. She raced up the stairs and was breathless when she reached the top and gulped in several mouthfuls of fresh air. The snow was heavier now but hopefully not so bad that the buses weren't running.

The white blanket hid the bombed houses from last summer and also made the smell of burning and smoke slightly less unpleasant. Hopefully, it would help douse whatever flames were still burning.

The bus was waiting, almost invisible under its snow covering, and Joanna and several other relieved ladies scrambled on. It was freezing inside but as long as it got her home, she was happy to endure the cold.

The bus lurched and slid but arrived safely at the end of her drive. She jumped off and thanked the bus conductor and the driver for getting her back in one piece. The snow was over the edges of her winter boots and her feet were wet and cold. By the time she pushed open the back door, she was numb from head to toe. Her face was so cold it was painful.

'Ma, thank goodness you're back. We heard the bombs dropping on Ramsgate and were so worried,' her son said and hugged her. Not something he did very often.

'I was perfectly safe in the tunnels. We even got tea and a sticky bun. Is Liza back?'

'She is, but there's bad news. Half a German plane fell on the house next door to Dr Willoughby. I've tried ringing but the operator doesn't know if the line's down because of the weather or the bomb.'

'Charlie was spending the day with him. There's nothing we can do but pray, my dear, and wait until we hear something.'

14

Charlie wrapped her hands in tea towels and got on with clearing the kitchen. The snow was drifting in through the glassless windows, so she pulled the blackout curtains across – not perfect but certainly better.

After sweeping the floor, she carefully pulled out all the splinters and larger pieces of glass embedded in the material that had hung down from the sides of the Morrison shelter. She dreaded to think how injured they might have been if these hadn't been there. She'd found a wooden crate in the scullery, lined it with an old sack, and dropped the glass into this. Everything got recycled and glass was particularly valuable.

The tablecloth that had gone over the Morrison shelter had been shaken outside to remove the worst of the glass and then she'd brushed off the rest. She looked at it carefully but wasn't convinced it would be safe to put it back. There was a clean one in the linen cupboard and she used this instead.

The front door opened and James called out, 'Nobody hurt, thank God. They're organising the removal of the plane and my neighbour and his wife are staying with friends until engineers can evaluate the damage to their house.'

Charlie removed the tea towels from her hands and was ready to greet him.

He appeared and without a second thought she walked into his arms. His kiss was hard, his lips cold, but she was bathed in an unexpected heat.

He raised his head and saw what she'd been doing. 'You should have left this to me. I didn't expect you to do it.'

'I know you didn't, but you were busy saving lives and the least I could do was tidy up the kitchen. I would have put some cardboard in the windows but I didn't know where to find anything suitable.'

'There's some at the back of the garage. I'll fetch what we need.'

Half an hour later, the kitchen was as it should be, all splinters of glass removed from every surface, including the tiled floor.

'I can't remember the last time I mopped a floor. I've certainly never done this one,' James said with a smile as he put the bucket and mop back in the scullery.

'I can't imagine what other floors you might have done – do tell?'

'Medical students were more dogsbodies than anything else and I did my share of cleaning up.' He grinned. 'I've no intention of going into detail but you can imagine what—'

'Please, there's no need to elaborate. By the way, the telephone isn't working.'

'Not to worry, the car's snowed in so I couldn't answer any emergencies even if I wanted to. The bloody Germans bombed Ramsgate as well as the base. I could be of use there but as I can't go, I'm not going to dwell on it.'

'I'm sure Mary will be all right.'

His eyes widened. 'God, I'd not even given her a thought. The tunnels under the town mean that everybody can get to safety so I'm confident she and her sister will have come to no harm.'

To pass the time, they played cards, dominoes and listened to the wireless, which Charlie enjoyed, but the nearer it came to bedtime, the more her stomach roiled. She trusted him, of course she did, but being alone in the house at night with a man made her nervous.

'You go up, darling, I put a hot water bottle in your bed and lit the fire an hour ago. I've got a lot of paperwork to finish. Get up whenever you want – I'm an early riser but that doesn't mean you have to be as well.'

'I'm so used to being up at six o'clock, I expect I'll wake then anyway. Goodnight, James, apart from the explosion, I've had a wonderful day.'

He made no attempt to stop her, kiss her goodnight, and she wasn't sure if she was disappointed or relieved. She stopped at the door and turned.

'I can't wait to be your wife. I'm looking forward to cooking lunch for us tomorrow. This weekend has been like a practice run for when we're married.' She took a deep breath and her fingers closed around the door frame. She wanted to say something to him, but it was really hard to get the words out.

'We haven't talked about children, but I do want them, this is the perfect place to bring up a family.'

His knuckles whitened, she saw him swallow before he managed to answer. 'I want children too. I hope you know how happy you've made me. Most men of my age are already settled with a young family and I thought I'd never be so lucky. I love you, and I promise you'll never regret your decision.'

'I know I won't. I never thought I'd get married after what happened. Not just because of my fear but because I didn't think any man would want me. I'm soiled goods...'

His chair clattered back and he was beside her in two strides. 'Don't ever say that again. What happened wasn't your fault and if the man wasn't already in jail – well – I think you know what would have happened to him.'

He pulled her close and she breathed in his familiar scent and relaxed into his embrace. 'You make me feel whole again. When we... when we're intimate it will be like the first time for me. I love you so much and never thought I'd ever be able to say that.'

He kissed the top of her head and gently pushed her out of the door. 'There's no need to worry about another raid as even the Luftwaffe won't be flying tonight. Sleep well, my love.'

Charlie almost floated up the stairs. Tonight, she knew without a doubt that she was ready to be James's true wife.

* * *

James needed a drink, maybe several drinks. He kept a decanter of whisky for special occasions in the cabinet in his study and he retrieved it and poured himself a double measure. He downed it in two swallows and then tipped out another generous glug.

Until he'd met Charlie last year, he hadn't really understood when other chaps had droned on about being in love with a woman, insisting that having a special person in one's life was the most important thing. He'd thought it romantic nonsense but now he could eulogise for hours about how much he loved her, how perfect she was, how happy she made him, how he'd willingly die for her. He thanked his lucky stars – he wasn't sure there was a God to thank – that the girl he'd thought he loved had left him for his best friend five years ago.

What he'd felt for that girl was a pale shadow of the real thing. When he walked into a room, he saw Charlie's eyes light up and he felt the same about her. They could sit in companionable silence for hours or talk about nothing much at all.

He swirled the amber liquid around the glass. He was already a little lightheaded as he wasn't a heavy drinker. No one else touched his whisky so he decided to tip the contents of his glass back into the decanter – if he could manage to without spilling it. 'Waste Not Want Not' was on posters and in magazines and wasn't he doing exactly that?

The house was quiet, peaceful even, and for the first time it felt like a real home. April seemed a long time away. A bit less than two months – ample time to arrange things and put into place any domestic changes Charlie wanted. They had to speak to Mr Evans, the vicar, as soon as possible and properly set the date. The church was only a hundred yards from his house, so however bad the weather tomorrow, they could attend and snatch a few words with Evans before or after the service.

James ignored the papers he'd said he was going to deal with and after banking up the fires, riddling the range and filling it with coke, he turned off the lights and retired.

* * *

James woke with a jolt some hours later. Charlie was calling for him.

He fell out of bed and in his pyjamas and bare feet hurtled down the stairs to find her in the kitchen holding a large, wet, scruffy ginger cat. He could hear it purring from where he stood.

'I heard something crying and thought it was a baby. Silly of me, as no baby would be outside the back door. I opened it and this bedraggled creature rushed in and jumped into my arms.'

James laughed. 'Seems like we've got a new member of the

family. I'll put some newspaper down and find a flea comb, he's bound to have them. We also need—'

'A piece of wet soap to catch them with as you comb them out.'

'Exactly. I think we should offer him something to eat first. I'll give him a quick check whilst you find him some food.' He went to remove the cat from her arms. It turned from a purring moggy into a demon feline and James was badly scratched before he could remove his hand.

'Bad pussy cat,' Charlie said, laughing at him as James literally licked his wounds. 'He doesn't like you, does he? You get the food; I'll hang onto him. He might be more receptive to you if you feed him.' She grinned. 'He might be a she. What shall we call it?'

'Ginger cats are usually toms. Lucifer seems appropriate. He's a devil cat, so the name fits.'

James opened a tin of spam – not something he was fond of – and cut half of it up on an old plate. He found a chipped bowl and filled it with water. Charlie had spread a sheet of newspaper on the table and was running her hands gently up and down the skinny cat.

'Lucifer has no lumps or bumps that I can feel but he's very thin. I don't see any fleas either. Maybe it's too cold for them.'

The animal started to growl as James approached but then caught a whiff of the food and the growl turned out a purr. He smiled. 'Thought so. Here you are, there's more but not until later.'

The spam vanished in seconds and then half the water. Whilst the cat was eating, James examined him and agreed there were no fleas.

'He's a stray. There are a lot of them since the war started. People can't afford to feed their pets or have been bombed out. I know a leaflet went out asking vets to put down any animals that owners couldn't keep to save on food.'

'Not rehome them? How awful. I'm so glad I heard Lucifer outside. He deserves to have a good home with us.'

'Mary doesn't like cats so I'm not sure how this will work. I've a feeling she'll leave.'

'Then let her. If the woman from the village can start immediately, that would solve half the problem and maybe she'll agree to prepare you something to eat for the days you're at home, but you shouldn't be standing around here in bare feet, James, there might be slivers of glass that I missed. Why don't you go up and get your slippers and dressing gown on and I will dry the cat and make us both some cocoa.'

He did as suggested but before returning to the kitchen – where he could hear her talking to the intruder in that soppy voice women used when speaking to babies and animals – he went into the front garden and brought in a flower pot that had contained dahlias during the summer. A dirt box would be needed and the contents of this pot would be ideal.

Fortunately, although cold and snow covered, it wasn't that heavy. Charlie applauded his foresight. The cat was curled up on an old blanket on a chair in front of the range and ignored both of them.

'I'm hoping he won't use this but will ask to go out and come in. I'm going to wash my hand again and find some antiseptic. Cat scratches can turn nasty, and God knows where his claws have been lately.'

'Don't be such a baby, Dr Willoughby, I've had far worse working on the farm and didn't even stop what I was doing to tend to them.'

They took their cocoa upstairs. Lucifer was shut in the kitchen but had the scullery where his dirt box and water were to wander into. The other half of the tin of spam was also cut up and waiting for later. He told her not to get up first as the house would be cold. 'I'll see to the cat, get the fires going and so on, you come down when it's warm. Shall I bring you up an early-morning cup of tea?'

'No, I don't want you waiting on me. I'm a light sleeper so will hear you go down. I'll give you half an hour to get organised and then join you.'

He waited in the passageway until she was safely inside the bedroom before going into his room – in a few weeks it wouldn't just be his room but theirs and he couldn't wait.

* * *

Joanna had to wait until Sunday morning before news of what had happened in the village reached the house. Joe rode Star to the newsagents, where one could always find out what was going on.

She was eagerly awaiting his return – not because she was worried he might have come to grief on the horse, but she wanted to know if anyone had been hurt and if, as the chair of the WVS, the Women's Voluntary Service, she or her stalwart ladies would be needed.

'Well, my dear,' she greeted him as he stomped in, his nose red from the cold, 'is it good news?'

'It is, Ma, the house next to the doctor's had half a German bomber in the kitchen wall but nobody was hurt and the remains have already been removed and the back of the house propped up.'

'What about Charlie?'

'She's tickety-boo.'

'Excellent. I really don't want to walk through the snow to church this morning so I thought I'd hold an informal service in the ballroom that everyone can attend. We can sing a hymn, have two readings and a few prayers.'

'Grandma will be pleased. I'll do a reading, I'm sure Liza will too. Jean's bound to know how to play something like "All Things Bright and Beautiful" and we all know the words to that.'

'Would you be a darling and speak to your sister and Jean whilst I prepare a few words?' Joanna said. 'Please let the girls know to be in the ballroom at eleven. No excuses will be accepted. It's nondenominational so the two Catholic girls have nothing to object to.'

The household gathered willingly, sung lustily and joined in the prayers. She ended the short gathering by thanking them for their hard work on the land and suggesting that some of them might like to volunteer, in their spare time, to be fire watchers or join the WI or WVS and help knit socks, gloves and hats for sailors and pack parcels to be sent to prisoners of war via the good offices of the Red Cross.

The telephone was still not working but Joe had said he'd seen the engineers shinning up a post in the village so it should be back in action shortly. Elizabeth had enjoyed the short service and was in a good mood, so Joanna thought this might be the perfect moment to tell her about the planned move.

Jean was busy, with the help of the girls on domestic rota, preparing Sunday lunch for everybody. 'Forgive me for getting in your way, but I'm going to make some coffee for my mother-in-law and myself. Would you mind if I took us both a piece of the delicious cake you made yesterday?'

Her friend smiled. 'Going to tell her ladyship about the house in the village? She might hear about it from one of the old biddies who come to visit occasionally so it's a good idea to tell her. Don't worry, I'll bring the coffee and cake through in a minute.'

The coffee had been in the hamper from Fortnum and Mason and was kept for very special occasions and this was one of them. Joanna smiled to herself as she headed for the sitting room. Elizabeth might be almost eighty years of age, but she was nobody's fool and would know at once that something was up when the coffee appeared.

Therefore, it might be best to tell her straight away and then the coffee and cake could be celebratory – or at least she hoped it would be.

'There you are, Joanna, I'm desperate for news. After spending a decidedly unpleasant two hours in the bowels of the house last night, I want to know if the wretched Nazis did any serious damage.'

'One house only in the village but several bombs were dropped on the base and in Ramsgate. As far as Joe could discover, there were only minor casualties and very little damage.'

'Splendid. Is that my newspaper? I do so love to read the news rather than hear it on the wireless. The dreary man makes everything sound so depressing. He'd be better off becoming an undertaker in my opinion.'

Joanna took the chair opposite her mother-in-law, slipped off her sturdy brogues and curled her feet under her bottom. Elizabeth didn't approve but had become used to this breach of etiquette and no longer tutted and fussed.

'I have something I need to tell you. I'm not sure you're going to be as happy as I am.'

'Finally! I was wondering when you were going to inform me that you are in the process of purchasing The Manse,' Elizabeth said.

'How long have you known?'

'Mrs Thomas told Mrs Fisher and she told me when she came here last week. Don't look so worried, my dear girl, I think it exactly the right thing to do. This house is too big and too expensive to run and to be honest, the novelty of having a dozen noisy young women sharing our home has somewhat palled.'

'You did tell me you wanted to die here, that Harcourts had lived here for hundreds of years, so I was concerned.'

'I have changed my mind. A lady of my age is entitled to do that. We will all be far more comfortable in a smaller, more manageable house.'

Joanna beamed, wanted to get up and hug the old lady, but knew that would be a mistake. 'The house will be legally mine any day, but it's been sadly neglected and I intend to have it fully modernised before we move. Depending on the availability of materials and men to do the work, I'm hoping we shall be living elsewhere by next year.'

Elizabeth laughed. 'Good gracious, Joanna, one could build an entire house in that length of time. Surely what you want doing can be achieved far quicker than that?'

15

Charlie woke refreshed and joyous and for a moment didn't know why. Lucifer. They had a cat and he was waiting downstairs for her to come and see him. Then a gurgle of laughter escaped. She was happy because she loved James and was no longer dreading sleeping with him, not because they'd rescued a stray.

She was sure he hadn't gone down but that didn't matter. She was fizzing with excitement and wanted to do all the things a wife would do for him. She flushed at the idea of what this involved... and not just making meals and keeping the house running smoothly.

They both wanted children and she was already quite old – twenty-three was positively ancient to be getting married – so having a baby was something she really wanted to do.

She'd pulled on her thick slacks and twinset and she was ready to descend. She paused outside his door to listen. Did he snore? Not a sound from his room and she hurried past, smiling. This was another thing she'd learned about her future husband.

The cat was standing just inside the kitchen door, his tail erect, purring, and he rubbed himself around her legs and she scooped him up. 'Who's a lucky boy then? Haven't you found yourself a lovely new home?'

He rubbed his whiskery face against her hand and she fell in love with him. 'I'm going to call you Lucky, not Lucifer. That suits you much better.'

She put him down and he stalked to the back door. She let him out and shivered. The temperature had dropped several degrees and was now too cold for snow. The only good thing about such beastly weather was that they couldn't work outside and the Luftwaffe hopefully wouldn't come.

When James appeared, freshly shaved and looking even more handsome, if that were possible, Lucky was back inside and devouring a plate of bread and dripping. The range was hot, the kettle boiling and breakfast ready. He strolled across and she walked into his open arms. His kiss was wonderful and her heart was pounding when he raised his head.

'Good morning, my darling, I thought we agreed I'd get up first and get things ready for you.'

'I know, but I wanted to see how Lucky was doing. Look at him. He's settled as if he's lived here for years.'

He raised an eyebrow. 'Lucky, not Lucifer? A better choice, I like it. I'm hoping we can speak to the vicar this morning about having our wedding on the 19th.'

'I wouldn't mind if it was earlier, but we can't get married during Lent and we certainly won't be organised by the end of this month, so after Easter is fine.'

'We could do it in four weeks if you want to?'

'Do you really think we could get everything done by then?' She held up her hand and counted on her fingers. 'There's the reception, invitations to send out, a bridal gown for me, honeymoon to book...'

'I don't care if you get married in your jodhpurs as long as we get married. I don't want to rush but having you here this weekend has made me even more eager to begin married life. And Lucky arriving has changed things, hasn't it?'

'He has, but probably not in the way you're thinking. For me, it showed that I'm the lucky one to be marrying you. I can't think of any other man who would have accepted a stray cat so readily.'

'I'm not sure I'd been quite so relaxed about it if Lucky had been a female. There might well have been a litter of kittens on the way and nobody wants to take in an extra animal at the moment.'

'Well, there are three Sundays between now and the 28th,' Charlie said. 'Just enough time to call the banns. I hope we can still have the reception at Goodwill House as it would be so much easier there.'

'The reception and everything else seems relatively straightforward but where are you going to get something to wear?'

'Jean was a court dressmaker before she came to us. I'm sure if I ask nicely then she'll make me something. She once showed me two trunks of beautiful material that had been stored in the attic for decades and I think Lady Harcourt would let me have a length.'

He brushed her cheek with the back of his hand. 'Are you quite sure? A few weeks ago, you didn't even know if you ever wanted to marry me.'

'I've never wanted anything so much in my life. I'll become Mrs Willoughby, the doctor's wife, and can finally put my past behind me. When my mother died a few weeks after I was born, my father rejected me, which is why I grew up with my uncle. For all I know, I might be an orphan now or indeed have a stepmother and several younger siblings.'

'We don't need any other family – we've got each other.'

After breakfast, James wrote down all the necessary details for the vicar whilst Charlie washed up. She'd always despised housework; however, taking care of James and herself was quite different and she couldn't wait to be in charge of this well-equipped and modern kitchen.

* * *

Mr Evans was delighted with their news and pencilled them in. There was no one from Goodwill House in church today so she couldn't share her exciting news with her friends.

They slithered their way back to his house – The Rookery now seemed like home to her and it would be the first real one she'd ever had.

'I wonder how long it will be before my telephone's working,' James said as they went in through the front door. This question was answered as it began to jangle. He dropped his coat over the banisters and hurried to pick it up.

'Yes, Mary, I fully understand.' He was quiet for some time and his housekeeper was obviously explaining things he needed to know. 'Yes, I'll ask Charlie to pack up your belongings and I'll bring them in to you the next time I'm in Ramsgate. It's unlikely to be today or tomorrow as it's just not safe to drive. Yes, I'll do that too. I can't tell you how happy I've been to have you look after me for the past five years, thank you so much for your loyalty and support.'

Charlie knew what the conversation was about just from listening to his side of it. Mary had decided to retire immediately. 'Is something wrong? Why is she leaving so soon?'

'Her sister slipped and badly sprained her ankle and Mary needs to be there to look after her. But I rather think she'd always intended not to come back. This is working out far too smoothly.'

'You didn't tell her we're getting married, but I don't suppose it matters now.'

'Not matter? It's the most important thing in the world to me.'

His eyes had a glint in them but she didn't resist when he swept her up, held her close, and kissed her with a passion he'd not shown so far.

Charlie got on with preparing what would be their first lunch together that she'd cooked. She shooed him out of the kitchen and he retreated to his study to finally deal with his neglected paperwork.

The delicious aroma of roasting chicken filled the house. The potatoes and parsnips were crisp and golden and the cabbage and carrots keeping warm on the range. There was just the gravy to thicken and they could eat. She was singing to herself as she finished off the gravy. This was what it would be like when she was married. She couldn't wait.

* * *

James was drawn to the kitchen by the smells. 'I can't wait. You said you were a good cook and you obviously are. When will it be ready?'

'Ten minutes,' Charlie said. 'Lucky has been meowing hopefully. He's so thin we've got to feed him up. Once he's back to his proper size, I'm hoping he'll catch his own meals.'

He looped his arm around her neck and kissed her. She tasted of gravy and chicken – a heady scent for a hungry man. Reluctantly he released his precious girl as the telephone demanded his attention a second time. 'Dr Willoughby. How can I be of assistance?'

'Thank God, Willoughby, I've been trying to contact you all morning. Where the devil have you been? We need you here. My registrar has mumps, and I can't operate without you.' It was Sir Harold Falconer, his boss from the hospital.

'I'll do my best, sir, but I can't guarantee I'll arrive unscathed.

The roads are lethal and no traffic has got through today so far.' He found this abrasive, bad-tempered man difficult to deal with but Falconer was the best surgeon he'd ever worked with. This man could be leading a team at any of the London hospitals but had chosen to remain in his hometown. God knows how many Ramsgate residents owed their lives to him.

'Good man, I knew I could rely on you. We've got a compound fracture, an appendectomy, a gall bladder and a possible perforated ulcer.'

'I thought you didn't work at weekends for routine ops.'

'Damn and blast it, man, stop blathering and get yourself over here. I've got a dinner in London tomorrow so won't be here.'

This robust response had been heard by Charlie and she giggled. He looked at her, held the receiver away from his ear, and pulled a face.

'Willoughby? Answer me, damn it. When will you be here?'

'I'm on my way, sir. If I don't kill myself, I'll be there in an hour.' He hung up and smiled ruefully.

'I was so looking forward to our lunch. I'll make you a hot chicken sandwich and you can take it with you.' Charlie didn't complain or insist he should stay but understood immediately that his work had priority.

'I'll stay overnight at the hospital as I have to be there first thing tomorrow anyway. I'll grab my bag. Can you make me something in a couple of minutes?'

She could and she did. He left with a hot, delicious-smelling sandwich in a greaseproof paper wrapper and a Thermos tucked under his arm. Her loving words were ringing in his ears as he drove away. This was how it was going to be every day in less than four weeks.

The drive to Ramsgate was horrendous. He skidded a dozen times but, by some miracle, managed to arrive at his destination in one piece. He parked in his usual place and sat for a few minutes whilst he devoured his warm lunch and drank the flask of tea that she'd found time to make for him.

As soon as he stepped into the hospital, he pushed all thoughts of Charlie aside and became a professional surgeon ready to do his job.

They got through the list by eight o'clock that evening and Falconer shook his hand and thanked him. 'Good man, I know I can rely on you. I'll be back from Town Wednesday.'

'That would be the day I have my surgery in Stodham so I won't be here even if you're not.'

'You will damn well do as you're told, Willoughby, if you want to continue to operate here.'

'I'm not sure that I do. I'm getting married at the end of the month and to be honest, I'd much rather spend time with my new wife than with you. I'm resigning my position. You're an expert surgeon but a very unpleasant man.'

Until he'd spoken, he hadn't known he'd even been thinking about giving up what he thought was the most important thing in his life. Stodham villagers needed him just as much as the hospital did. They'd been sadly neglected whilst he'd concentrated on his work here.

'Good God, young man, you can't leave me in the lurch like this. I'm not going to be here tomorrow.'

James smiled. 'I rather think that you will have to be, sir, as I certainly won't. Goodbye.'

He collected his possessions from the break room, thanked the theatre staff and dashed off before the irascible Sir Harold could chase after him. To be sure this couldn't happen, he left via the side door.

The snow crunched under his feet and he thought that driving back in the dark in these conditions was decidedly foolhardy but he wanted to be with Charlie and give her his good news.

It took even longer to make the return journey and if he'd had to attempt the steep hill which led down to the sea, he'd never have managed it.

His hands were stiff from gripping the steering wheel so tightly by the time he reached the village. He noticed that both pubs were shut – things must be bad if either of them was closed for trade. As he pulled into the garage – the doors were always left open when he was out – he hooted loudly, hoping Charlie would hear and open the door without him having to bang on it.

Closing the doors was difficult as they'd frozen in place. After a great deal of heaving, swearing and kicking, he eventually got them shut. He was smiling as he approached the front door, congratulating himself on a job well done, when Lucky jumped into his arms, he lost his balance and tumbled backwards into the hedge.

'Bloody cat, what were you thinking? You could have killed both of us.' The cat, unbothered by this sudden descent to the ground, began to purr and nudged his chin with his head.

He heard the front door open as he was gathering his wits and his breath.

'James, whatever are you doing in the hedge with the cat?' Charlie was laughing so the question wasn't serious. 'Do you want me to take Lucky from you or pick your bags up from the snow?'

'Actually, darling, I'd rather like a hand. I'm firmly embedded in this bloody hedge...'

'James Arthur Willoughby, your language is appalling. I'm tempted to leave you where you are as a punishment.' Still laughing, she reached down and grabbed his free hand with both of hers – the other one was holding the cat steady – and he regained his feet easily with her help. She was surprisingly strong for a girl.

'Good thing the ARP warden isn't around as we'd be in for a rocket for leaving the front door open and letting so much light out,' he said as he slammed it shut behind them.

It was wonderfully warm inside and the wretched cat, having caused the chaos, wriggled free and stalked into the kitchen, still purring loudly.

'He likes you now. I think he might be as pleased to see you back as I am. What are you doing here? I was just making my cocoa and about to go to bed.'

He explained and she threw herself into his arms with a squeal of delight. A highly satisfactory few minutes later, they came up for air.

'You gave up what you love for me? I can't believe it. I couldn't love you any more even if I tried.'

'You could do one thing for me, sweetheart.'

'Anything.'

'Whilst I'm sorting myself out, could you find me something to eat? I've had nothing since the sandwich and tea hours ago.'

16

Joanna was initially concerned by Charlie's request to have the reception at the end of the month and not at the end of April. However, when she heard the reason, she was happy to help.

'The arrival of a stray cat and the departure of a housekeeper have turned your lives upside down. I'm so pleased that you and Dr Willoughby have decided to marry so soon. Having him as a full-time doctor will be so much better for the village.'

'That's true, my lady, but James loved being a surgeon and I didn't ask him to give it up for me. I just hope he doesn't regret it.'

'My dear, I can assure you that Sir Harold would take him back in a heartbeat if he wanted to return. Surgeons of Dr Willoughby's calibre are hard to come by. If he misses that side of his medical life, then there's nothing to stop him returning to it.'

'I'll stop worrying then and just enjoy the next few weeks. Jean has kindly agreed to make me something to wear. It was so kind of you to give me that length of silk as a wedding present. I'm going to be the most beautiful bride because of you and Jean.'

Joanna smiled. 'You'd be a beautiful bride even if you married in your dungarees and gumboots. I'll miss you and I know that Sal and Daphne will too.'

'Daphne won't have time to miss me as she and Bob are getting married three days before us. Bob has found her a cottage close by and his commanding officer has agreed he can live there with her unless there's a flap on.'

'Goodness, I didn't know that. Have you let Mrs Ramsbottom know what's happening?'

'We wrote a joint letter and posted it yesterday. She should have it by the end of the week. Daphne wants to carry on working if they can find her somewhere she can get to on her bicycle. If they can't, then she's going to resign as I have.'

'Then it's a good thing that Sal has her new friends, or she'd be rather on her own.'

'Will you take in two more to fill the empty room?'

Joanna decided to take the girl into her confidence as she was sure she wouldn't gossip about what she was going to be told. Charlie listened and then nodded.

'This place is far too big even with all of us here. I won't tell the girls if you don't want me to, but I'm certain they won't mind as long as Mrs R is going to keep them together.'

'Last time we spoke, Mrs Ramsbottom told me that there's an empty rectory in the next village which will be ideal for a hostel. There are a dozen girls scattered about the neighbourhood as well as the twelve living here. The plan is to put you all together.'

'That sounds absolutely spiffing. Would you like me to give them the good news or do you want to keep it a secret until it's finalised?'

'Yes, by all means let them know.'

Jean would be making tea soon and as Elizabeth had remained in bed today on the advice of her personal maid, Joanna thought she would take some up to her.

Biggins had an unnerving tendency to curtsy whenever she spoke to her and nothing she could say would convince the maid that only royalty required a curtsy. Biggins approached Joanna in the grand hall.

'Her ladyship still has a bit of a temperature, my lady, so I thought it best if she remained where she was for the rest of the day. I don't think we need to call the doctor just yet, but one can't be too careful with a patient of Lady Harcourt's age.'

'Indeed we can't. One of her friends called just before the weather deteriorated and she was suffering from a head cold. I think my mother-in-law might well have picked one up from her.'

'A nice hot drink and a couple of aspirin will be enough for now.'

'I'll come and see her soon – you must let me know when she's feeling up to visitors.'

'I'm sure she would appreciate a visit at any time, my lady. At the moment she's still reading the *Sunday Express* and it's all over the bed – nasty inky thing. I don't hold with newspapers on a Sunday. It's the Lord's Day and the only thing we should be reading is the Bible.'

This was the first time Biggins had indicated she was an old-fashioned Christian. Joanna wasn't so sure she'd have employed the woman if she'd known she was so straitlaced.

'Everybody's entitled to their opinion, Biggins, but at Goodwill House people are free to believe what they want.'

Instead of being offended, the elderly lady nodded. 'That's what I like about this place, my lady, I'm allowed to have my beliefs without criticism and I wouldn't dream of saying anything to those lovely girls of yours.'

'Has Lady Harcourt mentioned to you that we'll be moving to a smaller house in the village in a few months?'

'She has, my lady, and very happy I am to hear that. This is a fine big house but I think we'll all be happier somewhere more convenient.'

'Good. I'll bring up a tray of tea for you both.'

If she'd suggested she was going to ride a camel through the drawing room, the maid could not have been more shocked. 'My word, that will never do. It's my place to fetch and carry for my lady.'

'If you're quite sure, then I must get on as I've several letters to write. Please tell my mother-in-law that I'll be along later.'

In fact, she had no correspondence to attend to but made her way to the study, which was now her domain again, and thought she would write a second letter to John. She wasn't going to post it, but it would make him seem closer if she wrote to him.

Could he have already received her letter? Would he toss it in the bin or write back? Maybe she'd never know.

My dearest John,

I think about you all the time and treasure the moments we spent together. Every time I hear about the bombs being dropped on Malta I shudder at what you must be going through.

I pray that you are safe and will be able to return to England after you've completed your tour of duty.

It's strange, my love, to be writing such a letter at my age. Women in their thirties should be sedate matrons, preparing to be grandmothers, not thinking about an erstwhile lover.

I daren't speak to Elizabeth about you as she would work out immediately that we were more than friends. I've nobody to talk to about what we shared – Sarah and Angus know but I don't see my daughter at all as she's so busy saving lives in London.

The only other person who knows about us is the detestable Lord Harcourt. I told him because I wanted him to understand I could never be more than a friend to him, and he decided this was my way of telling him I wished to be his mistress.

Needless to say, I no longer have any contact with him.

I won't be posting this letter, but if you ever do return to me then I'll show you this so that you will know that you were constantly in my thoughts.

All my love now and for ever,

Joanna

* * *

Charlie now went straight from work to The Rookery to see James as he no longer spent three nights in Ramsgate. Her days were shorter because of the horrible weather and the dark nights. She also wanted to see Lucky and make sure he wasn't being neglected. Miss Turnbull, the terrifying receptionist James employed for his surgeries, had already said she hated all cats and had threatened to leave.

Lucky thought it was his right to wander wherever he wanted and was a big hit with the waiting patients. It was just the receptionist who didn't want him in there. Surgery would have finished by now, but James might be out on a call. The garage doors were closed so that meant he was home. She wheeled her bicycle to the side of the house and made her way around to the kitchen and let herself in. There was no need to knock any more.

'Darling, did you have a wretched day pulling turnips or something equally nasty?' He was as happy to see her as she was to see him.

She flew into his arms. 'No worse than usual. Where's Lucky?' She accepted his kiss but was more interested in the absence of her cat.

'He's out somewhere. He'll—'

There was a furious scotching at the door and frantic meowing as if Lucky was being attacked. Laughing, she opened the door. 'Silly animal, no need to make such a fuss.'

As always, he jumped into her arms, purring like a sewing machine, and James complained that he was now second in her affections.

'He gets more kisses than I do. Worst decision I've ever made allowing him into the house.'

'I love you, too, but he's so attractive and I just can't resist his furry charms.'

'Put him down and have your tea. I'm afraid I've not got the best news.'

'Oh dear – has Mrs Thompson decided she won't work with the cat in the house?' This woman was the new daily lady who'd taken over from Mary on Monday.

'No, I could manage without her, but Miss Turnbull has departed in high dudgeon after the cat laddered her last pair of stockings.'

'Then I'll do it instead. I've already told Mrs Ramsbottom that I'm leaving in two weeks, so I don't think it makes any difference if I resign now.'

His eyes gleamed and she knew exactly what he was thinking but, instead of being shocked, horrified or nervous, she just laughed.

'No, James, that will have to wait until we're married. I won't be staying here overnight. I'm quite sure Lady Harcourt will be happy for me to remain there until the 28th.'

'Thank God! I wasn't going to ask you to stop so precipitously but I can't tell you how relieved I am that you're going to.'

The cat was now sitting on the table turning his head from side to side as if listening to their conversation. James reached out, picked him up and put him on the floor. 'I've told you, young man, tables aren't for cats.'

Lucky didn't scratch or bite him as he had done the first time they'd met but was looking at James balefully as if he didn't like being told what to do.

'I think you're fighting a losing cause; cats aren't like dogs, you can't train them. Has he started catching his own food yet?'

James leaned down and scratched the cat's head and received a nudge and a purr in return. 'Unfortunately not and we're running out of spam.'

'We'll think of something. Now, I need to see your diary, know your routine. I'll drink this tea quickly and then you can show me the ropes. I take it there's a surgery tomorrow or you wouldn't be in such a panic.'

'I'm holding one every weekday morning and doing calls in the afternoon. I've also let Manston know that I'm available if anyone needs stitching up and they don't want to send them to hospital.'

James wasn't keen on her pedalling back in the dark but as she said she'd travelled that way so many times she thought her bike could find its way home without her assistance.

'I'll be here at eight o'clock. We haven't discussed my remuneration – I would like to be paid for my work.'

He grinned and smoothed her hair from her face. 'You will, but only until we're married. Would be no point in me paying you then.'

She pushed him away more firmly than she'd intended. 'So you think I should work for nothing and then have to go cap in hand every time I want to buy something? No – absolutely not. We'll agree on an hourly rate and then this will continue as long as I'm working for you.'

His eyes narrowed as he digested this unpalatable fact. Charlie had been financially independent ever since she'd left her uncle's farm five years ago and didn't see why that should end just because she was going to be a married woman.

'Don't look so grumpy, darling, I'm not suggesting we have secrets from each other. Just that I want to feel I'm contributing to this marriage. I know until the war started women were expected to stay at home and concentrate on domestic issues, bringing up the children, but everything's changed now.'

He smiled a toe-curling smile and she didn't know what she'd said that had caused him to look so happy.

'That's the first time you've addressed me as darling. I actually don't give a damn about the money. I was just shocked that you were so vehement about being independent. Do you have a bank account?'

'No, just a post office book.'

'Then we can either open an account in your name or I can make mine a joint account. Which would you prefer?'

'Goodness me – I don't need to share your bank account. Whatever would the bank manager think? I'm quite happy with my post office savings book – I can pay in and get out money whenever I want.'

'If you're quite sure, sweetheart, then I'll leave things as they are. I'll pay you the same as Miss Turnbull.'

She had supper with him as Mrs Thompson had made a tasty vegetable stew with suet dumplings. There was no dessert, but he had been given a cake by one of his grateful patients which did just as well.

'Do you get paid in kind very often?'

'I do, I expect the full amount from the better off but those at the other end of the scale I'd treat for nothing if necessary. When my mother died, I inherited a small fortune which paid for my medical training, the practice and this house. I'm not exactly rich, but we won't go without.'

'I've got just under fifty pounds in my book. You didn't know you were marrying a wealthy woman, did you?' Charlie laughed.

James chuckled. 'As you'll have to go to the post office in order to get the cash to pay yourself, it'll be simple enough to put it into your little savings book. The cleaner has to be paid and the chap who comes in to keep the garden tidy and so on.'

'That's not a problem. Life would be so much easier if there was an actual bank in Stodham, but we can't have everything, can we?' She glanced at the grandfather clock ticking away loudly. 'I've got to go. They'll be sending out search parties soon.'

'Lady Harcourt knows exactly where you are and wouldn't be remotely bothered if you didn't go back at all.'

'That's as may be, my love, but home I shall go.' Her smile was enchanting. 'Although this house is my real home. I've never had one that felt completely mine. I'm going to be counting the days until I can move in here permanently.'

He was counting the days, too, but not for the same reason as her. He'd never wanted to make love to a woman as much as he wished to make love to her.

'Be careful on the ride back, darling, I don't want to be called out to patch you up.'

'Don't fuss, James, I'll be perfectly fine. Please don't come out with me, there's no point in both of us being cold.'

He kissed her and let her go. He didn't notice the cat was missing until he was about to turn in. He knew he wasn't indoors and yelled his name down the garden and at the front but no response.

The telephone rang and he forgot the cat and rushed in to answer it. At this time of night, it had to be an emergency of some sort.

'James, have you been looking for Lucky? He must have

followed me and he arrived at the back door of Goodwill House ten minutes ago.'

'Thank God. I didn't realise he'd gone out until I was about to go up. Is he okay?'

'He is now. I'd gone up and Lazzy started howling at the front door. Jean was just turning off the lights downstairs when she heard him scratching on the door.'

'I'm sorry, sweetheart. I wonder why it took him so long to arrive. It's only a couple of miles from here to Goodwill House.'

'Unfeeling brute.' She was laughing, so he knew she didn't mean it seriously. 'I'm just amazed he got here at all and so is everyone else. He's been fed and I'm allowed to take him upstairs with me. I'll bring him back when I come to work in the morning.'

'Goodnight, darling, I love you.'

'I love you too, goodnight, my love.'

17

Charlie arrived before it was fully light. James was waiting for her and the cat. Lucky was snuggled inside her coat but jumped down as soon as she got off her bicycle. The animal streaked off down the garden and they both laughed.

'Ungrateful beast, after I've carried him all the way here.'

He slung his arm around her shoulders and walked her inside. 'I've made real coffee. It's the last of my beans so let's not let it go cold.'

'How spiffing. Is that toast I can smell too? I left without my breakfast today as I wanted to get Lucky home.'

As they munched toast and marmalade and drank the fragrant bitter brew they both loved, James asked if Charlie had managed to speak to Lady Harcourt or Mrs Whatsaname, the land girl area organiser.

'Lady Harcourt has said she will let the authorities know I've resigned my position. One of the village ladies is laundering my uniform so it can go as spares for anyone who wants it. I can't tell you how glad I am to be in civvies again.'

'About that, as you'll be the second most important female in the village, I'm sure that you're going to need to increase your wardrobe.'

'Good heavens, I'm only going to be the local doctor's wife – I'm quite certain there are half a dozen other women with more important husbands.'

He puffed out his chest and attempted to look impressive. 'I'll have you know that as a surgeon...'

Charlie giggled and indulged his nonsense. 'You aren't a surgeon any longer so you can't use that to improve your position in Stodham society. Let me think, the vicar is probably on a par with you, but I think a solicitor or the owner of a string of factories is definitely above you in the hierarchy.'

'As far as I'm concerned, my darling, having you in my life makes me the happiest man in the village even if I'm not the most important.'

She moved into his arms and he tightened his hold. Their lips had barely touched when something heavy banged against the kitchen door. They jumped apart.

He flung open the door and Lucky came in dragging a rabbit – fortunately it was deceased.

'Clever boy, you've brought us a lovely dinner. I'm sure you'll get some to eat as well.' She smiled at him. 'I'll have this skinned and cleaned in no time. If I do it immediately, I can put it in the slow oven so it'll be ready for lunch.'

'If you do that then I'll dissect it. That, after all, is my expertise. Don't get any blood on your clothes, it might alarm my patients.'

He could hear her laughing as he lit the fires in the surgery and the waiting room. The telephone was on the small desk where Charlie would be sitting so she could answer it without having to leave her post. The appointments book was open on the desk and he'd got out the relevant patient records for her, although only a handful actually booked. Few locals had a telephone and why would they make the trek twice if they didn't have to? Therefore, the majority of the waiting room would be filled with those who just turned up. In future sorting the records would be Charlie's task – well it would if she wasn't skinning and cleaning a rabbit every morning.

After checking everything was ready, James wandered back into the kitchen to find it empty. He'd only been gone five minutes – if that – but the carcass of the rabbit was waiting for his attention.

'Good God, that was quick.'

'I told you this is something I'm good at. I'm just giving Lucky the offal and getting the vegetables we're going to need.' She came in holding a couple of onions, carrots and potatoes. 'I've not been to the end of your garden. As onions are in such short supply then I'm guessing you have a vegetable plot as well as half a dozen chickens.'

'Not only that, I also have a share in a pig.' He smiled at her expression. 'Don't worry, it's not been fattened up here. I should have told you about it as we have to keep all waste food, vegetable peelings and so on and Terry comes to collect it every few days.'

'I did notice the slop pail and guessed that's what it was for. They do the same at Goodwill House.'

He left her to it and dashed back to his surgery. This and the waiting room were on the right side of the house, his sitting room, dining room and study on the left. The downstairs WC was available for any patient that needed to use it and he thought that some of them only came to the surgery just for the luxury of using a flush lavatory.

The most delicious aroma of rabbit stew was drifting down the passageway and he loved the fact that they were going to eat something that had been prepared by her.

He was about to go in search of her when she emerged from

the kitchen, her cheeks slightly pink from the heat, the cat stalking behind her, tail erect and purring loudly.

'Should I run through how things work in the surgery?'

'No, thank you, I already know as you explained more than once yesterday.'

James laughed, not taking her sharp comment to heart. 'Okay, point made. Yell if you need me.'

'I'll do no such thing. Raising one's voice in front of others would be unconscionable.' Charlie pursed her lips, trying hard not to laugh.

'I love you, and if I find myself unable to restrain myself and kiss you in front of the patients, I apologise in advance.'

* * *

Everything went smoothly, in fact, the atmosphere was better and his patients far more relaxed than they'd ever been with Miss Turnbull in charge. The last patient, an ulcerated leg, left at one o'clock. Perfect timing.

The waiting room was immaculate, not a magazine out of place, the chairs neatly ordered and no sign of his fiancée or his cat. His mouth watered at the thought of what was waiting for him for lunch and he wandered into the kitchen – he'd never used the dining room as he didn't entertain. No doubt all that would change once they were married.

The table was laid and Charlie was just dishing up. 'I'm salivating, I hope there'll be enough for supper too.'

'By the time it's finished you'll be sick of it, and then Lucky can eat the rest. I think he's already looking better, his coat shinier, don't you?'

'He certainly eating enough to be gaining weight. I'm hoping he might bring us a pheasant next time.' James had already washed his hands so sat down at the table. 'I don't know how he caught a rabbit as they don't come out much in the winter.'

'I did ask him, but he was reluctant to reveal the secrets of his success.'

* * *

Charlie loved working for James, cooking for them both and watching their other family member, Lucky, continue to improve. Two weeks before the wedding, she was having the final fitting for her wedding gown.

'You can look now, Charlie, it's finished. What do you think?' Jean had worked as a court dressmaker and was an expert seamstress.

Charlie turned and looked into the full-length mirror. A stranger stared back at her. Daphne had arranged her hair in a French pleat which would allow the stunning antique veil to be put on easily. As it would be worn on her wedding day, she'd applied a little lipstick herself, and the lovely cream silk gown with a high neck and long sleeves was perfect. The sophisticated hairstyle and the dress had transformed her.

'It's beautiful. Thank you so very much. It seems such a pity that I'll not wear it again.'

'You won't, Charlie, but maybe your daughter will.' Jean smiled and picked up something from behind the chair. 'Lady Harcourt wanted you to wear this.' She held up the long lace veil attached to a stunning pearl tiara.

Charlie held her breath whilst Jean reached up and fastened it in place. 'I look like something out of a magazine. I didn't think I needed a headdress but this completes the outfit perfectly. How kind of her to lend it to me. I promise I'll take good care of it.'

'It's the something borrowed that you need and it's also old, the gown is new, so you just need something blue.'

'I'm sure I'll find something. I can't believe it's only ten days until I marry and I leave here.'

'We've got the farewell party for Daphne first. It won't be the same here without you two,' Jean said and Charlie hugged her.

'We'll miss you, too, but I'll be living down the road so hopefully we'll still meet often. James and I are going to Daphne's wedding next week. I'm looking forward to meeting her family.'

'I hope she's going to be able to attend your ceremony even if her new husband has to be back on duty.'

'I'd be devastated if she and Sal weren't there. We're going to stay in touch, remain good friends. We'll only be an hour's drive away and the war won't go on forever.'

'Things are going so badly for us in Africa at the moment,' Jean said. 'If Rommel—'

'Please let's not talk about something so depressing when I'm standing here in my lovely wedding gown. I'm so lucky to be marrying a man who doesn't have to fight in this terrible war.'

'Shall I keep everything up here until the day?'

Jean lived on what used to be the nursery floor and had made it her own domain. Miss Biggins shared the space and very cosy it was too.

'Yes, I don't really have room in my wardrobe, and I don't want it to get creased.'

'Let's hope we don't get an air-raid on your wedding day, there've been a lot of them lately.'

'I'm sure we won't. Fortune smiles on a bride on her big day, doesn't it?' Charlie said. 'The last time the siren went off, we had a waiting room full of patients. James and I just use the Morrison shelter at night but during the day everybody has to go down to the cellar and it's damp, cold and unpleasant.'

'I'm surprised he hasn't done something to make it better if his patients have to use it.'

'He's promised to make improvements if he can find anybody to do it for him. Remember, he only held one surgery a week there and spent most of his time at the hospital. There wasn't really any need to do anything until now. Lucky has caught all the mice so at least that's one good thing.'

After her fitting, James was waiting for her downstairs; they were going to spend the rest of the day together. He was on call for any local emergencies but as it was Saturday, there wasn't a surgery.

Charlie was tempted to slide down the curved banister but as he was standing at the bottom of the stairs, she resisted the temptation. But she and Daphne had made a pact to do it before they left Goodwill House to start their new lives.

'You look happy, darling, I take it your ensemble is what you wanted.'

'It's better than I dared dream, James, but I'm not going to tell you any details as you will have to wait until our wedding day like every other groom. Shall we go?'

'I've managed to persuade Lady Harcourt to allow me to pay for everything she's done for you, for us, I should say, but it was a hard struggle.'

'She's so generous and kind. I wish she could be as happy as we are. I don't think I could survive if anything happened to you.'

They'd left through the front door and were now walking towards his car. 'The marriage to the previous Lord Harcourt wasn't a happy one and it was a relief for her when he died at Dunkirk,' James said. 'She has the twins, her mother-in-law and Jean and is about to move somewhere more comfortable than this place. I'm sure she's content with her life.'

'Sometimes she looks so sad. I expect she's missing Betty. It was awful that someone so young died from measles last year.'

'I agree – remember I was there. Shall we change the subject to something more cheerful?'

As they drove away, a tall young man was walking towards the house. Charlie wondered who he was and felt a moment's regret that in less than two weeks what went on here would be none of her concern.

* * *

Joanna loved the feeling of excitement and anticipation in the house as the wedding of Charlie and Dr Willoughby approached. It was marginally warmer, most of the snow had melted and all the girls were back at work. Although their days were, of course, much shorter than they would be in the summer.

'Ma, there's a bloke outside wants to see you. He won't give his name and he won't come in,' Joe said to her as she finally sat down for a much-needed cup of tea halfway through the morning.

'I suppose I'd better come and speak to him. If the dog's outside, then I'm in no danger.'

Jean snorted from the far end of the table where she was chopping up vegetables for the evening. 'He didn't growl at those Germans so I wouldn't rely on his opinion.'

'Well, I'll not find out sitting here. Hopefully, my tea will still be hot enough to drink when I return.'

She didn't ask her son to accompany her, but he did and she was glad. He was now taller than her by several inches and had to shave at least twice a week if he wanted to look smart.

Unbidden, a thought of John slid into her head. What would her children think if he came back? This time, she wouldn't keep the relationship secret from any of her family – if they didn't like or approve of her being involved with John, then what would she do?

This wasn't the time or the place to think about the imponderable. The young man waiting to speak to her was dressed well but not as a gentleman. He was a complete stranger but looked vaguely familiar.

'Good morning, I am Lady Harcourt. How can I be of assistance?'

'My lady, I'm sorry to drag you out into the cold but I daren't come in. I've come to see my mother but I don't know that she will want to see me.'

Suddenly everything fell into place. 'Jean, my friend and housekeeper, is your mother? You look like her. Please go around to the front door and I'll let you in that way. I can assure you that Jean won't be aware you're here unless you wish her to know.'

'You go in, Ma, I'll take him round. The door's not locked. Do you want me to show him to the study?'

'Yes, that would be splendid. You haven't told me your name, young man?'

'I'm Tony Bairstow, my lady.'

Lazzy seemed to have accepted this young man as a friend and trotted along behind Joe, wagging his tail. If she went in, then Jean would ask what was going on – that would be awkward, so Joanna decided to go in through the front door as well.

She caught up with the two of them as they reached the portico. 'I'll take it from here, Joe, thank you. I shouldn't go into the kitchen for a while as I don't want you to lie to Jean.'

'Right, I was just going to collect the eggs if there are any.'

It was as cold in the grand hall as it was outside, but Joanna didn't apologise to the uninvited visitor. She wasn't altogether sure if he was friend or foe at the moment.

The fire in the study was always lit and she went up to it and rubbed her hands in front of the flames.

'Once you're thawed out, Mr Bairstow, you can put your outdoor garments on the chair over there. Please, take a seat next to the fire and tell me why you're here and why Jean might not wish to see you.'

He didn't hang his head, or wring his hands, but looked her straight in the eye. She liked that about him and began to feel a little more hopeful about this conversation.

'It's like this, my lady, my father was a drunken bastard. He knocked seven bells out of my mum and as I got bigger, he threatened to start beating me.' Tony paused to gather his thoughts. 'Mum took matters into her own hands and one night we escaped out of the window. She took me somewhere I'd never been before and left me with strangers. She said I wasn't safe with her and that I'd be better off living elsewhere.'

'I see. I didn't even know that Jean had been married or had a son.' He ignored her interruption and continued.

'She was right, I was happy with these folk. They treated me well, like their own son, but I always wanted to find my mum and see if she was all right or if that bastard had caught up with her.'

'Why now?'

'Uncle Jock died several years ago and Auntie Doreen passed recently. You're probably wondering why I'm not an enlisted man – I'm deaf in one ear so they wouldn't have me. I did an apprenticeship and am a skilled mechanic and engineer.'

He was silent for a few minutes and she waited for him to continue his story.

'My mum had kept in touch with Auntie Doreen and I was given the letters last week by the solicitor.' He smiled and there were tears on his cheeks. 'She sent money, gifts for Christmas and birthdays, but they never told me they were from her. I thought my mum had forgotten about me. If I'd known, I'd have come and found her years ago. I hope I'm not too late.'

'Why would you think that?'

'Because I never wrote back or thanked her for her gifts. She might think I didn't want to know her.'

'I'm sure she'll be delighted to see you. Why else would she have kept in touch?'

He nodded and seemed a bit more cheerful. 'I got the house – I've put two homeless families from the East End in it – it'll still be there at the end of the war if it doesn't get a bomb dropped on it. As soon as I read the letters, I handed in my notice and came here. Do you think she'll want to see me?'

Joanna nodded. 'I'll fetch her immediately or you can come with me.'

'I'll stay put if you don't mind. Just in case you're wrong. I don't want to embarrass her.'

'I'll get her. I expect you'd like something to eat and a cup of tea – most things seem better with a cuppa.'

18

Joanna almost ran to the kitchen, wanting to share the wonderful news with Jean that her son had come to find her.

'Tea and cake for two is it, Joanna?'

'Yes, how did you know I'd invited him in?'

Jean smiled. 'You'd not have stayed out without a coat for so long and you didn't come back this way. Who's the mystery man?'

'It's your son, Tony, he didn't know you'd kept in touch until his foster mother died. That was just two weeks ago.'

The brown tea pot fell to the tiles and instead of smashing, it bounced. This had to be a good omen.

'Tony's here? In the other room? I can't believe it. I thought I'd never see him again.' Jean picked up the tea pot and examined it. 'Not even a chip. I'll make the tea.'

'Yes, but he wouldn't come through as he thought you might not want to see him.'

Jean gulped and hugged the pot to her chest. Tears rolled down her cheeks. She was incapable of speaking.

Joanna ran to the sitting room. 'Quickly, Tony, your mother

wants to see you this minute. She's too overcome with happiness to even make the tea.'

He had been pacing the floor and his smile of joy brightened the room. She took his arm as he seemed unable to move.

'Come, she needs your arms around her so she knows it's really you.' She guided him to the kitchen and then pushed him gently through the door. She closed it quietly behind him. The girls must be told not to go in there so the two of them could share these precious moments only with each other.

Daphne saw her at the door to the ballroom and hurried across. 'Is something wrong, my lady?'

'No, but Jean has a visitor, someone she's not seen for years, and no one must go into the kitchen.' She saw they'd got the urn on and were busy making their own tea. A tin of biscuits stood ready.

'I'll make sure they stay in here. Liza's playing bridge over there. She's really good at it and she and Jill always win.'

Joanna smiled. She hadn't even known her daughter played bridge. She must have learned to play with the Mr and Mrs Evans at the vicarage. She returned to the sitting room where she'd left Elizabeth ages ago. The old lady was agog with curiosity and Joanna quickly explained what all the fuss was about.

'Well, Joanna, I always suspected Jean had an interesting past but I must say I didn't think she'd got anything as fascinating as an abandoned son and a brutal husband. I wonder if Baxter is her real name if her son is called Bairstow.'

'It's tragic that young man's foster parents kept her letters from him or they would have been reunited years ago. I do hope this doesn't mean that Jean will leave us. She's an essential part of the family now.' As soon as she'd said this, Joanna felt ashamed to be thinking of herself and not of her friend's happiness.

Elizabeth was about to reply when they heard the rattle of the tea trolley and Jean was behind it, her son walking proudly beside her. Both looked radiantly happy and Joanna blinked back tears.

She wasn't a demonstrative sort of person but moved swiftly across the room and embraced her friend. 'I'm so happy for you both. Tony, I do hope you can stay with us for a while?'

Before she could step back, she was enveloped in a bear hug. The last man who'd hugged her had been John. 'Mum's told me how you took her in, made her part of the family and I'm so thankful that you did.'

Suddenly he released her as if she'd become red-hot and the poor young man turned an unbecoming shade of beetroot. He'd obviously seen the look of horror on Jean's face at his actions.

'And now you're part of the family too. You met my son, Joe, and my younger daughter, Liza, is playing bridge in the ballroom with the land girls.' She turned and smiled at Elizabeth. 'This is my mother-in-law, Lady Elizabeth Harcourt. I'll leave you to get acquainted.'

As Joanna left them, she wondered if this reunion was a sign from above that she might be able to get her dearest wish too? She wasn't superstitious, wasn't particularly religious, but in that second Joanna strongly believed that John would come back to her one day.

Joe was in the kitchen and she quickly explained the circumstances and he rushed off to fetch his sister. She paused at the door, taking in the scene with delight. Tony was sitting on a footstool beside Elizabeth and they seemed to be having a lively conversation. Jean was watching, occasionally wiping her eyes, and she looked ten years younger.

Her friend became aware that Joanna was there and joined her just outside the room. They embraced a second time. 'I'm so happy I could burst. I wish I'd told you about Tony but talking about him made it worse for me. I knew where he lived, could have gone to see him, but Doreen told me he didn't want to see me and blamed me for abandoning him. I believed her – how I wish I hadn't. We've missed so much time together.'

'He's here now and you can put all that behind you. I only spoke to him for a short while but I know he's a good man, you'll not be separated again.'

They embraced fondly and Joanna was delighted for her friend.

* * *

James asked Charlie to stay the night, not in his bed, but in the spare room, but she refused.

'I don't want people to gossip and say that we pre-empted our wedding vows. It was different last weekend because of the weather.'

'But we'll still spend the day together tomorrow as planned?'

'I'll cycle down in time for breakfast and then we can go to church. Mr Evans will be reading our banns for the third time. Then the following Tuesday we're going to Chelmsford for Daphne and Bob's wedding and then we'll be getting married ourselves that Friday.'

His heart thudded at the thought of finally having the woman he loved at his side.

'I can't wait for you to live here. You haven't really looked everywhere in this house yet. Apart from the four main bedrooms, there's the attics and the nursery rooms above that. To be honest, I don't think I've been up there myself more than a couple of times.'

'Goodness me – do you think there might be exciting things lurking in the attics?'

'Plenty of spiders, but I doubt there's anything very exciting.

The old chap I bought this from was a major in the Indian Army who retired here.'

'Where is he now?'

'Dead. I should have phrased that better – I bought it from a cousin who inherited his estate. Shall we go and have a look now whilst it's still light enough to see?'

'I take it there's no electricity on the top floor?'

He shook his head. 'I think the last time there were children here must have been just after this house was built and electricity would have been a novelty then.'

Lucky was encouraged to come with them but seemed reluctant to leave his comfy place by the kitchen range. Charlie picked him up and he didn't object. When James opened the door to the nurseries, the cat jumped from her arms and crouched low, his tail swishing from side to side and his ears pricked.

'Don't look so worried, darling, our cat will soon clear out any unwanted visitors.'

She stared at him. 'I'm not scared of a few rats and mice – don't forget I'm a farm girl. My expression of dismay is at how this room has been left.'

He looked around and understood. There was a swinging cradle, the covers still on it, toys and games abandoned on the floor.

'I wonder if something horrible happened to the children who slept in here. It seems as though the parents couldn't bear to come up or have it tidied. Do you want to—' James started to ask. She understood his question before he said it.

'Absolutely not. Our children won't sleep in here but will be with us. Although we could make this an attractive place for them to play. That rocking horse is an antique but looks in good condition. I always wanted one when I was little, but my aunt said if I wanted a horse, I could ride a real one.'

'There's a paddock attached to the rear of this property so if you want to have a horse or pony at some point then we have room for one,' James said.

Her eyes rounded. 'If you really mean that, Lady Harcourt wants to sell her horse, Star – I've ridden her a few times and she's absolutely perfect. Gentle and willing and goes as well in harness as she does under saddle.'

He hadn't expected her to take him up quite so readily, but he'd made the offer and he could hardly back down now. 'The mare can be your wedding present from me. I know nothing about horses but am prepared to learn as long as I don't have to ride one myself.'

'Well, in that case, I don't want to explore up here, what I really want to do is see the land you've just told me you've got. If it hasn't been looked after, it might well not be suitable for Star at the moment.'

He was about to tell her that he'd get a man in to have a look but stopped himself just in time. Charlie had grown up on a large farm and probably knew more about this sort of thing than any farm labourer that might still be working in the area. Most of them had enlisted, which is why the land girls were so vital.

'It's a good thing I put my gumboots in the car. I hope you own a pair as I think we're going to need them. It's likely to be very muddy after all that snow.'

Sooner than he'd wished, he was tramping down the garden, the cat loping along beside them, heading for the gate that led into the paddock.

Charlie stopped to look in the walled vegetable garden. 'This is very similar to the one at Goodwill House, but much smaller. So much easier to grow vegetables successfully if you can keep the rabbits out.'

'Again, I take your word for it, sweetheart. I grew up in London and know as much about farming and the countryside as you probably do about general surgery.'

She giggled. 'Fair point. However, I can teach you all you need to know about the countryside but you can't return the favour even if I wanted you to. On that subject, darling, I would like to learn basic first aid just in case one of your patients needs assistance when you're occupied. Liza Harcourt has passed most of the preliminary exams in the St John's and is going to train to be a nurse when she's seventeen next year.'

'Sarah Harcourt did the same and was better qualified than most nurses by the time she left to be a doctor. She used to accompany me on my visits, observed many operations, and was always destined to be a first-class physician.'

'Well, I want to be able to do at least as much as she could in an emergency.'

'I don't think I'll have time to start teaching you the basics until we're married, but it's something we can do in the evenings.'

'Thank you. Is that building a stable block?' Charlie pointed to the tiled, brick-built, single-story building ahead of them.

'I've no idea as I've never been down here to look at it.' She pulled a face and he laughed. 'I know, I've lived here five years and really should have walked the boundaries or whatever a landowner does. I do know I own just over five acres in total. I'm a busy man – I don't have time for wandering about the place.'

She punched his arm and he flinched dramatically as if she'd hurt him but she wasn't fooled. Her delightful laughter rang out in the quiet field, sending a flock of something black – probably rooks as his house was called The Rookery – flying, squawking loudly, into the air.

'I can't believe anybody, even a "busy man", can live somewhere and not have explored his surroundings. I can see I'll have to take you in hand, Dr Willoughby, or we'll be at odds.'

He put his arm round her waist and not a moment too soon as her feet slid out from under her and without his support she would have ended up on her backside in the mud.

'Thank you, your help's most appreciated. This area in front of the stables would need to be something harder, not squelching mud like this.'

The building, she informed him, had two loose boxes, a tack room and a fodder store. There was also a small barn where she told him they could keep the hay and straw.

'What do you think? Will it do for your wedding present?'

Her smile said all he needed to know. 'It's the best present I could have. Thank you. Star will have a new home and Joe can still come and ride her whenever he wants to.'

* * *

Charlie returned to Goodwill House to find a new member of the household. Daphne was waiting upstairs to tell her about it.

'How exciting. I'm so happy for Jean. Have you met this young man?'

Daphne shook her head. 'No one has so far, but I think he's going to be here for a while.'

'Another man will be good for my reception. I expect he'll be swamped by the girls all wanting him to dance with them.'

'That's the other thing. Bob's just been told he's being posted back to Manston to be in charge of a bigger team.'

'Does that mean you're going to stay at the farm where you're working now?'

'I hope so. There's a cottage close to the base, it's where one of the WAAF girls lived briefly last year when she got married, and we're renting that. He can get to the base in minutes, it's so close.'

'That means we can see each other whenever we have a few hours free. What's happening about your wedding and so on?'

'His CO has added an extra two days' leave so we can both be here for your do. I can't believe it's only three days away,' Daphne said. 'Bob's picking me up on his motorbike on Tuesday, but I'm not looking forward to the ride in this weather.'

'Beastly on the back of a bike. Why don't you come back with us on the Thursday? Bob can ride his motorbike and you can travel in comfort.'

'He won't like it but I'm sure he'll understand. Yes, thanks, I'll return with you. The cottage is vacant, and I've got to go there after work tomorrow to make sure it's habitable.'

'Shall I meet you there?' Charlie said. 'Surgery finishes by lunchtime and even with the paperwork, I'll be able to leave when you do.'

'That would be so kind. What will I do if it's damp?'

'Light a fire and just be glad you've got somewhere to live and a wonderful husband to live in it with you.' This sounded a bit sharp, but Daphne didn't take offence.

'You're right. There's a war on, lots of folk have lost everything and I shouldn't complain. We're spending one night at The Saracens, a smart hotel in Chelmsford, where are you two going?'

'The Royal in Ramsgate, as long as there isn't an air-raid. Otherwise at home. Now Mary isn't there, I don't mind if we don't go away.'

It was late when Charlie finally settled down to sleep. They'd talked for hours and admitted they were both were excited and nervous about the prospect of their first night as married women.

* * *

Wednesday morning, Charlie and James set out for Chelmsford at dawn, only able to drive so far because Lady Harcourt had allowed him to fill the car with the petrol her dead husband had stored before the war. James also had a full can in the boot for the return journey.

'This is like a practice run for our do on Friday, sweetheart,' he said as they approached the outskirts of London.

'Not really, we only have to walk to church and drive to the reception. We also don't have any family attending the ceremony – apart from that, I suppose one wedding is very much like another.' She immediately regretted the less than jolly reply, but it was too late to take the words back. She squeezed his arm.

'I'm so sorry, I don't know why I'm so snippy at the moment.'

His smile was warm and completely non-judgemental. 'Don't worry about it, my love, it's pre-wedding jitters. Hardly surprising that you're on edge.'

'I don't understand it as I'm really looking forward to being your wife.'

'And I to being your husband but it's a much bigger step for you than for other young women. This is hardly the right place for me to say this but if you just want to share my bed, nothing else, then that's how it'll be. It's up to you entirely. Put aside all the girly gossip about "wedding nights", as ours can be whatever we want it to be. Darling, we've got the rest of our lives to know each other in every way possible and there's absolutely no rush.'

It was as if a weight she hadn't known she'd been carrying was lifted from her chest. Her eyes filled and she blinked furiously. 'I didn't realise I was so nervous about being intimate with you until you said that. I really do want to be your true wife, to have your children, but knowing it doesn't have to happen on our wedding night is a huge relief.'

He steered the car to the side of the road and she thought for a moment it had broken down. When they were stationary, he turned off the engine. 'I should have talked to you about this, this is my fault that you've got so wound up. For God's sake, it's my job to notice these things. I want to make love to you but more than that, I want you to want to as much as I do when it happens.'

He pulled off his leather driving glove and rubbed away the tears from her cheeks with his thumb.

'I love you so much, James, I didn't know I could love you more but after what you just said, my heart's bursting. We're going to be so happy.'

He cupped her face, tilted her chin and kissed her tenderly. Then he replaced his glove, turned on the engine and engaged the gears. He pulled out without looking over his shoulder. This small error of judgement told her just how moved he was, made him seem more vulnerable, and she knew everything was going to be perfect when they were married.

They agreed that London was depressing, pedestrians walking with their heads down, nobody smiling and a pall of smoke and dust hanging in the air from a recent air-raid. This was particularly noticeable as they drove through the East End and her heart went out to those who'd lost their homes, their loved ones, their possessions.

'There seem to be more people in uniform than there are civilians, James,' she remarked as they eventually drove onto the open road heading for Chelmsford.

'Hardly surprising, my love, as most of the men are in the services.' He looked sad and her heart lurched. Was he thinking that he too should volunteer even though doctors were exempt from call-up?

'I'm so lucky that you can do your bit for the war at home. It must be so difficult for those married to servicemen.'

'I've convinced myself that I'm needed here and that being an army medic would be a waste of my talents.'

Her hands unclenched, but then he continued.

'That was when I was working mostly as a surgeon. Things are grim in Africa, they don't have enough doctors or medical staff, especially experienced surgeons like me, I might well have to volunteer at some point.'

Charlie's heart dropped. She couldn't bear it if her beloved James was away on the front line, but she said nothing. This was his decision to make.

19

Joanna had told the girls the ballroom was out of use until after the wedding reception on Friday. There were a few grumbles, but she ignored them. They'd been living in luxurious surroundings, with excellent food, for the past few months and some of them were still seriously in arrears with their board and lodging money. As far as she was concerned, they were lucky to be with her and not having the use of the ballroom for a few days was a minor inconvenience.

Liza was enjoying her employment as a nanny at the vicar's house, the days weren't onerous, and the hours were excellent. This gave her daughter ample time to continue with her St John's studies and with attending WI and WVS meetings. Joanna was a little concerned that the work set by Mr Kent was being ignored.

Joe, who still attended lessons two or three times a week at the tutor's house in the village, reassured her. 'Mr Kent told me Liza will pass the exams in the summer with flying colours. He said that I can take my Highers next summer and not wait till the following year.'

'I'm so proud of you both, I'm sure your mother would have been too,' Joanna said.

'I doubt it, Ma, she wasn't interested in either of us and certainly had very little education herself. I wish I knew who our father was because he's the one that's given us our brains.'

'Then it's fortuitous for both of us that you arrived in Stodham and that your grandmother didn't want to look after you. I always wanted a big family and to be blessed with three such wonderful children is something I never thought to have. I'm a very lucky woman.'

Joe beamed and hugged her. 'We're the lucky ones. Being a Harcourt will open doors for both of us. I should get a commission when I join the RAF. I'm hoping they'll take me as soon as I'm seventeen.'

Somehow she managed to remain smiling but inside a sick feeling replaced her happiness. Every day, dozens of brave RAF air crew were killed. She'd been told that the life expectancy of a pilot was horribly short. Two of the WAAF who had billeted with her last year had married pilots and both were now widows.

Was John one of the casualties of war? Was this why he'd not replied to her letter? No – she wouldn't even consider that as a possibility. The lack of correspondence was because he'd moved on with his life as she'd told him to and he no longer wanted to be involved with her. That was the reason she'd heard nothing.

She put aside these depressing thoughts and tried to think of something happy. She glanced at the overmantel clock – it was almost two o'clock and Daphne would be walking down the aisle and Bob would be waiting for her.

And on Friday, just three days away, she'd be sitting in the church watching Charlie and Dr Willoughby say their vows and then the wedding party would return here for a celebration.

'Joe, does the suit that Jean altered for you still fit?'

He accepted her change of conversation as he was well aware of her feelings about him becoming a pilot when he was old enough.

'She's had to let down the trousers and the sleeves of the jacket. It won't fit me for much longer as I seem to be filling out as well as getting taller.'

'I expect there are still such things to be had in London – it's far too dangerous to be there now but, if things calm down a little in the summer, the three of us will go and see what we can find. We shall stay the night at the Savoy and hopefully can spend a few hours with Sarah whilst we're there.'

'I reckon where Liza and I used to live has been flattened by now. We'll not go back there even if it hasn't. A trip to the Smoke is something else to look forward to. By the way, I like Tony. It's good to see Jean so happy. Did you know that he's fixing the central heating boiler?'

'I didn't know that. I do remember my late husband complaining that it gobbled up fuel at an alarming rate, so I doubt we'll be able to use it until the war's over.' She laughed. 'But as we won't be living here, doing all that work seems a bit of a waste of time.'

'I should have said, he's converting it to run on wood. We've got lots of that. I'll be sad to see Star go, but she'll only be in the village with Charlie, so I can go and see her whenever I like.'

'They won't be taking her for a while, there are a few things they need to do first. And it'll be much harder to fetch timber from the woods once she's gone, so why don't you spend what time there is left using the cart?'

He grinned. 'I'm already doing that, Ma. I'll have the barn full soon. Then it just has to dry out and I can start chopping it up. Anyway, Charlie said she won't take Star until I've finished.'

The telephone interrupted their conversation and Joanna hurried off to answer it. It was her future son-in-law, Squadron Leader Angus Trent. She could think of only one reason he would be ringing and it wasn't a good one.

* * *

James sat beside Charlie in the freezing church surrounded by people neither of them knew and regretted having made the long drive. Seeing the happiness of the couple surrounded by a loving family brought it home to him, as nothing else could, how different his wedding was going to be on Friday.

He'd lost touch with those he'd thought of as his close friends when he was living in London – and although he'd told Charlie some of them would be coming, no one would be attending. After leaving the hospital so abruptly, nobody from there was coming either. He rather thought that his previous boss, Sir Harold Falconer, had made sure all of them were working and couldn't, even if they wanted to.

The bride and groom exchanged a chaste kiss and then retreated to the vestry to sign the register. They would then process triumphantly down the aisle and the guests would follow.

'I'm so happy for them, and they might never have got back together. The church is packed and I didn't realise Daphne had such a large family or so many friends,' Charlie said quietly.

'I was thinking the same, sweetheart, it's going to be quite different for us. I wish we had families who could support us but...'

'We don't need anyone else. Against all odds, we found each other and we're going to be even happier than Daphne and Bob.'

James loved her optimism. 'I'm not sure how you work that out, my love, as I've never seen a happier bride and groom. Mind you, I've not attended more than half a dozen weddings in my life.'

There would now be a slight hiatus until the bride and groom reappeared and, as they were sitting at the back of the church, he and Charlie wouldn't be required to leave the pew for some time.

'We're starting our married life in your wonderful house, can spend every day together knowing neither of us are in any real danger. Bob's ground crew, a lot safer than air crew, but he's still going to be working at Manston, which is a very dangerous place to be at the moment.'

Until she'd spoken so fervently, he'd not actually come to a decision about enlisting as an army medic. 'You're absolutely right. We don't need family, we've got Lucky and soon we'll have Starlight as well.'

She leaned in closer and whispered in his ear, her warm breath sending shockwaves of excitement racing through his body.

'We might have a baby by the end of the year. You keep reminding me that you're a medical man – tell me, how long will it take me to have a baby?'

'I assume that you're asking how long it might take for you to conceive, not how long it will take you to deliver.'

She punched his arm and he laughed. 'You know exactly what I mean – don't be so pedantic. I'm beginning to realise that marrying such an old man is going to be a disadvantage when it comes to holding a sensible conversation.'

He couldn't help himself. He pulled her closer and kissed her thoroughly. The old couple sitting in front of them were horrified by this. He grinned at them, unrepentant.

'We're getting married on Friday.'

'That's as may be, young man, but this is God's house and such an unseemly display is quite disgraceful.'

Charlie leaned forward. 'Don't refer to Dr Willoughby so disrespectfully. This is certainly God's house, and God *is* love, so I'm sure he'll approve of ours.'

He hid his smile behind his hand. He loved the way she jumped to his defence – in fact, he loved everything about her.

Fortunately, Daphne and Bob were now ready to exit the

church and the congregation stood up, meaning the judgemental old couple had to face the front and thus end the conversation.

'It's a shame we can't throw rice or confetti but there's a war on, in case you hadn't noticed, and waste not want not.' She managed to keep a straight face as she said this but he didn't and laughed, making the grumpy couple in front glare at him.

'Behave yourself, James, this is God's house, you know, and nobody's allowed to laugh or kiss their partners.' She said this loud enough for them to hear. Not content with this, she continued, 'Of course, if you've just got married or if the vicar has told a joke, that's all right. I'm sure the Almighty is immediately aware of the difference – after all, he is God Almighty.'

The old man's neck flushed scarlet. He had to stop Charlie before the poor old fellow had a coronary.

'That's enough, darling, I think you've made your point.'

She looked at him, tilted her head and her eyes glinted dangerously. What the devil was she going to do now? Then she giggled.

'It's so easy to tease you, my love, and I couldn't resist. I'm not going to say anything else apart from I love you and Friday can't come quickly enough for me.'

They trooped out and were directed to the church hall. None of the guests wanted to hang around outside and watch the photographs being taken – it was far too cold for that.

'Doesn't it look pretty?' Charlie said as they walked in. 'I love streamers and balloons and all the greenery's lovely too. Look at that – they've got a three-tier cake and it's iced and decorated.'

James had spotted this centrepiece of the buffet table and like her was curious as to how they'd managed to bypass the strict regulations that said cakes couldn't be iced. He was pretty sure that dried fruit was also unavailable.

'I'm not taking off my coat just yet, it's far too cold. I'm hoping it will warm up when we're all here,' she said and he agreed.

He took her hand and they made their way through the throng to admire the cake. 'Good heavens,' she said laughing, 'it's not a cake at all, it's a cardboard replica. How clever.'

One of the ladies behind the food table overheard her remark and nodded. 'We've got a lovely madeira cake under the bottom tier and two Victoria sandwiches in the kitchen. Everybody will get a slice of wedding cake, even if it's not what they used to have.'

'I'm sure it'll be quite delicious. We're getting married on Friday and our wedding cake will be a sponge as well. The spread looks absolutely delicious. I hope ours is half as good.'

The woman beamed at the praise. 'I'm Daphne's auntie – she told me all about you and I'm sure your reception will be wonderful. Here, have a cup of tea to warm you up a bit. We daren't put on the paraffin heaters as they smell something terrible and are likely to poison us.'

'Tea would be wonderful, thank you so much.'

Eventually the hall warmed up and as coats and scarves were removed, a more celebratory atmosphere prevailed. Now the party frocks and smart jackets were on show, the guests were smiling and enjoying themselves.

'We need to check in at the B&B before nine o'clock, sweetheart,' James told Charlie as they paused, breathless after completing a dance recently come over from America, a lively jitterbug. The record on the turntable was something by Glen Miller's band.

'Do you know how far it is from here?'

'I have the address and I'm pretty sure it's no more than a five-minute walk.' He'd carefully selected this guest house as walking about in the dark with only the tiny beam allowed from his torch wouldn't be easy.

'In which case I'll ask Daphne, she's coming over to speak to us, she's bound to know exactly.'

'Have you had a good time, you two?'

James kissed Daphne on the cheek, and Charlie hugged her. 'Wonderful, I just hope our do is half as good.'

'It's been lovely, hasn't it? Don't forget you're giving me a lift to my new home tomorrow morning.'

'We haven't forgotten. Shall we pick you up here?' James thought the village hall was an easy place for them to find each other.

'Yes, thank you. Mrs Cranfield's, where you're staying tonight, is just round the corner from here. Bob and I are leaving now, I want to change into my going-away outfit, and then we'll come back to say goodbye and head for The Saracens for the night. What time tomorrow, James?'

'Ten o'clock? Is that too early?'

'No, perfect. Thank you so much for driving all this way. We really appreciate the effort.'

After the happy couple left, the party ended. Creeping out from behind the blackout curtain covering the door was a nuisance but essential. James's concern over inadequate torch lights was unnecessary as it was actually brighter outside than it had been during the day. Not a glimmer of light could escape tonight because it was a full moon – a bombers' moon – and he heard several people mention this as they left.

He and Charlie were making their way across the street when the siren began to howl. The search lights lit up the sky, the ack-ack began firing, and the unmistakable drone of approaching bombers filled the air.

* * *

Charlie clutched James's arm. 'Where are our fighters? Why aren't they up there?'

'God knows. More important is where the hell do we go? No one mentioned the whereabouts of a public shelter.'

'Follow us, you two, there's a shelter just around the corner,' a man called as he ran past.

She hung onto James's hand and together they raced behind the helpful man and his wife.

An ARP warden shone his torch towards them. 'This way, be quick, I'm going to shut the door in a minute.'

They almost fell down the steep concrete steps into the smelly interior of a large communal shelter. It was full, mostly with faces she recognised from the wedding. There were a few in night-clothes, clutching their precious documents on their lap, and even a cat and small dog sitting shivering on the laps of their owners.

There were no spaces left on the benches, so they'd have to stand. There were candles in jam jars for illumination but even the pungent smell of burning wax couldn't mask the overpowering odour of an unemptied Elsan. She didn't envy those who had to sit at the far end, next to the curtain that screened the privy. Maybe arriving last had been a good thing.

The warden pointed to the steps. 'Sit on them, you'll not want to be standing all night.'

They did as instructed. James sat sideways so he could lean against the wall and she snuggled into his arms.

'Gosh, I hope we're not here all night,' she whispered to him. 'I really don't want to have to go behind that curtain.'

'I doubt any bombs will be dropped on Chelmsford as the planes will be heading for London.'

A man sitting on the bench nearest to them disagreed. 'We've got Marconi's, Hoffman's and The Arc Works as well as the rail yard. Them Nazi buggers will know how important those are to the war.'

'I'm sorry, I know nothing about Chelmsford as we're just here for a wedding.'

'Fair enough. Mind you, mate, we've only had a few stray bombs dropped so far but it'll happen, we all know that.'

'Then let's hope tonight isn't the night it does.' James pulled Charlie closer and she was glad of his warmth. The concrete steps were cold and uncomfortable but they were better off in their outdoor clothes than those in dressing gowns and nighties.

After an interminable time, the warden opened the door and slipped out. A few moments later, he was back. 'All quiet out there. The guns ain't going and the lights are off. I reckon you can go home if you want but you might be back again later. The all-clear ain't gone.'

James was on his feet immediately. 'Let's go, sweetheart, the B&B might have somewhere more comfortable for us if we do need to shelter again tonight.'

Being last in meant they were first out. Her bottom was numb, her legs stiff, and she was glad to be on the move.

'It's well after nine, James, what if the landlady has given up on us and gone to bed?'

'Then we'll have to sleep in the car. Don't worry, I've got a couple of rugs in there.'

The moonlight made it simple to find the house they wanted and he knocked loudly. The door flew open and an elderly grey-haired woman in dressing gown and curlers beamed at them.

'There you are, then. Guessed you were down the shelter. Come in quick, I'll get you a nice cup of tea before you turn in.'

The tea warmed Charlie and she began to relax a little. As she enjoyed a second cup, James asked an important question.

'Do you have a shelter or do we go back to the public one if the siren goes again?'

'It's under the table in the dining room. I've a Morrison shelter. I don't bother myself but you two can pop under there if you want to.'

'You remain in your bed even if you can hear the bombers overhead?' Charlie was horrified.

'I do, love. If one's got my name on it, then so be it. My Alf, bless him, dropped dead last year, and I'm on me own. No kiddies, no family, that's why I take in guests. A bit of company is what I miss.'

'If you don't mind, we'll sleep under the Morrison. Then we won't have to move if the siren goes a second time.' The old lady looked shocked. He hastily continued. 'We're getting married on Friday.'

'Then that makes sense, love. There's pillows and blankets, you'll be warm enough.' She nodded. 'No fire in there, I don't use that room, but you'll be in your clothes and have your coats. You won't need a fire, will you?'

'We won't, thank you.'

'I put bottles in your beds a while ago. I'll nip up and get them. Put the kettle on again, love, then I can top them up for you.' She bustled off, leaving Charlie and James alone.

'I'm so tired I could sleep anywhere and curled up with you under a table seems perfectly acceptable.'

'I think it will be more comfortable and warmer than in the bedrooms. This house is freezing. Only the range in here provides any heat.'

The kettle was whistling when the landlady returned and she filled one bottle for herself and the two for them and left them to it.

'I'll be literally sleeping with you for the first time, James.'

'So you will. Think of the scandal if this gets out? Handsome young doctor sleeps with his fiancée out of wedlock.'

She laughed and so did he. They were so well suited, shared the same sense of humour, loved animals, and wanted a big family. She glowed all over, as she settled into his arms for the night, thinking of what was going to happen so that a baby could come along.

20

Joanna waited for Angus to say why he'd telephoned, hardly daring to initiate a conversation. He didn't sound upset, had plenty to tell her about her daughter, and her heart settled to a more regular beat.

'I'm so busy with the wedding preparations, I don't have long. How can I help you, Angus?'

'Sorry, I'll get to the point. I thought you'd want to know how Sarah's getting on first.'

'Of course I did, and I'm thrilled that she's doing so well and likely to complete her training and take her final exams far earlier than any of us expected.'

'There's a desperate shortage of doctors and as long as she continues to pass exams, both practical and written, it seems she can qualify a year early.'

'How exciting – does that mean that you'll be getting married at the end of next year?'

'I sincerely hope so. Now, I wanted to tell you that I gave you the wrong information. Sergeant completed his tour of duty successfully in Malta and has returned to England. I haven't the foggiest where he is now – the letter you wrote will be chasing him all over the shop so I doubt he's got it yet. Just thought you'd want to know.'

Joanna gripped the edge of the table to hold herself steady. 'That's really good news. Do you think I should write again or hope the letter eventually catches up with him?'

'I can't tell you any more than I have. If I discover his whereabouts then I'll let you know.'

'Thank you so much for taking the time to ring me about John. I'm intending to come up to London in the summer with the twins. We really must get together for lunch when we're there.'

'I'll make damn sure Sarah has a day off. I'll go in and throw my weight about a bit. She won't like it – but what's a chap supposed to do?'

Joanna replaced the receiver. Her worst fear had been that John hadn't responded because he was dead. As she obviously wasn't listed as his next of kin, she'd only hear if Angus saw his name on the fatality list.

She wasn't exactly sure what happened when a pilot had completed the required number of sorties, but she seemed to recall being told they were then posted somewhere quiet for a few weeks before being returned to active duty.

She would just have to be patient and hope he eventually received her letter. Whether he would respond favourably or not no longer seemed so important now that she knew he was alive.

Things were going well for her family and her small band of land girls and the deprivations and damage caused by the war for thousands of others, mainly those living in the big cites, seemed a long way off from Goodwill House and the peaceful village of Stodham.

Daphne had now left and would be living near the base from tomorrow. Then, on Friday, Charlie would also be gone.

'Excuse me, my lady, Mum said there's someone come to the back door to see you.'

'Thank you, Tony, did she say who it might be?'

The young man shook his head. 'I answered the door and I think he's possibly a builder as he's wearing overalls covered in plaster.'

'I'm coming. How are you progressing with the boiler?'

'Should be working by tomorrow ready for the big do. I had to make a couple of bits for it, which is why it's taken so long.'

'I'm so glad you came to find your mother and I do hope you can stay. I've never heard her sing before.' Joanna smiled at him. 'As a duet you sound really professional. Do you think you could sing at the reception?'

'Don't see why not. Liza has a lovely voice too, could I ask her to make it a trio? I can play the piano.'

'Of course you can ask my daughter. I'm certain she'd love to perform with the two of you.'

'I've put the bloke in the office at the far end of house. Bit cold, but I wasn't sure where else he should go.'

'Thank you, I'll take him to the study if he is who we think he might be.'

She had been eagerly awaiting a response from the builders who had so expertly demolished the Victorian wing after the fire last year. She hoped they could do the refurbishment and alterations to the house she'd bought and intended to move into later this year.

The young man waiting to speak to her was a stranger, but from his clothing she thought Tony was correct in thinking he must be a tradesman of some sort.

'I'm Lady Harcourt, how can I be of assistance?'

He didn't seem at all awed by her title and grinned. 'Me and my dad have been working on the conversion of the rectory for the Land Army. We heard that you were looking for someone to do the same at The Manse.'

'Good heavens, how word travels in this neighbourhood. Yes, you're quite correct. I've had plans drawn up of what I want – would you like to see them and then you'll have some idea if it's the sort of work you're looking for?'

'That makes sense.'

'Then perhaps you could introduce yourself.'

'I'm Billy Hoskins, me dad's Tommy Hoskins.'

'I'm delighted to meet you, Mr Hoskins. Shall we go somewhere warmer to continue this conversation?'

'It is a mite chilly in here, that's for sure. We builders work outside and don't feel the cold, but it's different indoors.'

She rather liked this young man. She noticed that he had a slight limp, which was no doubt the reason he wasn't in uniform. The plans were on the desk in the study and she spread them out for him to look at.

He didn't speak for five minutes and she watched him run his finger over various parts, nodding and smiling occasionally. 'Right, ma'am, this is exactly what me and my dad are best at. We don't build from scratch but are dab hands at renovating and refurbishing.'

'That's excellent news. Do you do everything yourselves or do you bring in plumbers and electricians and so on?'

'Me dad's a plumber and I'm the electrician. This house already has mains water and drainage, but I reckon the wiring will need looking at. I won't be able to get my hands on new bathroom fittings, can't be had for love nor money at the moment.' He looked at her speculatively as if expecting her to be outraged at the thought of having something second-hand.

'As long as it works and isn't damaged then I don't mind how old it is,' Joanna said. 'Actually, now I come to think of it, there's a barn full of things that might be of use. I seem to remember there's a beautiful Victorian WC, hand basin and bath somewhere amongst the other items.'

'One of them with blue flowers?'

'Yes, exactly that. My late husband took out the Victorian bathrooms and installed something more modern. My son's outside somewhere if you would care to have a rummage through and see if there's anything you could use?'

He beamed. 'I'll do that. We'll be finished at the rectory by June so could start, if you want us to and you accept our estimate, in July. I need to have a look at the house. Can you arrange for someone to be there to let me in?'

'Again, my son Joe can do that. It's only a couple of miles from here and he has an excellent bicycle. Perhaps you could arrange a time for your visit when you speak to him outside? I do know it's difficult for you to give a precise time for when the job will be done as it all depends on the materials and so on. I would like to move either before or after Christmas.'

'That sounds about right. If you're happy with recycled and second-hand, then that makes things easier.'

Joanna went to bed that night bubbling with excitement and anticipation. John was alive and in her heart she believed that he still loved her and would return one day.

* * *

James delivered Daphne to her new home before taking Charlie back to Goodwill House for the very last time. Tomorrow she would be his wife and he couldn't be happier.

'I can't believe the next time I see you it will be when you arrive at the church, darling. I hope you're as excited as I am.'

'You know I am. If I was a bottle of pop then I'd be fizzing over the top. I just hope you don't get any emergencies you can't ignore in the next three days.'

'The local midwife rarely needs my help, and the St John's are on standby. The good thing about it being such a tight community here is that everybody knows everybody else's business. I forgot to tell you that I think most of the village will be attending the service. It appears that our union is very popular.'

'I should think so too,' Charlie said. 'It's certainly very popular with me. Did you know that Jean's son, Tony, is acting as chauffeur for me tomorrow? I'll be arriving in the Bentley.'

'I'll be waiting. I know it's unusual, but I'm glad that you're walking down the aisle on my arm.'

'So am I. I didn't want a big fuss; I could have asked Daphne and Sal to be bridesmaids but just the two of us suits me perfectly.'

'It will raise a few eyebrows in the congregation but it's our wedding, not theirs. I take it Lady Harcourt and the twins will come with you in the Bentley.'

'Actually, they'll be here first then Tony's coming back to collect me. Jean will travel in the car to make sure when I get out my veil and gown are as they should be.'

He escorted her to the back door, where they exchanged a long and passionate kiss. He didn't go in but drove away immediately. He was seeing a handful of urgent cases this afternoon and needed to get back.

* * *

The last patient had just left when James heard a car pulling up outside. He frowned. It was already dark and there were things he needed to do for tomorrow and he really didn't want any visitors and especially not one who arrived in a car.

With a sigh of resignation, he stepped between the blackout curtain and the front door and opened it just as the visitor, a man in a smart coat and trilby hat, was raising his hand to knock.

'Dr Willoughby?'

'I am he. Can I help you?'

'I hope so. I'm Sebastien Somiton, I believe that you are hoping to marry my daughter tomorrow morning.'

James was rarely lost for words, but for a few moments was unable to give a coherent answer. 'Then I suppose you'd better come in.'

He stepped aside and the man, who looked to be only in his fifties but was probably older than that, took a step forward but then remained facing the blackout curtain as if waiting for someone to move it for him. James ignored him.

The car, a Rolls-Royce, was blocking the road.

'Put the car in the drive and then come in. Use the front door. I'll put the kettle on.' The shadowy figure of the uniformed chauffeur raised a hand in acknowledgement and jumped back into the car. James left him to it.

Somiton had realised nobody was going to move the curtain for him and was now inside. This man had sent his newborn daughter away like an unwanted package and had had no contact with Charlie until today. Therefore, he already disliked the man and his behaviour in the few minutes since he'd arrived had done nothing to change his opinion.

The entrance hall was empty. Where the devil was he? Although the house was large by ordinary people's standards, no doubt it seemed like a farm worker's cottage to someone like this unwanted visitor.

James headed for the kitchen and pushed the kettle onto the

hotplate of the range. Surely the man would hear the rattling of crockery and do the sensible thing and come into the kitchen? It beggared belief that Charlie's father couldn't bring himself to enter a kitchen.

He was about to call out – he was damned if he was going to actually look for him – when there was a hideous yowling and Lucky streaked into the room, his tail like a bottlebrush and his fur standing on end.

The missing man arrived in hot pursuit. 'I'll kill that bloody cat. Look at my cheek – he pounced on me and scratched it. I'll probably catch some dreadful disease.'

There were three deep gouges on the left side of his face which needed medical attention. James put aside his dislike and became a professional.

'Please, Mr Somiton, sit down here. I'll get my medical bag and deal with the injury.'

As he was collecting what he needed from the surgery, he heard the front door open. 'If you wait in the hall, I won't be a minute.'

'I'll do that, Dr Willoughby. Thank you for inviting me in.'

James smiled at the grey-haired man who was holding his peaked cap in his hand. 'My cat attacked Mr Somiton and I'm just going to deal with it. Why don't you sit in the waiting room here? There's coal in the scuttle and if you give fire a poke, I'm sure it'll come back. I shouldn't come into the kitchen at the moment.'

'Give the cat a medal.' The chauffeur grinned and did as he was asked.

Lucky was now back on his chair by the Aga and curled up and asleep as if nothing untoward had occurred – and if it had, he was making it quite plain it was absolutely nothing to do with him.

James tipped some freshly boiled water into a dish and then, using squares of lint, carefully cleaned the scratches. The patient said nothing so neither did he until he'd finished.

'They don't need any sutures, the dressing I've applied will keep them clean. I'll give you a couple of aspirin for the pain.'

Still no response from Somiton. Whilst he'd been dressing the wounds, James had checked the man's pulse, which had been regular and strong, so he wasn't in shock. Probably a cup of tea would do the trick.

He took a mug and a piece of cake in for the chauffeur who'd made himself comfortable and was sitting next to the fire, reading a discarded newspaper.

'Here you are. Do you know why your employer has turned up tonight?'

'He wants to stop Miss Charlotte from marrying you.' The man took a slurp of his tea, nodded his appreciation, and smiled. 'Fat chance of doing that, I should think, after seeing you. He never married again, has no other close family apart from his two nephews – one of whom is in jail for raping two women – and I think he wants to bring Miss Charlotte back so she can take care of him in his dotage.'

'I thought he had a brother – the one who took my future wife in when she was a baby.'

'He did, but he died from a heart attack a few months ago. Probably the shame.'

'Thank you for being so frank. Have you got a hotel reserved for tonight?'

'The Royal in Ramsgate. God knows how I'm going to find it at this time of night with all the signposts taken down and it too dark to read a map.'

'How did he know to come here and that it's our wedding day tomorrow?'

'Some Masonic friend of his told him when he was in London for a big do the other day. Think his name was Falconer.'

James nodded. That explained everything. Falconer was exactly the sort of friend Somiton would have.

'I'd offer to have you here, but I really don't want him under my roof any longer than necessary. I'm going to speak to him now and he'll be leaving immediately afterwards. If you turn right out of my drive, go through the village without turning off the road, it will take you to Ramsgate. Follow it down the hill and the hotel's on the corner. Car parking is to the left facing the promenade. It's easy enough to get to even in the dark.'

'Thank you. I'll finish my tea and then get the car started.'

James didn't care if Somiton had overheard this conversation, but he hoped for the chauffeur's sake that he hadn't. As he approached the kitchen door, he heard the cat growling and increased his pace.

Not a moment too soon, as Somiton had a heavy cast-iron pan in his hand and was approaching Lucky with murder in his eyes.

In two strides, he was beside the man and forcibly removed the skillet. 'No, you bloody don't. You've got the temerity to barge in here uninvited and are now attempting to harm my cat.'

'That animal's dangerous. It should be put down. Where's my daughter? I've come to take her back to Somiton Hall where she belongs. I'll not have her marrying a country doctor.'

'Charlie's reached her majority, can do as she pleases, you've had a wasted journey. Now, get out of my house before I throw you out.' He loomed over the man who flinched and retreated.

'I have powerful friends, I'll make it my business to ruin your life.'

James clenched his fists, his intention clear in his face, and the man's bravado faded and he scuttled out. Somiton tore the blackout curtain from its pole, letting light flood out into the street. A petty act from an insignificant man.

James slammed the door shut, hoping the village warden hadn't seen this breach of regulations. He picked up the torn curtain. Now he was faced with a dilemma – should he tell Charlie about this unexpected and unwanted visitor or pretend it had never happened?

21

Charlie missed Daphne's company the night before her wedding but had refused Sal's kind offer to sleep in the room with her that last night. Much as she loved Sal, her friend might have wanted to talk and she wanted her beauty sleep.

Before she turned out the bedside light she went upstairs for one last look at her gown so beautifully made by Jean. Nothing she'd owned before held a candle to it. Her clothes had always been made to measure, her shoes also, but not with as much love or expertise as Jean had shown with her wedding gown.

It would be sponged clean and carefully folded in tissue paper and put away in the hope that in years to come, a daughter or granddaughter might wear it on her own wedding day.

Charlie hadn't expected to sleep so well but woke refreshed and excited at seven o'clock, confident today was going to be the happiest day of her life. Until she'd fallen in love with James, she'd never really felt wanted, loved or truly content.

Now a wonderful, intelligent, kind, handsome man was marrying her and from today she would be loved and protected, finally have a real home. Although she'd lived all her life with her uncle, aunt and two cousins, she'd always been aware she didn't really belong there, wasn't a real member of that family.

Today was the start of a new life, a better life, and if she and James were fortunate, this time next year she might be holding his baby in her arms. After what her cousin had done to her, she'd thought she'd never marry or have children of her own. James had shown her that intimacy between a man and a woman who loved each other could be a wonderful thing.

Her pulse skittered and a wave of unexpected heat washed over her at the thought of being in his arms unclothed and becoming his true wife. Knowing that if she wasn't ready tonight to consummate the union he would wait had taken away her fear.

Daphne had positively glowed yesterday when they'd given her a lift to the cottage near the base. It hadn't been possible to talk but when Charlie had walked her to the door, Daphne had kissed and hugged her and whispered in her ear.

'It's lovely, you've nothing to worry about. Just let James take the lead.'

Well – that sounded like excellent advice. Her knowledge of the process was something she tried not to think about. Making love was what James had called it and that's what she was looking forward to.

This morning, she'd had sole use of the bathroom. Fortunately, Lady Harcourt had arranged for all the girls to have the whole day off so nobody would be getting up as early as her. Sal had given her some delicious-smelling bath salts; she wasn't exactly sure of the fragrance, but she thought probably rose or jasmine. For the first time since the restriction on the amount of water allowed in a bath, she ignored it. The system burbled and gurgled, not used to being asked to provide so much hot water all at once.

Charlie had pinned her hair on top of her head to make sure it didn't get wet and then stepped into the lovely, illegal, deep bath.

Having the water completely covering her was an experience she'd not had for years. She relaxed, luxuriated in the novelty and remained submerged until the water cooled.

She'd been in the bathroom so long that she could hear the girls getting up. They had their own washbasins, and the WC was separate, so nobody knocked on the door. It belatedly occurred to her that the Harcourt family might well want a bath as well this morning as they were attending the wedding in all their finery. Too late to worry about that – they would have to have a lick and a promise, as the hot water tank would certainly be empty and she wasn't exactly sure how long it took to heat up again.

Usually getting out of the weekly bath was an unpleasant experience as the bathroom was always cold. Today it wasn't and for a moment she was puzzled. Then inadvertently a naked thigh touched the radiator and she squealed and jumped away. It was red-hot – she touched it with the tip of her finger and winced.

The radiator wasn't just hot, it was dangerously so. She flung on her clothes – she wouldn't change into her wedding dress until an hour before she left – and still slightly clammy, she ran downstairs.

Everywhere was warm – not something she was used to. She raced to the kitchen and found Tony, Jean and the twins enjoying an early-morning cup of tea.

'I think your boiler might be about to explode, Tony, have you felt the heat of the radiators? I touched one inadvertently and it left a red mark on my leg.'

'Bloody hell!' Tony said and his chair crashed to the flagstone floor as he hurtled out of the room. Joe followed him.

'Thank goodness you came down when you did,' Jean said calmly. 'I don't suppose you want much to eat but I've prepared you a special breakfast. Soft-boiled eggs, toast and coffee.'

'Coffee? I really don't want to use up the last of Lady Harcourt's precious hoard. I'll be perfectly happy with tea as usual.'

'No, Charlie, Lady Joanna insisted. This will be the first and last wedding here and she wants it to be memorable for everyone, but especially for the bride.'

Liza had gone in the opposite direction to the other two and came back looking worried. 'You're right, Charlie, the radiators are dangerous. I'm going to go round and warn the girls.'

'No, I'll do that, you tell your mother and grandmother, that's far more important.'

On a normal day, Charlie would have politely tapped on each door and told the girls individually. This morning, she stood halfway down the passageway and yelled at the top of her voice.

'Don't touch the radiators – they are dangerously hot. Don't put anything on them to dry or you'll cause a fire and burn your clothes.'

She was answered by a chorus of thanks and good wishes. Satisfied nobody would be harmed, she returned to the kitchen. Joe was now back at his place eating toast as if the newly repaired boiler hadn't almost exploded.

'Has Tony been able to do something?'

The young man nodded, unable to answer as his mouth was full. 'Good thing you told us when you did, Charlie, otherwise it might well have blown up and then all his hard work would have been wasted.'

Jean laughed. 'My son's an engineer as well as a mechanic. He wouldn't let anything explosive happen here. You're exaggerating as usual, Joe.'

'The radiators were very hot, Jean.'

'That's true, Charlie, but Tony said it just needed a few minor adjustments. It might take an hour or two for them to cool down, but they won't ever be as hot as that again.'

Liza came back smiling. 'Grandma was cock-a-hoop about not needing the fire lit. Miss Biggins was actually smiling. I think the whole house will be smiling today. I nipped into the ballroom and there's no frost on the inside of the windows. It's not exactly toasty, but with more people in there this afternoon, it'll be perfect.'

All three ladies from the village, the ones who helped out with housework, cooking and so on, had turned up early as there was so much to do. Charlie went to look at the ballroom where the reception would be held as soon as she'd finished her special breakfast. She took a second mug of coffee with her.

Sal saw her walk past the dining room and joined her. 'You look ever so calm, I thought you'd be all over the place this morning.'

'I did all my panicking ages ago so am eager to start this new chapter in my life. Once things are organised and I'm settled in as Mrs Willoughby, I want you and Daphne to be the first to come to lunch.'

'Crikey, that's posh. I ain't never been invited to lunch before. I'm going to wear one of me outfits what Jean made for me last year. Not had no opportunity until today. I reckon the others will be jealous – at least them what have nothing to wear but their uniforms will be.'

'Thank you for doing that. If you've got time, would you help me to get ready? I would have asked you and Daphne to be my bridesmaids but didn't want a fuss.'

'I'd love to,' Sal said. 'When are you going to start?'

'It's nine now, the wedding's at two, so not until after lunch. Jean's making soup and sandwiches. Everybody seems to think I should be too nervous to eat but the reverse is true. I enjoyed my boiled eggs, and this coffee's scrumptious.'

'I ain't fond of it, good thing as there ain't none to be had. Me, I prefer a cuppa.'

Charlie stood open-mouthed, gazing at the transformation of the ballroom. She'd helped to decorate it a couple of times for events but never with more than paper streamers and a few bunches of balloons.

Sal enjoyed her surprise. 'Looks blooming marvellous, don't it? We made them paper flowers and that to go in the greenery. Looks a treat if I say so meself.'

Charlie gazed around at the arrangements and was overwhelmed that her land girl friends had gone to so much trouble for her and James. There were tables arranged around the space, all covered with white damask cloths. Several trestles had been put together to make the buffet.

'Golly, it's the best china, the plates have the crest on them. I'll be terrified something will be broken.'

* * *

Lady Harcourt had come to join them and had heard the girls talking. 'It is the Harcourt china and cutlery. However, I don't give a fig for it and if some gets damaged or broken then it's in a good cause. I'll be leaving here in a few months and I certainly won't be taking it with me. I'll probably donate it to charity.'

Sal had picked up one of the almost translucent plates and was admiring it. 'Blimey, my lady, this is ever so delicate. I reckon I can see right through it. It wouldn't last long in a normal person's kitchen. Wouldn't Lord Harcourt want it?'

Joanna didn't appreciate this suggestion from Sal. She was all for informality, but the girl should have known better. She was about to make it perfectly clear how cross she was when she closed her mouth and swallowed the words.

Her abiding dislike for Harcourt had caused her to direct her anger at Sal, who was only trying to be helpful. In fact, what she said made perfect sense, but doing it would be impossible as she had no wish to ever see him again.

'Thank you for your suggestion, Sal, it's a good idea but as I won't be leaving here until the end of the year, I don't have to do anything about it at the moment. You and your friends have made this ballroom look quite beautiful – I'd never have thought of crêpe paper flowers and the ones you've made are perfect.'

'Ta ever so, my lady, we wanted it to look nice for Charlie and her doctor. I just hope the blooming bus runs, otherwise we'll be late. No one wants to walk in their glad rags.'

'I think you might be one of the only ones not going in their jodhs and brogues. Why don't you come in the car with Jean and me?'

'If that's all right with you, my lady, I'd be tickled pink to come with you, Charlie.'

Joanna smiled. 'You don't have to ask my permission, girls, the Bentley's for the bride and groom.'

Charlie shook her head. 'We'll come from the church in James's car, thank you, my lady. I wouldn't want the other Lady Harcourt standing around outside the church getting cold.'

'If you're quite sure, my dear, it would certainly make life a lot easier if we can come back in the car as soon as you and Dr Willoughby have left.'

The postman had arrived with a bundle of letters but none were from John. Joanna took them to the study and filled the remainder of the morning dealing with correspondence. Aggie brought in a tray with her lunch.

'Here you are, my lady, Jean thought you might prefer to have it in here. Lady Harcourt's having hers in the sitting room.'

'Thank you, it's certainly easier to remain here as there are so many people bustling about in the kitchen at the moment. I really do appreciate the fact that you, Doris, and Edith have come in to help with this wedding reception.'

'Our pleasure, my lady, we wouldn't be able to see the bride if we weren't working.'

As the wedding ceremony was at two o'clock, Joanna and the rest of her family would have to be ready to leave at a quarter past one. The Bentley had to come back to collect Charlie and it would never do for the bride to be more than a few minutes late.

Winter weddings were not as enjoyable as those held in the summer months as one's ensemble had to be hidden by an overcoat. The finery would only be revealed when they got to the reception.

Elizabeth was already upstairs getting ready when Joanna went up. She was revelling in the warmth of the house – the boiler that supplied water to the radiators had been out of action for decades and she was both amazed and delighted that Tony had repaired it so swiftly.

Today the house felt alive, looked its absolute best, and this would be the biggest party that had been held here since she'd invited the entire village to the engagement celebration for Sarah and Angus.

She hoped that when the two of them eventually got married, when Sarah finished her training and qualified as a doctor, they would marry in Stodham Church. They couldn't have their reception here as she would no longer own this house, but The Manse was more than large enough for a reception and the grounds were extensive and quite lovely.

Liza was moving about in her bedroom, so Joanna knocked. 'It's me, darling, can I come in?'

The door was thrown open by her daughter in her underwear. 'You shouldn't appear at the door without your peignoir on. Someone might see you.'

'I don't know who? I knew it was you so I didn't think it mattered. I can't decide which frock to wear so you can help me choose. I've got shoes to match either of them and as I'll be wearing my best coat then my hat only has to go with that, not my frock.'

Draped over the bed were two gowns that at first glance would have seemed far too old for a girl of fifteen. But then Liza was already physically a young woman and also emotionally mature.

'I love both of them but I think the navy with polka dots is very smart. I didn't know you had that one, did Jean make it up for you?'

Liza looked a bit uncomfortable. 'I used my first wages to buy it. I went into Ramsgate with my friend Alice last Saturday and it had just come in.'

'Well done, it's the perfect choice for you. Your hair looks lovely arranged as it is. Did Jean help you?'

'No, I do it myself now. I always wear it up when I'm at work as the little ones tend to pull my hair if it's loose.'

'Then I'm redundant – I thought I might be able to help my daughter get ready for her first wedding,' Joanna said.

Liza hugged her. 'Don't be silly, Ma, I'll always want you. I intend to be independent like Sarah, you've both taught me that. In eighteen months, I'll be able to start training as a nurse and I want to be ready for that.'

'I believe that you'll be ready for anything life throws at you, my dear. I'm not going to ask if your brother needs any help as I know that would be unpopular. We have to be downstairs in half an hour.'

'You'd better hurry up then, Ma, as you're the only one not getting ready.'

Laughing, Joanna headed for her own room, where she'd already set out her clothes. She was wearing a heavy silk gown in a dark pink – she thought this colour suited her better than blue or green. She did nothing to her hair, just added a slick of pink lipstick, and was ready well within the allotted time.

Tony was waiting in the hall and from somewhere he'd found a peaked cap, dark suit and looked as if he was a genuine chauffeur.

'How splendid, it's a long time since I've been driven by anyone in uniform.'

He grinned and saluted. They were both laughing when her mother-in-law and the twins arrived.

They were almost unrecognisable as the two urchins who'd arrived at Goodwill House all those months ago.

'My word, you both look so smart. Joe, you look years older in that suit and Liza, you're definitely a young woman now. What do you think, Elizabeth?'

'I think that if we stand here talking then we'll be late and that will make the bride tardy. Come along, young gentleman and lady, escort your ancient grandmother to the car.'

They each took an arm and then the three of them sailed out of the house with scant regard for the fact that steps might be slippery. Her mother-in-law looked magnificent – she was dressed in a midnight-blue three-quarter length costume which had scarlet lapels and cuffs and her astonishing hat was the same colour as the ensemble with scarlet feathers.

There was room for only three on the commodious rear seat in the Bentley, so Joe pulled down the jump seat and sat on that. As long as he remembered to hold onto the leather strap, he'd be perfectly safe. If he didn't, he might well end up on the floor.

'I can't tell you how much I am looking forward to this wedding, Joanna. I know Charlie isn't family but for some reason she and her two friends have fitted into the household as if they belong. Do you know, I thought that maybe you would marry her handsome young doctor one day as, after all, he is your age, not hers.'

'I've no intention of marrying again. I don't think the age difference matters one bit, Elizabeth, as the two of them are perfectly suited.'

She'd spoken more vehemently than she'd intended as she'd been thinking about John. The age difference between them wasn't as great but she was older than him. For an older man to marry a younger woman was an accepted practice. She was certain that if she and John resumed their affair and the relationship became public knowledge, there would be finger-pointing and tongue-wagging because she was almost a decade older than him. This might have bothered her last year, but not now.

22

James was glad to have both Dolly, the maid who'd remained in his employ when his housekeeper had retired, and Mrs Thompson in the house on the morning of his wedding. Hearing them bustling about ensuring that his home was sparkling and pristine – including rooms that wouldn't be used – kept his mind from last night's unwanted and unpleasant visitor.

As he only had to walk a hundred yards to the church, there was no necessity for him to start getting ready, to change into his best suit, before one o'clock at the earliest. He decided he'd tell Charlie about her father turning up but not today as he'd no intention of saying or doing anything to make the day less than perfect for her.

He tried to keep himself busy writing out the invoices for the six patients he'd seen yesterday but after ruining several sheets of his expensive headed paper, he abandoned the idea. He listened to the wireless, but the news wasn't good, so he turned it off. Today, for just one day, he wanted to put all thoughts of the war aside.

His gas mask was hanging on a nail in his study. He frowned. When was the last time he'd taken it out with him? He thought it was still a legal requirement but nobody in the village had them hanging around their necks any more. Perhaps they did in big cities but if Hitler had been going to gas the population of Britain, he'd have done so by now.

Living in a small village in Kent, even one as close to Manston and the coast as this was, one could almost forget there was a war on. People living in the countryside were fortunate as they didn't have the constant bombing and could supplement the meagre rations allowed by the government with their own produce – something those in the big cities couldn't do.

James was jerked from his reverie by the insistent ringing of his telephone. He checked his watch – it was only eleven o'clock so he could go out on a call without fear of being late for his wedding. Everybody in the village knew he was getting married today and wouldn't be ringing unless it was a real emergency.

He snatched up the receiver. 'Dr Willoughby speaking.'

'Doctor, it's my Ethel. She's not due for another four weeks but she's in labour. The midwife said she needs you.'

'I'll be there in ten minutes.'

He grabbed his medical bag, shrugged into his coat, and shouted to Mrs Thompson. 'Emergency call, Mrs Thompson, the other side of the village. If my future wife rings for any reason, reassure her that I'll not be late for our wedding.'

Whilst he still had a supply of petrol, he could use his car, but he thought in a few months' time he would have to resort to a bicycle.

* * *

This was Ethel Roberts's fifth attempt to have a baby. She'd never carried a baby to term – this was the closest she'd got. Four weeks premature shouldn't be a problem as the last time he'd spoken to the midwife, Sister Jones, she'd said the pregnancy was progressing well and the baby was a good size.

The fact that she'd asked him to come was worrying. He screeched to a halt outside the neat semi-detached modern house where the couple lived. As he ran for the front door, it opened, and Mr Roberts, ashen faced, grabbed his arm.

'It's all going wrong, Dr Willoughby. Quickly, help my Ethel, I don't think she'll get over it if we lose this baby too.'

'Have you rung for an ambulance?'

'It'll be an hour and that'll be too late.'

The midwife was waiting on the landing. 'The baby's breech. I'd be grateful for another pair of hands, Doctor. We really don't want Ethel to lose this little one.' A midwife, and especially one as competent as Sister Jones, would normally deliver a breech birth without needing his assistance.

'I'm here to help, Sister, but you take the lead.'

He stripped off his jacket and tie, rolled up his sleeves then washed his hands in the china basin on the washstand. He pulled on his rubber gloves and was ready to assist.

Poor Ethel was distraught, crying and barely able to follow their instructions. She'd been through this so many times and must know how dangerous the situation was.

'You save my baby, Dr Willoughby, I don't care what my husband says. If you have to make a choice – choose the baby.'

'We're going to save both of you. Now, Ethel, whatever you do, don't push. We want you with your buttocks over the end of the bed. It will make the delivery easier for the baby.'

He and Sister Jones helped Ethel shuffle down the bed and put her feet on the lino. The midwife dropped to her knees and he stretched across in order to hold Ethel's legs.

The perineum expanded and the prolapsed cord slid into view. This was normal and as long as the thick purplish tube was pulsating, the baby was receiving life-giving oxygen from the mother's placenta.

'Don't push yet, Ethel,' he said to the panting woman in the bed. 'I'll tell you when you can.'

The baby had to be delivered slowly and Sister Jones knew what she was doing. He hoped he wasn't going to be needed. The baby's legs would be curled up and the midwife would need to hook her fingers over the legs and deliver them.

The legs slid out and then the rest of the baby apart from her head. He released his hold and carefully wrapped the baby's body in the warm towels waiting in front of the fire. The towels kept the baby warm but also gave the midwife something to grip, as a baby was a slippery individual.

He applied pressure on the supra-pubic area on the next contraction. If this didn't work, he'd have to deliver the baby with forceps. Thank God this wasn't necessary and when Ethel pushed, the head was delivered safely. The baby was blue but this was usual and as soon as the midwife cleared her nostrils and throat, the infant screamed loudly. There was a general sigh of relief.

Once the placenta was delivered, James changed places with the nurse and inserted a few sutures in a tear and he was free to leave.

'You've got a lovely, healthy little girl, Mrs Roberts.'

'I'll fetch your husband. He'll want to see his daughter,' James said as he removed his rubber gloves and dropped them into the waste bin.

'The ambulance is waiting outside,' Sister Jones said as he left the room.

'I'll send it away. Thank God we didn't need it.'

'Amen to that.'

'You'd better get a move on, Doc, you're going to be late,' Ethel called out from the bed with a tired but triumphant smile.

'Good God, I didn't realise it was so late!'

He came out of the house as fast as he'd gone in and the ambulance men snatched up the stretcher, thinking he'd come to fetch them.

'Everything is tickety-boo, chaps. I'm delighted to tell you you've had a wasted journey. Mother and baby are doing well.'

'You'll be in disgrace, Doc, I reckon your bride's being driven around the village right now waiting for you to turn up.'

He waved a hand in acknowledgement and jumped into his car. How those two knew he was getting married he'd no idea, they weren't even locals. He was glad he didn't have to pass the church to get home.

He'd never changed so quickly in his life. He was late, but not disastrously so. Charlie would only have been waiting for ten minutes – brides quite often arrived late and he hoped today was one of those occasions.

* * *

James arrived at the entrance to the churchyard as the Bentley pulled up. His heart was thudding, his hands clammy, but he wasn't late.

The young man who was acting as chauffeur jumped out of the car and opened the door. His future wife stepped out. He knew all brides were beautiful, but he was quite certain there were none to match her.

Jean emerged after Charlie and whilst he stood in awe, drinking in the beauty of the young woman standing in front of him, her eyes bright, her smile radiant, the housekeeper fussed with the veil and the gown.

'You look quite stunning, my darling, I'm the luckiest man alive to be marrying you today.'

He held out his arm and she moved gracefully towards him and slipped her hand through it. 'I hate to say this, my love, but you look a trifle dishevelled. Your tie's crooked and you've buttoned your jacket incorrectly.'

'Sorry, I only got back ten minutes ago. I'll sort myself out before we walk down the aisle.'

'No, soon as we're in the porch, I'll do it for you. I take it your emergency had a happy ending.'

'Mother and baby are both safe and well.'

'How absolutely wonderful – I can't think of a better way to start our married life than for you to have delivered a baby just an hour or so ago.'

It didn't take her long to make him presentable. Jean and Sal slipped past them and made their way to their seats in the congregation. The 'Wedding March' filled the interior of the old building and everybody stood up.

He escorted his lovely young bride down the aisle and was oblivious to everything apart from her. He spoke his vows loudly and clearly, as did she. When it came to the part of the service when the vicar asked if there was anyone there who had reason to dispute the marriage, he held his breath. There were no unwanted interruptions, rings were exchanged, and he was told he could kiss his bride.

* * *

Charlie walked back down the aisle on her new husband's arm as if she was floating. All she was aware of was the man beside her, the smiling faces of the congregation, not the cold, not the war, just pure happiness that finally, after a life devoid of love, she was now surrounded by it.

'Well, my darling Mrs Willoughby, shall we walk back to our

home and spend a few moments alone before heading for the reception?'

'I think Lady Harcourt has arranged for a professional photographer to take some pictures. We have to stand outside the church for those.'

'Absolutely not. It's far too cold for you to stand about in that flimsy gown. He can take all the snaps he wants at the reception.'

'Of course, my love, your word is my command. The fact that her ladyship has gone to all the trouble of arranging this means nothing compared to my following your every order.'

She smiled sweetly and he laughed, turning several heads. He understood her so well and they shared the same appreciation of the ridiculous.

'I can see I'm going to be a hen-pecked shell of a man. But you're right. It would be extremely rude not to freeze for an hour just to keep Lady Harcourt happy.'

As it happened, the photographer, an ancient man with an old-fashioned camera, was only too happy to postpone the wedding pictures until everyone was safely at Goodwill House.

'Suits me fine, Mrs Willoughby, it's a lovely old house and you'll both be more relaxed in the warm.'

'Excellent. We'll see you there later.' James took off his smart jacket and draped it around her shoulders and then they dashed down the path, along the pavement, and arrived at his front door much warmer than they had been.

Lucky was sitting on the front step as if he was expecting them. Charlie leaned down and fussed him but didn't pick him up. 'No, not today, young man, I'm not risking cat hairs and mud on my wedding gown.'

'Mrs Thompson must have let him out and forgotten to let him in again. He would have been out for hours if we'd not come here first.'

'Good heavens, James, I didn't think you were so soft-hearted. He'd have been fine. He was a stray, remember, his luxury life only started a few weeks ago.'

The house was deliciously warm. Although Charlie loved her silk wedding dress, she thought it might have been more sensible to have worn something better suited to the weather.

'Here, I'll take back my jacket and you put my overcoat on. Not very glamorous, but you'll be a lot warmer in the car.'

'I've been thinking, my love, that I'd rather stay here tonight. Would you mind very much cancelling the reservation at the hotel in Ramsgate?'

'We'd better check we've got something to eat in the house.'

'There's going to be a sumptuous spread for our reception and I'll ask one of the ladies from the village to pack us a hamper. Mrs T will have got in something for us to eat on Sunday.'

'Then I'll ring The Royal. Shall we have a cup of tea before we go?'

James was sometimes not very aware of how things he did could affect others. 'We can't do that. Guests will be arriving, and the bride and groom have to be there first.'

'Of course. My overcoat's in the closet over there. If you get that, I'll make the telephone call.'

'First I'm going to make sure that Lucky has something to eat.'

There was a scribbled note from Dolly left on the table. Charlie read it and wasn't sure whether to laugh. Lucky had bought in a pheasant and two rats – all dead, fortunately.

'James, I'm afraid we're going to have to manage with just Dolly. Our cat has driven away another member of your staff,' she called.

He was still speaking on the telephone so probably hadn't heard. Mrs Thompson had just dumped all three items in the scullery sink. Charlie wasn't bothered by rats but dressed as she was, she didn't want to risk handling them.

'Did you say something, darling?' he said from behind her and then saw what was in the sink. 'Bloody hell! At least we have something tasty to eat Sunday. I'll get rid of the rats. I don't think Lucky will want to eat them.'

'Did you read the note?'

'I did. I'm sure we can manage with just Dolly. In fact, I think having both of them was rather excessive.'

Whilst he disposed of the unwanted gifts, she tied a piece of string around the feet of the pheasant and hung it up in the pantry. She wasn't going to risk the cat having a nibble whilst they were out.

* * *

Ten minutes later, the newly married couple were in the car and arrived just after the Bentley. The Lady Harcourts seemed unbothered by the lack of etiquette on the part of the bride and groom.

'It's worked out rather well, Charlie, as the bus was just pulling in as we drove away,' Lady Harcourt said gaily.

Joe and Liza escorted their grandmother into the house first, and she and James followed. Lady Harcourt, Jean and her son were close behind.

'Golly, I could get used to being welcomed by this lovely warmth,' Charlie said as James tenderly removed his overcoat from her shoulders.

'You won't need this in here. Do we have to stand here and shake everybody's hands?'

'Probably, but I don't want to do that. We've already set tongues wagging by walking down the aisle together in both directions, so I hardly think it matters what we do now.'

The ballroom looked magical and even empty, the huge space

was pleasantly warm. James seemed distracted; something was bothering him.

'What's wrong, my love? Having second thoughts?' For an instant, he thought her serious and the horrified expression on his face made her giggle.

'Quickly, before anyone else gets here, there's something I've got to tell you.' He looked so serious her heart plummeted. He took her hand and led her to the far end of the ballroom where even if people came in, they would be unable to hear what they were saying.

He told her about the unexpected visitor he'd had last night and was obviously unsure how she'd react or even if he should have told her.

'I'm glad you got rid of him, he's nothing to me, you're my life and my family. I don't want or need anybody else.'

With a shout of triumph, James snatched her up and swung her around as if she was a child and then, with her feet still dangling, he crushed her against his chest and kissed her so thoroughly her head was spinning by the time he put her down.

His actions were cheered loudly by the guests assembled at the far end of the room. Her cheeks were pink, his eyes dark and there was a streak of colour along his cheekbones. He'd never looked more handsome or dashing.

'Come along, my darling wife, I think we've entertained our guests sufficiently for one afternoon.'

Their informality had set the tone for the reception and the atmosphere was relaxed, happy, and very lively. Charlie had managed to slip away and speak to Edith, and she'd kindly offered to pack up a hamper for them before the food was put out.

The photographs were taken in the grand hall and in the ballroom. There were individual pictures of Charlie and James but also group photographs with all the guests crowded in together.

About a dozen had been invited from the village and they trooped off to catch the last bus at seven o'clock.

'I'm having such a wonderful time, James, I really don't want to leave. We would have had to go when the others did if we'd been going to Ramsgate tonight.'

'One more dance, sweetheart, and then we must depart. Nobody expects the bride and groom to remain to the end of the reception.'

For a moment, she didn't understand, then her cheeks coloured. It was their wedding night and everybody knew what was going to happen. Six months ago, she'd have been terrified, insisted on staying, but things were different between them now. She was ready – if not exactly eager – to learn what happened between a loving couple in the privacy of their bedroom.

'We can leave now, my love, I don't need another dance.'

It didn't take long to walk hand in hand around the ballroom and say thank you and goodbye to those who had attended their reception. Daphne and Bob asked if they could have a lift to their cottage, which made their departure a little less embarrassing.

'I'll get the car started, turn it round and then you three can just jump in. It's going to be icy inside as the heater only works intermittently and not very well when it is functioning.'

They pulled up outside Daphne's cottage. 'I'll come and see you next week sometime, Daphne. I'll finish by mid-afternoon and so will you.'

'Yes, please do. We had a wonderful time at your wedding. It seems quite astonishing to me that we've both got married in the same week. Goodnight, James, Charlie, I know you're going to be as happy as we are.'

23

Joanna thought it had been a jolly good party but had left the young people to continue their fun and retired at ten o'clock. None of the land girls were working tomorrow but had all agreed to go in on Sunday morning instead. She believed that most of them were relieved not to have to go to church.

One might have thought that seeing not one, but two happy young brides with their handsome husbands would have made her sad, but the reverse was true. Until she'd met John last summer, she hadn't understood what happiness was. She hadn't been mistreated as a child, had attended a decent boarding school, but having quite elderly parents and being an only child, she'd never had the pleasure of playing with siblings or even been allowed to make friends with the local girls.

When David had seen her working at the bank where her father had been the manager and decided he wanted to marry her, she'd had no option but to fall in with his and her parents' plans. Nobody had asked her opinion, she was swept along by the romance of it all by this older, handsome aristocrat. She thought him her Prince Charming and she his Cinderella.

In some ways, this had been true – he had treated her like a precious object, not allowed her to lift a finger, do anything at all but sit around looking like the lady of the manor. He'd told her in no uncertain terms to be silent when his friends were there, to offer no opinions, just to look pretty and obedient.

Perhaps if she'd been able to give him the son he'd wanted, things might have been different, but she hadn't and they weren't. It had been a relief when he'd died at Dunkirk, even though she'd found the transition to head of the family difficult at first. Now, less than a year later, she couldn't even recall his face, let alone his voice.

John had been a revelation. He'd introduced her to physical love; she'd understood how things should be between a man and a woman and their brief liaison had been the best time of her life. With hindsight, she understood that it had been unkind of her to send him away, telling him that their worlds were too far apart, that the age difference was too great, that...

All nonsense – didn't they say that love could conquer all? She was a wealthy young woman and could do as she pleased with her money, there was no man to dictate to her.

John might be an ardent socialist, despise the upper classes, but he'd got a full scholarship to Oxford and had a first-class honours degree so was better educated than any of David's friends.

If he came back to her then they would work something out. Obviously, marriage wasn't something she'd consider, but a loving long-term relationship could surely be managed? A wave of despair swept over her.

This was a fantasy, a pipe dream, as no young man would give up his chance of a family of his own to tie himself to an older woman, however rich and however much he loved her. It would be cruel to ask him to. His position would be invidious, he wouldn't have a clear place in her family, her life, but be forever on the outside.

If a rich man took a mistress, he would install her in a smart house in Town and visit when he had time. His wife would pretend she didn't know, and the mistress would move in a different circle. There was no recognised place for a man in the same position.

She desperately wanted to see John, knew she would always love him, but now realised it would be better for him if he didn't resume the affair. She loved him too much to ruin his life and bitterly regretted having asked him to come to her. If he did arrive, then she wouldn't have the strength to send him away, so it would be better if her letter never caught up with him.

It did occur to her that he might no longer love her and have no interest in resuming the affair and probably that would be the best outcome for both of them. As Joanna hung up her glad rags, she smiled ruefully. In a few short weeks, she'd vacillated from desperate to have him with her at any cost to wishing she hadn't even written the letter. If she couldn't make up her mind about something so important, how could she continue to look after her family during the remaining difficult war years?

From tomorrow, she must concentrate on her duties, her family and put her selfish wishes and dreams to one side. Tony could drive the family to see The Manse and then they could all be involved in the changes she wanted to make. She'd only viewed it from the outside before purchasing and had yet to see the interior. Of course, the architect had inspected every inch in order to draw up the plans.

* * *

Today was the first of March, Joanna realised, as she headed for the kitchen the next morning, half expecting there still to be the chaos from yesterday's wonderful wedding reception. The house was eerily quiet – where was everybody?

Tony was sitting at the central table in the kitchen and jumped to his feet as soon as she walked in. He really was the most polite and charming young man.

'Good morning, my lady, Mum's in the ballroom checking that everything is as it should be. The tea's just brewed, shall I pour you a cup?'

'I know the girls have the day off but I did expect some of them to be down as it's already past eight o'clock.'

'The party went on until the small hours, my lady, I doubt any of them will be down before lunch.'

'Oh dear, I do hope that doesn't mean Jean has extra work to do today.'

Jean walked in and overheard her. 'I told the girls that if they wanted to continue to dance then they had to leave the place tidy before they went to bed. I've just been to look and the ballroom's perfect. I think Sal and her two new friends took care of everything.'

'I hope you told Aggie and the others not to come in today after their sterling work yesterday.'

'I did. They took home enough to feed their families today as well as the extra money so were very pleased. I'm not cooking today – it'll be leftovers for lunch and omelettes and jacket potatoes for supper. Things will get back to normal on Sunday.'

'I'm sure you must have told me this, but I'd forgotten,' Joanna said. 'This makes what I'm going to suggest absolutely perfect as you won't be busy in here today. I'm hoping that Tony will agree to drive us all to see the house we'll be moving to quite soon. I want everybody who's going to be living there to have some input in the decoration and refurbishment.'

'I'd be happy to drive you, my lady. Joe's out doing the horse and chickens and Liza's helping him.'

'I just need to speak to my mother-in-law when she comes down as I'm quite certain she'll want to be included in the outing.'

'Even the weather's smiling on us today, Joanna, a bit grey but not as cold and we might even get some feeble sunshine later on,' Jean said as she expertly toasted two slices of bread simultaneously.

Joanna settled at the table and when she'd finished her breakfast spoke directly to Tony. 'Do you have any long-term plans?'

'Not really, my lady, I don't have a job as I resigned from my previous employment, but I'll have no difficulty finding work when I'm ready.'

'I'm hoping that you'll consider making your home with us here. Your mother's part of my family and as her son, you are too. There are several factories on the outskirts of Ramsgate and you'd be only a few miles from them when we move.'

He beamed and Jean's face lit up. 'There's nothing I'd like more than to be in the same house as my mum. Thank you for accepting me.'

Jean wiped her eyes on the edge of her pinny. 'I've always dreamed that one day Tony and I would be reunited and now it's happened, I'm quite over the moon with joy.'

Tony looked equally overcome with emotion. He cleared his throat noisily. 'I'll pay my way; I've got more than enough in the bank to keep me going for a couple of years without paid work. That said, my lady, I'll not stand around idly whilst I'm here.'

'There's absolutely no necessity for you to do anything you don't want to, Tony, but I'm sure Joe will find you dozens of maintenance jobs that we haven't been able to get anybody in to fix.' She smiled at them both, pleased to share in their happiness. 'What you've done with the old boiler and driving the Bentley is more than enough. You'll certainly not pay for your board and lodging.'

Later that morning, Jean, the twins, Elizabeth and Joanna climbed into the Bentley and were driven in style through the village and down Kingfisher Lane to where The Manse was situated. Their new home.

* * *

James was stretched out, Charlie asleep in his arms, scarcely able to believe that things had turned out as well as they had. He'd been gentle, taking things slowly last night and, to his astonishment and delight, she'd responded to his touch in a way he'd never anticipated.

Why would any man want to take his new bride somewhere strange, where they were both nervous and uncomfortable, when they could spend a blissful night in their own bed?

Their legs were entangled, her hair trapped under his arm, but he didn't want to wake her by moving. Then the matter was decided for him as the cat landed on the bed and began to clamber over them, purring and meowing as he did so.

Charlie attempted to sit up and yelped. 'Move your arm, I want to say good morning to my cat.' Hardly romantic, but seeing her so relaxed, behaving as if being naked with him was the most natural thing in the world was something he'd not expected so soon and was a wonderful start to their life together.

'I'll see to the fires, get the range going and make us both some tea. You stay where you are, darling, I'll bring it up.'

She'd flopped back on the rumpled pillows, the epitome of a woman well loved. 'I'm just too happy and too lazy to move. Hurry back, my love, I don't think either of us need to get up just yet.'

They didn't stir from the marital bed apart from for the necessary bodily functions and Charlie went down to let the cat in and out and pile the leftovers onto the tray.

The Champagne he'd been keeping cold in the pantry was drunk, curled up sandwiches and cold sausage rolls were consumed. Nothing had ever tasted so delicious in his opinion. The cat had shared the feast and was now asleep on the rug in front of the fire.

'I'm afraid we've set a precedent, my love. Cats shouldn't be allowed upstairs and certainly not on a bed but Lucky now has free access to both.'

'I don't mind if you don't.' He suddenly remembered something he'd put aside which he should have given her last night. He jumped out of bed. He was at the door when she called out to him.

'Are you going down in your birthday suit? Don't you think you should put on your dressing gown just in case?'

He turned and leaned nonchalantly against the door frame. 'In case of what, my darling girl? Another unexpected visitor?'

She was a little tipsy and giggled. 'If you'd opened the door to my father as you are, I think he'd have passed out with shock. I don't care, but I'd be careful you don't tread on something unpleasant. You never know what Lucky might have fetched in for us.'

'I'd look even more ridiculous with slippers and nothing else on. I'll take the risk.'

He could hear her delightful laughter as he went downstairs. He wanted to rush back and make love to her again but that could wait until he'd retrieved his bounty.

It was perishing on the ground floor as only the kitchen range was alight. What he wanted was in his study – it was a box of very expensive Black Magic assorted chocolates. They'd been put aside as he'd intended to take them with him to the hotel in Ramsgate, but because they'd remained here, he'd forgotten all about them until now.

He took the stairs two at a time and bounded into the bedroom and flung himself under the covers. 'Here you are, my darling, chocolates.'

'Your feet are icy, don't you dare put them anywhere near me again,' she said with another giggle.

Inevitably the chocolates were forgotten but as the box hadn't been opened by the time they did get around to eating them some hours later, there was nothing wrong with them at all.

When James woke on Sunday morning, he was alone in bed. He pulled on his pyjama bottoms, pushed his feet in his slippers and found his discarded dressing gown. He wasn't worried about her absence as he could hear her talking to the cat in the kitchen. What he didn't realise until he walked in was that she was dressed and busy making breakfast.

'Good morning, husband, I've made bacon, eggs and fried bread. I've plucked and dressed the pheasant and it's ready to go in the oven later. The vegetables are peeled and in cold water in the pantry.'

He'd got a thumping headache as he wasn't a heavy drinker and had polished off most of the Champagne – she'd only had one glass and even that had made her silly.

'Don't sound quite so cheerful or so loud, wife, as I imbibed far too much Champagne last night and am feeling a little worse for wear.'

Charlie faced him, tilted her head on one side and pursed her lips. 'You also need a shave – but have your breakfast first and then you've got about half an hour to sort yourself out before we go to church.'

'Church? I'm not bloody going to church so soon after our wedding. I...'

She was giggling. He'd been teased again. 'Horrible wench. I thought you the sweetest of young women yet here you are upsetting your poor husband who's got a hideous hangover.'

'Serves you right. I certainly don't want to go to church today – can you imagine the sniggers and pointed looks we'd get if we did go? What I would like to do is dress the table in the dining room and make our first meal together as a married couple really special.'

'I like the idea of that, but you won't do it on your own. As you've already taken care of the main course, I'll organise the dessert.'

She raised her eyebrows and shook her head.

'I'll have you know that I'm no slouch in the kitchen. I know there's a shortage of things, but I asked Mrs Thompson to get in some extras, so I'm hoping there'll be the makings for a sherry trifle.'

'Trifle? Now I'm impressed. I don't suppose there are many surgeons who can turn their hand to one of those.'

By one o'clock, the whole house was filled with the appetising aroma of roast pheasant, roast potatoes and parsnips and rich redcurrant-flavoured gravy. He'd lit the fire in the dining room immediately after breakfast so the room was pleasantly warm.

'You know, darling, this is only the second time I've eaten in here. I've never invited anybody to dine or had anyone here apart from employees and patients.'

'That's not entirely true, my love, because I've been a frequent visitor and even stayed here for three weeks when I had concussion last year.'

'I didn't consider you a guest or a visitor, so you don't count,' James said. 'Last year you were my patient initially and then my future wife.'

Her eyes widened. 'So I wasn't mistaken when I thought you

were interested in me? Why did you draw back after I returned to Goodwill House?'

'I sensed you had reservations about being more than a friend and didn't want to scare you away.'

She threw herself into his arms and for a few heady moments, they both forgot about the lunch that was waiting for them. Reluctantly he stepped away – if they continued, the meal would be ruined and they'd end up in bed.

'It might be better if you carved the pheasant in here, James?'

'If we leave it on the table, the cat will get it. Haven't you noticed he's been watching from his chair?'

Charlie glanced over her shoulder. 'Naughty puss, I'll give you some when we've finished. The carcass will make a wonderful soup and the leftovers I'll make into a pie.'

Talking about something as mundane as cooking discharged the atmosphere but he had a strong suspicion that his magnificent trifle might well be left until teatime.

Lucky was given a few scraps to keep him happy and was then shut out of the dining room so they could eat their meal in peace. The pheasant was perfectly cooked, the flesh moist and pink and how it should be, the gravy delicious and the vegetables that accompanied it perfect.

'We couldn't have eaten better if we'd gone to The Royal, darling, you're the most exceptionally talented cook. No – I think you deserve the title of chef after doing this.'

'It was wonderful, wasn't it? I don't knit, I can't sew very well but I am a good cook and gardener.'

'You get top marks in every department, darling. Do you want to leave the trifle...'

'Are you suggesting that we don't have the dessert after all the trouble you've gone to make it for us? Another thing you might not know about me, my love, is that I have a sweet tooth.'

He grinned. 'You ate half the chocolates last night, so I should have realised. I'm still a bit concerned about having all this food where the cat can get at it.'

'He can't open doors, can he? Anyway, you've got a perfectly good meat safe in your pantry and I'll put everything in that.'

It didn't take long to clear the table and put out the dessert plates and cutlery. He suggested that she wait in the dining room.

'I want to make a grand entrance with my trifle. I managed to get another treat for us – a small tin of coffee. Do we drink that with the trifle or have it afterwards with the last few chocolates?'

'We'll have it together. It's not often we get a chance to overindulge on luxury items and, after all, it's our honeymoon, isn't it?'

Charlie raced upstairs to fetch the chocolates and when she returned, the coffee was made and he was ready to take it all in on a tray. The reaction was everything he could have hoped for.

'That looks absolutely spiffing. You've whipped the cream and swirled it most professionally on the top. Are those tinned peaches in between the layers of sponge and custard?'

'They are indeed. There was cream in the pantry and I added some to the milk when I made the custard. Just Birdseye powder, not the real stuff, but I'm sure it'll taste almost as good.'

'Did you make the cake?'

'I don't see anyone else here who might have done it, do you?'

They ate almost half of it, and it was so saturated with sherry that it had gone to her head. The coffee should sort that out, but he didn't mind if she was a bit sozzled. In fact, she was even more entrancing.

24

Charlie was loving every minute of being a wife. She'd honestly believed five years ago that she'd never be able to have a loving relationship. Look at her now – blissfully happy and as eager to tumble into bed and make love as her wonderful husband was.

Pottering about in her very own kitchen making him something delicious to eat was a joy, even doing housework was a pleasure. James was so appreciative of everything she did and wolfed down each meal she put in front of him.

'That game pie was the best I've ever eaten, sweetheart, where did you learn to cook like this?'

'I spent most of my time in the kitchen with the cook as I wasn't wanted in the family rooms. I loved it there and Mrs Brooks taught me everything I know. I'd love to see her again – she was still working for my uncle and aunt when I left there.'

'Then why don't you write to her? I'm sure she'd love to hear from you and to know that you're so happy after what happened.'

'I still write to the vicar's daughter and I could send a letter there and ask her to give it to Mrs Brooks when they meet at church on Sunday.' There was something that puzzled her about her friend Millie Metcalfe. 'She will be the same age as me – I wonder why she's still unmarried and living at home.'

'Is she an attractive young lady?'

'Not beautiful, but pleasant-looking and with a lovely smile. We were best of pals at school, she was a popular girl, so I really don't understand why she hasn't got married. I suppose there aren't many unattached young men available since the war started, so that might be the reason.'

'Why don't you invite her to come for a visit? It shouldn't be too difficult for her to get from Guildford to Ramsgate even nowadays.'

'Thank you for suggesting it, James, but I don't want to share you with anybody just yet. I've got Daphne if I want a friend to talk to.'

He put down his newspaper, brushed the crumbs from his trousers and slipped on his jacket. 'The first patients will be here in half an hour, Charlie, are you going to be ready by then?'

'I wish we could have had longer without having to work. Perhaps you could take a few days off in the summer to go away somewhere, have a real holiday.'

'It's not easy when you're the only doctor in the neighbourhood to slope off for more than a night.'

'You were spending three nights a week at Ramsgate Hospital until recently so that's not true, is it? If your patients could manage without you then I'm sure they can do so in the summer.'

'True enough, sweetheart, I promise we'll go away when the weather improves.'

By the end of the first week of her married life, Charlie had settled into her roles as a wife and receptionist for the local doctor. Everybody addressed her as Mrs Willoughby, and she loved being called that. She made a point of flashing her wedding and engagement rings at every opportunity.

James treated her professionally whilst they were working and initially she'd found this difficult but soon understood they had to keep their personal and professional lives separate as much as they could.

Dolly was revelling in being the only domestic employed at The Rookery. From being a shy, quiet and not very enthusiastic under maid, she'd blossomed into something else entirely. The girl didn't work at the weekend, which suited all of them.

James had noticed the difference too. 'Whatever have you said to Dolly? She's worked for me for two years and until this week I've never seen her smile or move at more than a snail's pace.'

'I've increased her wages by ten shillings a week and told her that she is now a junior housekeeper. I've given her the little office that Mary used to use; she feels very important and appreciated now.'

'Does the woman from the village still come in to do the laundry once a week?'

'She certainly does, we could manage without her, but she relies on the income, so I want to keep her on as long as she wants to do it. Dolly's now doing the ironing and I'm teaching her how to keep household accounts. Although she left school at thirteen, she's certainly not stupid and is going to be a real asset to us until she leaves to get married herself.'

'Then I'll leave all domestic matters in your capable hands, my darling,' James said. 'The old chap who takes care of the chickens and the vegetable garden should have arranged for the stable block to have been cleared. It's not raining or snowing so shall we wander up there and see if it's what you wanted?'

'Yes, that would be splendid. I've spoken to Mr Pickering and there should be a load of hay, straw and some hard feed arriving sometime next week. Once that comes, all I have to do is collect Star.'

'I promised Lady Harcourt that Joe could keep your horse until he'd finished collecting the timber they need to run the central heating boiler. I suppose that we'll be going to church tomorrow morning so you can ask Joe when you see him if it's all right to bring Starlight home.'

He sounded so despondent about going to church that she laughed. 'You don't have to come with me, my love, I'm quite happy to go on my own. I don't believe you were a regular attendee so nobody will expect you to have become a devout Christian just because you married me.'

'Thank God for that.' He looked puzzled when she started to laugh but then joined in. 'Religion is ingrained into us; I meant no disrespect. I'm not exactly an atheist, more a sceptical agnostic.'

'I'll just wash up the breakfast things and then we can inspect the stable.'

* * *

Charlie was more than happy with the work that had been done to get the stable yard usable and she and James walked around the hedge that enclosed the paddock to check for any gaps. There were none.

'All I need to do now is speak to Joe and wait for the delivery from Fiddler's Farm.' A flash of red caught her eye at the far side of the field and she pointed. 'Did you see that? I think Lucky's over there hunting.'

'Let's hope he brings us back a rabbit or a pheasant. I really don't want any more rats or mice.'

'Don't be so ungrateful, Dr Willoughby, Lucky's bringing us gifts and as far as he's concerned, all of them are equally valuable.'

His eyes flashed and he gave her a wicked smile. Then she was in his arms, and she was weak with desire by the time they both drew breath. He looked hopefully towards the small barn.

'I know what you're thinking, but you can forget it. Even if there was hay in there, I'm certainly not going to... to do what you're thinking anywhere but in the privacy of our bedroom.'

'Alfresco lovemaking is something I'm looking forward to when we take a holiday in the summer.' His expression was innocent and for a horrible moment, she thought him serious.

'I can't wait to skip in my birthday suit around the meadows in full view of anyone who happens to be walking past. I do hope we don't get arrested for indecent exposure.'

He ruffled her hair and kissed the top of her head. 'Be careful what you wish for, my darling,' he whispered into her already overheated ear.

'If you weren't quite so large, husband, then I'd kick you in the shins. We'd better go back and have a calming pot of tea.'

In fact, as soon as they'd taken off their outdoor garments and gumboots, he picked her up and bounded up the stairs as if she weighed no more than a bag of feathers. They didn't emerge from the bedroom until late afternoon and then had to creep about the house with a torch, drawing the blackouts.

Lucky came in dragging a large rabbit and didn't seem at all bothered by having been forgotten for so long. They retired early and made love again, each time better than the last.

Charlie preferred to sleep with her nightgown on, so James compromised and wore his pyjama bottoms. He fell asleep quickly and she lay beside him, listening to his breathing. Her heart was bursting with happiness, there might be a war on, but she had James to take care of her and knew she was safe.

She ran a hand reflectively over her flat stomach. Was there a baby already growing inside her? She wasn't exactly sure what symptoms she should feel or how soon they would appear – she did know that her monthlies would stop. They were due at the end of next week, so maybe she'd know if she was carrying his child in a week's time.

'Can't you sleep, darling? Do you want me to make you a hot water bottle or some cocoa?' James asked sleepily.

'No, thank you, my love, just hold me in your arms and I'll fall asleep immediately. I love you.'

'I love you too, my darling, now go to sleep.'

* * *

Joanna had been rather disappointed by the interior of the house she'd bought but Tony had reassured her that when the improvements were made, it would be exactly what she wanted. He said that he'd take care of installing the new boiler and was already liaising with the builders she'd contracted to do the work in the summer.

Elizabeth, surprisingly, had been very enthusiastic about moving and even her maid had managed to smile a few times at the thought of having her own room and not being obliged to share the nursery floor with Tony and Jean.

Starlight was leaving Goodwill House today but as she was only going to the village to live with Charlie, it wasn't too much of a wrench for any of them. Joe had been given permission to cycle down whenever he liked and take the mare out for a hack.

Saying any sort of goodbye was something Joanna preferred to do in private. Therefore, she'd come out early and given the horse half a carrot. 'Goodbye, Star, I know you'll be happy in your new home.' She patted the animal's neck and left her munching happily in her stable.

There had been an air-raid last night and they'd spent an uncomfortable few hours in the shelter in the cellar. She yawned, there were WI and WVS meetings in the village hall that afternoon so there was no possibility of having a much-needed nap.

There had been no fresh snow for a week, the last fall hadn't thawed as the temperature remained stubbornly above freezing. She had her stout boots on, a thick coat, gloves, hat and scarf so decided to take a brisk walk in the hope it would clear her head and wake her up.

It wouldn't be sensible to venture from the drive, which had been cleared by Joe and Tony, as some of the drifts on either side were over six foot high. The drive was no more than a quarter of a mile long so walking from one end to the other wouldn't be too arduous. The girls had already departed for their various workplaces, as had Liza, the others would be eating breakfast, and it would also mean she wasn't going to be gone so long that they would send out a search party.

The ground was crisp and slippery underfoot and twice she nearly lost her balance but she was enjoying being out of doors. She was almost at the road end when she heard the distinctive roar of a motorbike approaching at speed.

Her heart jumped. Silly, but the sound reminded her so poignantly of John. Daphne's husband also rode a motorbike, but it sounded quite different to the one that her lost love had ridden.

Joanna stopped in the centre of the drive, wanting to see it flash past. It didn't go past, but instead it skidded around the corner, heading straight for her. She was temporarily paralysed. Everything happened so fast. The rider saw her and swerved, putting both feet down to steady the bike, but it was a lost cause. She watched in horror as the bike ploughed into the snowdrift and the man sailed over the handlebars and vanished beneath the drift.

Her feet moved of their own volition, and she was scrabbling over the snow a few seconds later. Even then, she didn't realise who it was, was too worried that her stupidity had injured the visitor.

Then John's head and shoulders emerged from the snow. 'Bloody hell, that wasn't quite how I envisaged our reunion.' He was laughing as he spat out the snow. 'I got your letter last night and wangled a forty-eight-hour pass.'

She was numb – not just from the cold seeping into her clothes but from the fact her wildest dream appeared to be coming true.

'I'm so sorry, I hope I haven't broken your bike.'

He heaved himself to his feet, looking more like a snowman than an RAF pilot, and grabbed her hands, pulling her up beside him.

'Sod the bike. Did you mean what you said in your letter?' His voice was gruff; despite the snow, she could see the hesitation on his face.

'I meant every word,' Joanna said. 'I love you; I want you in my life, but I just can't see how we're going to make this work.'

'I love you too. I've never stopped loving you, and I don't care about any obstacles you might care to throw in our way. This time, I'm not going to leave you.'

He put his arm around her waist and lifted her free of the drift and then joined her on the drive. 'Don't move, I'm going to rescue my bike. I need it to get back to Hornchurch if I don't want to be AWOL.'

She couldn't have moved even if she'd wanted to. She was mesmerised by the young man in front of her. He'd changed since last summer – looked older, tougher somehow. Being a fighter pilot, as he now was, would do that to a man.

He dragged the bike free, fiddled about and then miraculously it roared into life at the first kick of the starter.

'Come on, my lady, your chariot awaits.'

Joanna had never travelled on the back of a motorbike and

wasn't sure she wanted to now, but had no option. Once she was settled, he lifted his feet from the ground, and they were off.

It was an extremely unpleasant experience and one she hoped she wouldn't have to endure again. She thanked God that she was only obliged to clutch onto him for so short a distance.

He stopped in full view of anyone who might be looking out of the windows at the front of the house. 'The house looks so much better without the Victorian annex. Why are the drawing room windows boarded up?'

'I'm really not going to discuss the state of my home with you whilst sitting on the back of this horrible bike in the freezing cold,' Joanna said. 'Please put it in the barn so we can get warm and have a sensible conversation.'

He didn't reply but expertly guided the bike the remaining few yards into the open barn where the girls kept their bicycles. As the noise of the engine died, he put his boots back on the ground, but still remained silent.

She slithered from the seat behind him and waited for a response. With slow deliberation, he pulled off his leather gauntlets, removed his flying helmet and goggles and then swung his leg over the pillion and turned to face her.

'You haven't changed at all, Joanna, and I can't tell you how happy I am to see you and how much I've missed you.'

She was going to say the same, but he grabbed her by the elbows and the next thing she knew, she was being thoroughly and passionately kissed. His lips were icy when they touched hers, but this changed as the kiss deepened.

After a wonderful, delirious few minutes, she was weak with desire and without his bulk supporting her thought she might have slithered to the ground. The romantic interlude was shattered by Joe.

'Bloody hell, Ma, I never expected to see you doing that with him or with anyone, to be honest.'

The instinct was to move sharply away from John but he had other ideas and, keeping his arm firmly around her waist, turned them both to face her son. She'd been expecting him to look horrified, angry even, but he was grinning.

'John and I are very good friends...'

Her son laughed. 'Blimey, I'd say you're a bit more than that. Good for you. You've got my support, but I can't see Grandma being happy.'

'It's none of her business, Joe, what your mother and I do with our lives. That said, I'm glad that you approve as you're going to be seeing a lot of me in future.'

Joanna listened to this exchange, feeling slightly left out. Why was it that men tended to talk over the heads of women?

'John, if you don't mind, I need to put on something dry. I hope you've got spare clothes in your panniers?'

His smile was for her alone and in that moment she no longer cared what any of her family said. This was the man she loved and intended to have in her life regardless of the scandal it might cause. Sarah approved and now she had her son's blessing, too.

'I have, Joanna, if you want to go in first and speak to the rest of your family, that's fine by me. I'll hang about here for a few minutes whilst I get my kit.'

She stepped away but then turned and kissed him. 'We've got so much to talk about, but I really can't do it when I'm wet through to my underwear.'

He was still laughing as she hurried inside but couldn't see what had amused him. Then a wave of heat spread from her toes to her crown. She understood, but prayed that her son hadn't.

25

Joanna hastily changed into a dry camisole, warm slacks and a pretty peach-coloured twinset. Her pearls would look perfect with this ensemble, but she really didn't have time or the inclination to fiddle about putting them on.

Where would John be sleeping tonight? He could hardly join her in this room, so she'd go to him, which meant he needed to be somewhere they were unlikely to be overheard or interrupted. Heaven knows what Elizabeth was going to say but her mother-in-law would just have to get used to it. After all, she'd said she'd had several lovers when living in the south of France for all those years so was in no position to comment.

She didn't pause to check her appearance in the full-length mirror – something David had always insisted that she did in order to ensure that not a hair was out of place, not a stocking seam crooked, or her lipstick smudged.

John loved her as she was and wouldn't care about the things that had been so important to her dead husband.

He was halfway up the stairs, carrying an overnight bag, when she emerged from the passageway in which the family rooms were situated.

'Take the room at the end of that corridor, John, one of the ones that you used when you were here before.'

'Do you want me to be with you when you tell Lady Harcourt?'

'I don't think so, but once I've explained how things are...'

He reached out and brushed her cheek. 'How are things? My head's been spinning ever since I read your letter. Joe and I always got on well and now that I'm one of the Brylcreem boys, a seasoned fighter pilot, I can do no wrong in his eyes.'

'Well, darling, that's two members of my family that approve. I couldn't have got in touch with you if I haven't told my daughter and her fiancé – Squadron Leader Trent. I'm certain that my younger daughter will be happy for me. That just leaves my mother-in-law.'

'She might surprise you. She told me a few stories from her time in France that certainly made my hair curl.'

'She told me, too, of course no details, but I certainly think she had several liaisons. One thing she made perfectly clear was that to have affairs somewhere where one is not known was quite different from doing the same thing where you have a reputation to keep intact.'

He looked at her speculatively. 'Are you telling me that your reputation is more important to you than I am?'

'Don't be ridiculous – nothing is more important to me than you.' This wasn't quite true. 'My children come first, naturally, but nothing else is of any consequence.'

John wiped his brow as if relieved. 'Phew! Then there's only Liza to get onside and everything's tickety-boo.'

'I don't care what Elizabeth says, I'm sure with your undoubted charm you'll win her over in time. I doubt that the women of the

Women's Institute and Women's Voluntary Service will be so forgiving.'

'I don't give a f—'

'No, John, I draw the line at that sort of language. Hurry up and get changed and then come to the small sitting room.'

A large glass of brandy would steady her nerves before she had to explain the unexpected arrival of her former lover. She glowed all over at the thought that from tonight he would be very much not erstwhile.

Jean was waiting in the hall and rushed over and embraced her. 'I guessed that you and John had been involved but didn't want to mention it in case I was wrong. Joe told us. He couldn't keep it to himself. He's cock-a-hoop and I'm sure that Liza will be too. We all want you to be happy.'

'Thank you, my dear friend, for your support. I can't understand why so far no one has been scandalised by my wanton behaviour.'

'Go on with you, you're not the only young woman to throw her hat over the windmill. I promise you that nobody will hear about him from any of us.'

'I know that, but the land girls will soon draw the correct conclusion and gossip will be all over the neighbourhood by the end of the week.'

'Ignore it, just look down your nose and raise an eyebrow if anyone mentions it. You don't have to deny it – just look amused at their outlandish suggestions.'

'Church next week is going to be interesting. Now, John will be down in a minute, so could you please find him something to eat – he's bound to be hungry as he must have left before any of the canteens or mess halls were open.'

Elizabeth was watching the door as Joanna went in. 'Who is it? What's going on? I'm sure I heard a man's voice a few minutes ago.'

Joanna took a deep breath, swallowed, and told her mother-in-law everything. When she'd finished, Elizabeth nodded.

'My dear, I suspected that you'd had an affair with that handsome young RAF sergeant. I'd have preferred you to fall in love with Peter Harcourt as he is one of us, but I liked the young man and you have my support.'

'Thank you, that means so much to me.' Joanna flopped into the nearest chair as her legs were suddenly unable to hold her upright a moment longer. 'In a day or two it'll be all over the village and I'll have to resign my position in the WVS and leave the WI.'

'Then that will be their loss, my dear, and our gain.'

'Excuse me, ladies, might I join you or am I *persona non grata* in here?'

Joanna turned and walked into John's arms. 'You're welcome everywhere in this house. Elizabeth's given her approval. That's enough for me at the moment.'

He kissed her briefly and then, hand in hand, they walked across the room and sat on the chaise longue. Elizabeth was smiling and nodding.

'You make a handsome couple. It's fortuitous, is it not, that Joanna looks so much younger than her age and you look considerably older than yours, young man?'

John grinned. 'Indeed it is, my lady, we can all pretend that there's no age difference at all.'

'My word, I can't wait to tell my friends about this. They've been hoping to persuade Joanna to marry one of the many ineligible and inadequate gentlemen of their acquaintance. Imagine the faces of the congregation when the two of you attend church tomorrow arm in arm.'

'I'm an atheist, my lady, I don't go to church.'

'Absolutely delicious – is there anything else scandalous I can regale my friends with next time we meet?'

He nodded solemnly. 'I'm a member of the Labour Party.'

For a moment, Elizabeth was speechless, then she laughed. 'As long as you're not a Bolshevik, then I think there's nothing to worry about.'

* * *

Liza returned from her work as a nanny at the vicarage and was equally enthusiastic about the new member of the family. Joanna had already written to Sarah and the letter would be posted in the morning.

John remained in the sitting room with Elizabeth when the land girls were around and Joanna joined him for supper on a tray.

During the evening, he told her all about his life as a fighter pilot and explained why he hadn't answered her letter.

'It followed me about the place and I only picked it up last night. I'm not on the roster yet – I arrived at Hornchurch yesterday afternoon. The adjutant took pity on me and gave me two days' leave.'

'Are you going to be stationed at Hornchurch for long?'

'Nobody is stationed anywhere for very long, but I'm there for the moment. As long as I can get petrol, I can be here in a few hours. I've not met this Angus Trent but no doubt I will once I've been there for a while.'

'It would be wonderful if you got posted to Manston, then we could see each other far more often.'

'I expect I'll be at Manston once I'm active again, but we only stay to refuel and rearm and then fly back to Hornchurch.'

'I hate that you're a fighter pilot but promise I won't complain,'

Joanna said. 'I suppose it would be worse if you were in the navy or fighting with the army in Africa.'

They sat and talked, not something they'd done much of in their brief affair last year, and the more she knew, the more she loved him. Once the house was quiet, it was safe for him to emerge.

'This is all very clandestine, darling, but it adds a certain piquancy to our relationship.'

'It might seem amusing to you, but I find it all highly embarrassing having to creep around my own house like this.'

'Then don't.'

'I don't want to parade you around like a trophy. Someone will see you at some point but the longer my private life remains that, the happier I'll be.'

John gathered her close and she rested her cheek against his shoulder, knowing this was where she was meant to be. 'We'll make this work, my darling, I give you my word.'

ACKNOWLEDGMENTS

I would like to thank Boldwood and the fantastic team who work there to make my books so well received by thousands of readers. I am supported, valued, and motivated by Boldwood and wouldn't want to be anywhere else. Especial thanks to Mills, the eagle-eyed proofreader, who saw a historical error that none of us had noticed in my last book.

BIBLIOGRAPHY

Chronicle of the Second World War edited by Jacques Legrand and Derrik Mercer
A to Z Atlas and Guide to London, 1939 edition
Oxford Dictionary of Slang by John Ayto
Wartime Britain by Juliet Gardiner
How We Lived Then by Norman Longmate
The Wartime Scrapbook by Robert Opie
The Land Girl Manual 1941 by W. E. Shewell-Cooper
Land Girls and Their Impact by Ann Kramer
Land Girl by Anne Hall
The Women's Land Army by Bob Powell and Nigel Westcott
A Detailed History of RAF Manston by Joe Bamford and John Williams with Peter Gallagher Fonthill
BBC Archives: World War II
Call the Midwife by Jennifer Worth
A Doctor of Sorts by V. J. Downie
A Doctor's War by Aidan MacCarthy

MORE FROM FENELLA J. MILLER

We hope you enjoyed reading *Wedding Bells at Goodwill House*. If you did, please leave a review.

If you'd like to gift a copy, this book is also available as an ebook, large print, hardback, digital audio download and audiobook CD.

Sign up to Fenella J. Miller's mailing list for news, competitions and updates on future books.

https://bit.ly/FenellaMillerNews

Why not explore the rest of Fenella J. Miller's wonderful Goodwill House series...

War Girls of Goodwill House
FENELLA J. MILLER

New Recruits at Goodwill House
FENELLA J. MILLER

Duty Calls for Goodwill House
FENELLA J. MILLER

Land Girls of Goodwill House
FENELLA J. MILLER

Wartime Reunion at Goodwill House
FENELLA J. MILLER

Wedding Bells at Goodwill House
FENELLA J. MILLER

ABOUT THE AUTHOR

Fenella J. Miller is a bestselling writer of historical sagas. She also has a passion for Regency romantic adventures and has published over fifty to great acclaim. Her father was a Yorkshireman and her mother the daughter of a Rajah. She lives in a small village in Essex with her British Shorthair cat.

Follow Fenella on social media:

Sixpence Stories

Introducing Sixpence Stories!

Discover page-turning historical novels from your favourite authors, meet new friends and be transported back in time.

Join our book club Facebook group

https://bit.ly/SixpenceGroup

Sign up to our newsletter

https://bit.ly/SixpenceNews